BOOKS BY ROBERT J. SEIDMAN

Notes for Joyce: An Annotation of James Joyce's Ulysses
(With Don Gifford)

One Smart Indian

Bucks County Idyll

Robert J. Seidman

SIMON AND SCHUSTER
NEW YORK

Designed by Eve Kirch
Manufactured in the United States of America

1 2 3 4 5 6 7 8 9 10

Library of Congress Cataloging in Publication Data

Seidman, Robert J.
Bucks County idyll.

I. Title.
PZ4.S4585Bu [PS3569.E532] 813'.5'4 79-23721

ISBN 978-1-4391-8325-0

To Binnie

Bucks County Idyll

Carroll Management Corporation

 "I don't want to be pushy or anything. But what the hell are we doing here?"

Stephanie smiled and waved the *Triple-A Guide* at Nick. "We're on vacation."

Nick Young watched people moving across the huge enclosed quadrangle and lectured himself, "Don't be a grump. A whole new city's at your feet. Enjoy it." But Nick wasn't certain he'd follow his own advice.

They passed out of the courtyard in the center of Philadelphia's City Hall, leaving giant stone goddesses, gorgons, and eagles staring furiously at their backs.

"What do you think this Carroll guy will be like?"

"I don't know." Stephanie Harrold tried not to anticipate things. She didn't like spoiling the surprise and hated being tied down to her own bad guesses. This made the Philadelphia trip an adventure, without plan or ending. All she knew was that, at her own urging, they were answering an ad in the *New York Times* about a housesitting position. But now, prompted by Nick, she let her mind wander: Carroll was probably older, a pure-bred Main Liner, a not too successful lawyer who settled on management as a not too taxing way of making a living.

"I don't trust a guy with two last names."

Walking south on Market Street, Nick looked around and recognized the street was still up for grabs. Next to a posh men's haberdashery stood a noisy, doorless arcade stocked with a line of ringing pinball machines and a facing line of pinging electronic games. The noise and flashing lights and smell of popcorn worked like a magnet, pulling in a flotilla of landlocked sailors.

"Two generations of machines." Nick pointed. "That's kind of funny."

"The sailors all look about fourteen."

They passed under the marquee of a Quadruple-X–rated movie house, its barker drawling, "See it all buddy. See it all." Nearby, a lounging hooker in very short shorts offered passersby the three-dimensional alternative.

They stopped in front of a sleek department store with a sunken brick courtyard and a glassed-in escalator which carried well-dressed people up to the mezzanine.

"Suburban chic meets urban funk. I love it, Steph. Makes me feel at home."

A slim well-dressed young man sidled up to them. "Want to buy a watch? Seiko."

"How much?" Nick asked.

"Twenty-five."

The young man looked around suspiciously as Nick lifted the watch out of its case and examined the dial. Stephanie edged away, putting Nick's body between herself and the hawker.

"No thanks. Not today."

"Good buy. I'll make it twenty."

"Not interested," Nick replied a little more harshly. He took Stephanie by the elbow and led her away a few yards. They stopped to let a clutch of matrons break around them.

"Oldest scam in the world. Buy or steal a cheap watch,

10

pry off the crystal, stick in a Seiko dial, and sell it for 300 percent profit."

A few steps below them in the courtyard, the young man offered his Seiko watch to a well-dressed businessman, who put out his hands as if to fend him off, then scurried away.

"Not a very high batting average. Must be new at it."

They peered into shop windows, then crossed Market Street and lost themselves in the Reading Terminal Market until, promptly at a quarter to two, they stood in front of the Philadelphia Saving Fund Society Building. The *Triple-A Guide* noted that "PSFS" had not only been one of the country's earliest skyscrapers but also been voted "Building of the Century" by the American Institute of Architects.

"What a wonderful building." She pointed to the large bands of glass with their softly rounded corners. "The book's right. Those windows do give it a 'sleek, streamlined look.' "

"Yeah, like old trains." But Nick liked the way those horizontal stripes of window gently eased the movement of the eye upward. "Must've made quite a splash in old Philadelphia when they started pushing it into the sky."

Bradford Carroll's office looked as sleek as the building. Narrow bands of shiny black started in a corner of the room near the window, turned that corner, ran along a wall toward an enormous rank of windows that looked down on the city and northward to the statue of William Penn atop City Hall. Penn, who was just above eye level, looked as though he stood only a few yards away. At any moment, Stephanie thought, he might begin to lecture on the subtle emanations of the inner light and infallible methods for negotiating with the Leni Lenape. In contrast with the baroque staginess of City Hall, Carroll's office had a cool, crisp angularity. His desk, which looked at least ten feet long, had vertical brass inserts like a pipe organ spaced at six-inch intervals across its front. The big sofa and two chairs were upholstered in a gray and white geometric print, softened only by the gray and dark red of the drapes. To Stephanie, the room was gorgeous; to Nick, it seemed kinky and pretentious.

The room's principal living adornment was a flashy secretary, a very thin ash blonde with a slight overdose of eyeliner and lipstick a shade too red, the color of bull's blood. Openly, without the slightest inhibition, she made a slow and complete study of Nick. The more embarrassed he became, the more bemused her smile. She made Nick feel like a kid in short pants.

In a throaty, cooing voice uncorrupted by Philadelphia accent, the secretary asked them, "Would you please wait here? Mr. Carroll'll be out in a moment."

They sat down in wide low-slung chairs. Nick snuck a glance at the secretary, which she returned with accrued interest. Then she made what they both would've termed a conspicuous exit. Something else caught Nick's eye then. "Catch that stereo, Steph." By the foot of a wall-length bookshelf stood an array of the most futuristic electronic equipment imaginable. The stereo was housed in glossy chrome-and-ebony cabinets, scribed with inlaid parallel chrome bars. Nick got up to take a look. He hovered over the equipment, shook his head and said, "That's some setup."

When he sat down, Stephanie said, "The whole place is quite a setup." Carroll's office made her revise her opinion of the man.

Then Bradford Carroll strode into the room. He was tall and moved with a long, quick, exact step. He looked about forty, roughly the same age as his secretary. At first he appeared to be rail thin, yet he had thick features—a strong jaw, prominent cheekbones, and a surprisingly fleshy face. The effect was lightened by fair, perfectly smooth tanned skin and silky corn-colored hair. He wore a cream-colored suit and carried a thick manila folder under his arm. Carroll fit well with his office, secretary, stereo. Stephanie knew immediately that he was "an appreciator." Her evaluation of sexual and aesthetic appeal told her she was safe, and so she could enjoy the attention.

For Carroll, Nick just didn't exist. There was no contempt in this dismissal, it was simply as though Nick were not sitting in that sharply angled chair.

Stephanie wanted to look over to catch Nick's reaction, but politeness dictated no peeking.

"Sorry to have kept you waiting," he said. The voice was perfect, rich without being phony, very sexy. Carroll slid into his seat behind the Wurlitzer desk. "Let me get to the point, Miss Harrold, Mr. Young. You answered an advertisement in the *New York Times*." He paused. "I assume you are the type of people my clients are looking for." Another pause. "My clients are anything but snobs. They are simply art collectors who must be certain that the couple who will occupy their house for an entire year will care for, appreciate, and of course enjoy their splendid collection." Nick could not relax; he recognized Carroll as the type who talks in complete sentences. "But that pleasure isn't the only compensation," Carroll continued, warmed by his own eloquence. "Peter and Amanda Berger insist that their sitters be well compensated for what is, after all, a serious and demanding job. The housesitters will receive a monthly stipend of $200. Household duties will be minimal —a gardener will come at least once a week, and two maids will clean the house. The sitters will have free use of the house and grounds. There will be other privileges, too, but there's no point in going into that now."

Carroll opened the manila folder and slid Stephanie a

bunch of eight-by-ten glossies of the grounds and the out-buildings, the stone farmhouse, the living room and its enormous walk-in fireplace. She skimmed through the pile and passed the pictures to Nick, keeping only the shot of the fireplace. The courses of massive boulders were outlined by pure white mortar; each stone seemed a jewel on display. The foot-thick black lintel which defined the front edge of the hearth was charred by use. The hearth, not the artwork on the walls, provided the room's focus, which made her feel more comfortable about the house. She could see herself sitting through a winter in front of a roaring fire, watching the flames of that natural strobe machine leap and dive in time to Dylan—no, perhaps, she thought, it was Mozart. That single photograph sold Stephanie on the farmhouse, sold her on Bucks County. Not that she was particularly resistant to the idea, but the photo transported her the rest of the way. This house plus $200 plus my $200 a month, she thought. That's not that much less than I'm making at the plant store. We could get by on that without much trouble.

Carroll, whose eyes remained fixed on Stephanie, pressed a button on the elaborately lighted console on his desk. "Obviously the Bergers have a remarkable collection. The right couple will have a wonderful time and learn an enormous amount in this environment." Nick sneaked a glance Stephanie's way which read, roughly, "What a condescending ass." She couldn't have agreed less.

The blonde secretary reentered with an extended flourish and, once seated, took down all their particulars—Stephanie was surprised that the woman could actually take dictation. Carroll inquired as to: age (Stephanie twenty-eight, Nick thirty); education (NYU and the New School for Social Research, respectively); bank and credit references (a few dollars in checking and a pittance in savings,

14

though fortunately in April they'd been mailed a Master Charge and hadn't thrown it away; she liked paying bills on time); pets (none; their Siamese had died recently); personal references (three, including Stephanie's rich stockbroker father). Carroll perked up professionally when she mentioned her relationship to William Harrold.

While the secretary transcribed, Carroll opened a thin mahogany box and pushed it toward Nick, who looked in and said no thank you. Carroll took out a long, thin, very dark cigar. Carefully positioning it between thumb and forefinger, he twirled the cigar deftly, searching for minute breaks in the wrapper. Satisfied, he ran his tongue generously over the end, then slowly introduced the cigar to his mouth.

"You'll be insured, of course." Carroll lit up lovingly, the flame leaping the gap between match and cigar. "Do you have any objections to being bonded?" He made being bonded sound like an erotic delight.

"I don't think so," Stephanie replied, almost blushing. She wanted that house, wanted it badly. Stephanie's temptation was to limit their questions to a bare minimum, but Nick added responsibly, "Just what does bonding involve?"

Carroll answered: "The Bergers' collection is worth millions of dollars. I can give the figures when and if they're needed. In case of a theft occurring while the sitters are in residence, the bonding is to cover their liability." Carroll said that as sweetly as possible.

As the interrogation/interview proceeded, it became clear to Stephanie that the Bergers conceived of the housesitting arrangement as an educational and charitable act. A subsidized education in a magnificent setting among one of the country's finest private art collections, two maids and one gardener thrown in, a darkroom for Nick. Their only duty, it seemed, was to soak up culture and wallow in

15

beauty. So even beyond her desire and need for this year-long paid vacation, the place began to stir the suburban princess in Stephanie: Already she was wondering what to wear. Meanwhile, Nick did his best to reserve judgment as he listened to the polished voice which pretended he didn't exist.

"There is a single restrictive condition of employment. And this must be met without reservation by the couple who'll occupy the farmhouse." Nick and Stephanie nodded tentatively. "Except for those days when the maids or gardener are on the estate, at least one of you must be in the house at all times."

"At all times?" they chimed in unison.

"Yes. They mean that altogether literally. Let me explain. There have been a number of robberies—not an alarming number, just a select few. The investigators suspect that a gang of art thieves is working out of Princeton, just across the river, as well as in Bucks County. This restriction is a simple but absolutely necessary security measure. It entails no—"

Stephanie interrupted: "Do you mean that if I went out to shop, Nicholas would have to stay inside the house until I got back?"

"If we wanted to go to the movies, we'd have to go one at a time?" Nick sounded incredulous.

"Precisely." The cigar glowed brightly.

Stephanie's instincts rebelled: Forget it. This is all too bizarre. But in her heart she had already laid claim to that huge stone fireplace. So it's a five-day work week, she told herself. Just like working, only better hours.

"Isn't this business dangerous?" Nick asked.

"No. As far as we can tell, there's absolutely no danger. The burglaries have all occurred in vacant homes. Not a single occupied house has been touched, and we have no reason to believe any will be. Obviously these thieves can't afford to have witnesses. That's why the Bergers are adamant about having one of the sitters in the house at all times."

"But how could you tell," Nick asked, "if a housesitter really was in the house?"

Bradford Carroll looked righteously indignant. "I've been asked to phone periodically to make certain that someone is in the house. I don't want to be too literal or fussy, but I would prefer—no, I would advise the sitters to answer the phone, say, by the sixth or seventh ring. Does that sound reasonable?"

"I can imagine moments when that will be inconvenient."

"When such moments occur," Carroll replied, his eyes bemused, insinuating, "the sitter should call my office back immediately."

Nick started to object, but Carroll continued, "The job is as I've described it. There's nothing I can do to change my clients' conditions. Of course you have to take time to think about your decision, to weigh the benefits and responsibilities as you see them. I have to meet with the others who are interested. Just call my secretary in a few days and tell her whether you've decided to apply for the job. In a week or so I'll get back to you with our decision. Do you have any more questions?"

Silence for a moment. Carroll puffed contentedly on his slim cigar. Stephanie studied the fireplace that lay in her lap. "No."

"One final thing," Bradford Carroll said. "The Bergers do not want to be disturbed while they're in France. I'll handle all correspondence between the Bergers and Bucks County."

Feeling he was on uncertain ground and looking for

holes in a proposition that had started to intrigue him, Nick said, "That also sounds strange to me. I mean, the people living in their house and guarding their art—"

"This is not a wholly unusual arrangement." Carroll cut off the line of discussion. "More important, these are the Bergers' conditions."

It sounded quite final. There were plenty of questions to ask Carroll, but Stephanie sensed they'd already overfilled their quota. She also sensed that Nick, for the first time, was genuinely intrigued by the proposition. The strangeness of it all was starting to interest him.

As they stood up to leave, Nick asked, "Aren't those Klipschorn speakers?"

Stephanie looked at Nick, wondering where on earth the Klipschorn business came from. She assumed Nick knew as little as she did about the stereo equipment. Carroll looked at Nick as though noticing him for the first time.

"Yes."

"And the new Bang and Olufsen turntable?"

"That's right."

Nick never ceased to amaze her. He had Carroll for his audience now. "But I've never seen such an extraordinary amplifier."

"There's a good reason for that. I built that unit myself."

"Impressive, Mr. Carroll. Very impressive."

On their way out, Nick signaled Stephanie not to laugh. As soon as the elevator door closed, they both started giggling.

"You know," said Stephanie as she kissed him, "you're the greatest." She hadn't realized how much tension Carroll's high-pressure salesmanship had produced.

"For you, kid, anything." Stephanie kept laughing. "Play to their vanity. Always to their vanity."

At the entrance to the New Jersey Turnpike, Nick breathed a small sigh of relief. Even with Stephanie's charms and his last-minute coup with the stereo, he figured they didn't have much of a shot at the farmhouse. Which was fine with Nick. He hadn't liked Carroll much. Bucks County would probably mean more of the same.

As Stephanie wedged the ticket into the top of the glove compartment, she asked, "So, what do you think about it?"

"I doubt we're in the running. I asked a lot of questions he didn't want to hear."

"It would be so nice, Nick. It'd give us a whole year rent free and time to figure out what we want to do."

"What do you mean we?"

Not wanting to get sidetracked on the complicated issue of the future, Stephanie retreated to her original question: "What if we did get it?"

"Well, I got to admit that pastoral beauty looks good. And the fact of my own darkroom doesn't bum me out. But I hate the idea of being cooped up in the house for a year, even in 'an exquisite eighteenth-century farmhouse.'" Nick quoted the copy from the *Times* ad in a bad British falsetto.

"Very funny."

"Plus I'm not crazy about not being able to contact the owners." Nick didn't want to admit that Stephanie would be so much more at home there than he. And down in a hidden corner of his being, Nick also worried about liking the place and the whole gentry trip; the last thing he wanted was to become "homogenized" and turn middle class like every other man she'd ever known.

"I just have this feeling, Nick, that we're going to get it, the housesit, I mean, and that it's going to be terrific."

"Ah, the certainty of privilege."

"Don't quote Karl Marx at me."

19

Nick smiled and braked as the large Cadillac in front of him started to swing out in front of an oncoming truck. The Cadillac barely squeezed back into the center lane. "Asshole. Adorno, not Marx, old pal. And I wasn't going to." Adorno had cunningly labeled Stephanie's habit of mind "the casualness with which privilege expropriates experience." Nick had first directed the quotation at Stephanie four years before during their early pre-love debate about who they were and what each of them wanted. (What an elaborate evasion that long debate had been, how very obviously they had wanted each other but kept checking, checking for the irremediable flaw that would have kept them apart.)

Long knots of traffic thinned out, the Cadillac sprinted ahead as the turnpike split into six lanes—on their left, the putrid marsh with its turbid, flammable river, on their right a scattering of rusty ships and billboards for Broadway shows.

As they sputtered up one of those long Connecticut hills at forty-two miles per hour, Stephanie realized she was almost twenty-nine, Nick thirty, and they still were drifting. When they'd started for Philadelphia, she had no idea she wanted a change. She'd been working in a plant and flower store in Woods Hole for over a year. Stephanie loved that store, loved the lush leafy beauty and the cool close damp. She loved all the care she aimed in the plants' direction and asked no questions about what, if any, surrogate function they served. Meanwhile, Nick worked on his photography, roofed on a building crew sporadically, and every weekend tended bar at The Fisherman. All that was OK for kids, but she could imagine it getting tiring for adults. Nick still entertained intermittent fantasies about Saying Something Significant through Film, in spite of his dreadful experience with a script about a Vietnam veteran's wife and her increasing disillusionment with the war. Stephanie had offered guarded encouragement about the script, but she had doubts about its commercial possibilities and didn't want to throw too much fuel on the film world romance. A friend of her father's put Nick in touch with a couple of independent producers who showed interest in the story, but nothing ever came of it except to sour Nick on the world of independent producers and make him incapable of hearing the word "package" without flinching.

As they rolled down a long hill, the valve lifters ticking erratically, Stephanie kept her own council: Already it was late April, the summer season was approaching, those three golden months from June through August inclusive, which jacked up the rent on their minuscule apartment from $150 to $650 per month. Their usual custom was to take the summer off, to travel, visit friends, to camp and hike, and twice in the last three years they had crossed the country. For three summers, after the passing moment of anxiety which Stephanie always suffered when faced with homelessness and dislocation, she had pitched in gladly, they'd broken camp and hit the road. But just two weeks earlier she had said to Nick, "Let's use a little of my money this year. After all, that's what it's for. I think David Burston would let us have the beach house in Chatham for only $400 a month."

"Twelve hundred bucks," Nick replied. "That money's for you, not for Burston."

"But I'd like to use it this way. Just the thought of packing up again and living in the Dodge. I want to be here in July, on the Cape, in a home."

They'd reworked the same arid untillable ground so many times before, they automatically stepped to their respective sides—the complicated entails on Stephanie's inheritance were once again opposed by Nick's equally rigid rules about accepting Stephanie's money. Nick had always bent over backwards to duck the inevitable gold-digging charge, which was precisely what Stephanie's father, William Harrold, wanted to believe about him. She felt pinned between these two intent male egos, the men almost oblivious to her, waging a war no one could win.

"Nick, when you said to Carroll how could anyone tell if someone was in the house, you meant how could the burglars tell, didn't you?"

"Yeah. That pissed me off. He thought I was trying to sneak out on him before we even got the job."

"Nick," Stephanie announced definitively, "I want to live in that house."

Outside Providence, Nick shook his head, slapped his cheeks lightly and rubbed his eyes with the back of his hand.

Only half-awake, Stephanie said, "Are you sleepy?"

"No, I'm OK." When he rubbed his eyes again, Nick brushed away the hair at his right temple. By moonlight, the scar had lost its lividness—a sickle-shaped pad of ivory skin just at the hairline, like some tribal memento of how different they were; it was the result of Nick's head-on collision with a Budweiser can in a fight in a parking lot.

Wide-awake now, Stephanie heard again that terrifying phone call: "Steph, don't get upset." She knew from his flat, matter-of-factness that something was hugely, desperately wrong.

"Are you hurt badly?" Stephanie's heart clogged her throat.

"I'm fine. A little cut on the forehead which caused a lot of blood—you know how scalps bleed." No, she didn't

22

know; it was Nick who had experience with such matters. "I'm fine now. They've already stitched it up, no concussion, no visual blur, my head's clear. Fine. Now come down to the hospital and bail me out of here. And, love, please don't be upset. I'm perfectly fine."

Driving like a maniac—downshifting and drifting through corners the way Nick had taught her—Stephanie remembered what his Aunt Mathilda had said: "If he hasn't been taken out by the time he's thirty-five, he'll live to be a hundred." One of the times he almost got taken out was outside Princeton, N.J., on a Triumph 500 motorcycle; a woman in a Chevrolet station wagon made a left turn into his body. The first time was two days after a football game when Nick urinated blood and they discovered a ruptured spleen. "What pissed me off," Nick concluded after relating these comforting bits of personal history to her, "was how well I'd run that day. A couple of good twenty-five-yard scoots and a sixty-three-yard touchdown— You should have seen it, Steph, I made the cut and suddenly my blockers were falling into place the way they do on the blackboard when they're little X's moving at O's in a skull session —the center hit the nearside linebacker, I went right off the ass of the flanker as he pulled even with the short safety, and that left the deep safety who'd been dumb enough to follow the fake. He was leaning to his right, off-balance, and I knew I could outrun him. I actually started to laugh. Unfortunately, they called it back because damned Moose —the center—was offside."

The bulging tires screeched and squealed as Stephanie laid into those corners. All the way she kept rehearsing her excuse for the cop: "My friend's in the hospital, very badly hurt. I've got to get there as fast as I can, officer."

On that wild race to the hospital Stephanie understood that you get to know people only in bits and pieces, which

23

she figured was one of the most enduring appeals of marriage. All that time together. And only time creates the possibility of intimacy. Of course she knew about Nick's juvenile delinquent stage: about his getting drunk and passing out and sleeping all night behind a hedge; about rumbles in the Hot Shoppe parking lot and drag races down Route 301. About his brief notoriety as "One Punch Young" for decking the big dude who came charging at him across the parking lot. ("The guy just couldn't stop," Nick said. "All I did was hold out my fist.") About his slugging the tyrant of a math teacher one week before graduation and having to finish high school in a special course.

The stories had a familiar quality because she'd read the books about J.D.'s and seen the movies and vaguely knew local kids in Rye who were up to the same insane stuff. The stories did shock and titillate her; to some extent, they added to Nick's mystery. But she had never actually lived with the hoodlum Nick because, by the time they got to know each other, even his street-fighting radical days were over and he was into his civilized revolutionary phase.

The emergency room looked as cool and functional as a morgue—all that white and those strange devices that hung down from poles with their gauges and bulbs and tubes, all the squat machines waiting to be wheeled over and plugged in.

She found Nick sitting up on a paper-sheeted hospital bed which crinkled when he moved. The whole right side of his head was bandaged, but what showed looked like uncooked liver.

The Doctor relayed the comforting news: "A half-inch gash in the frontal scalp—a concussion. There's no evidence of a fractured skull, but your friend sustained a very nasty head injury nonetheless. Another quarter of an inch and, who knows, he might not be here, Miss."

24

Nick explained on the way home. He called it "simple": a big white pimp car holding a handsome Eurasian woman, a desire to drive into the supermarket parking lot, yelling to the pimp car to back out of the driveway, and suddenly a tall guy in tapered white slacks, high-heeled leather boots and a black silk shirt swinging at Nick with a fist that turned out to be wrapped around an unopened Budweiser can. Nick figured the guy wouldn't be able to move in his high-heeled boots, so he danced just out of the reach of the swinging arm. "But the arm was mesmerizing me, Steph; I found myself thinking and watching while all this was going on. That's what got me. I kept thinking: What am I doing here? Silly as hell. Meanwhile, this guy is trying to kill me. The thinking slowed me up; then I realized I'd lost my instincts, had no urge to kill, not even to be in the fight. A sitting duck, just dodging and watching, all pure defense. Sock! I heard an ugly sound like suction as he bopped me one on the side of the head. I felt shocked that he'd actually connected. And still I'm watching, taking notes for some fucking journal. Weird. I didn't lay one finger on him. Didn't touch the bastard once." That made Nick furious. "He got me twice and I never touched him. Sick."

To relieve Stephanie's anxiety, if that was possible, Nick explained, "I've got no chance but to reform. If I ever did get into a real fight again, I'd get killed." Nick seemed a little sad and a lot perplexed that he'd lost his killer instincts.

"Oh, and I refused to press charges against Mr. Budweiser can man, which confused the cops who wanted to arrest the guy for 'Assault with a Deadly Weapon.' The pimp was probably even more confused than the cops." But even that pimp wasn't as confused as Stephanie was, having finally caught a glimpse of the old "crazy" Nick.

"Thank god we're home. I feel like my ass is going to fall off."

"You did a lot of driving."

"What time is it?"

"Three o'clock."

"What, about forty-five minutes for dinner, ten minutes for gas and a pit stop? We left at five. Ten hours. That's not bad time."

Stephanie needed a glass of water badly, so she made her way toward the kitchen—the flip side of the living room/dining room/bedroom of their studio. Since Nick stood in the doorway he had to turn sideways to let her by. This created an opportunity for snuggling.

"Want me to roll a joint?"

"Way ahead of you," Stephanie answered.

They changed positions—she squeezed by him to get to the refrigerator, which stood against the back wall. For such emergencies she kept a Marlboro pack full of what she considered elegantly thin joints stashed in the cheese compartment since a stoned hippie had once told her the female plants liked it cool.

She fetched the pack, backed a quarter step and leaned against the counter/cutting board/dish drainer combination. Lighting up, she took a long toke, then chased it with the much needed water. Nick smoked with the ease of a kid who'd been at it since he was ten; which he had. Stephanie looked at his fingernails; they were in pretty good shape.

"Well, tell me, Nicholas, the exquisite farmhouse, yes or no?" She struck a defiant pose, hands on hips, elbows out to the side. She realized she could span the width of their kitchen just by sticking out both arms. But she had to be careful not to thrust too quickly, otherwise she'd break a fingernail—or a finger.

Nick smiled sheepishly, the way he always smiled when wondering how Stephanie would feel about something he said. "What's the matter, you're down on our little love-nest?"

Looking up she saw her cake pans, casserole, pie pans, her one large mold and the blue Arabia platter all stacked up on top of each other. Nick's enlarger crowded the kitchen gear. The pegboard looked like a gallows on a busy weekend in the Old West. The broom handle supported the colander, while the colander held a corkscrew on one foot and tongs on the other.

"I love it here. Really, I've grown quite attached to our squalor."

"It may be squalor, partner, but it's ours." Nick took her in his arms and slowly, in step, they squeezed their way through the doorway out of the kitchen. They couldn't make their first turn until they were in the center of the living/dining area, and by then Stephanie was humming softly, in waltz time, "123, 123, 123."

Next morning at breakfast, Stephanie kicked off the debate again: "Nick, I really want to apply."

"Am I in your way?"

"It would be nicer if you wanted it too."

"What is this, thought control?" He attacked the white of his eggs. "You really must want this place bad."

"I do," she answered solemnly.

Nick looked into her hazel eyes to find that, once again, they'd changed color. More gray in them now— Probably picking up the overcast, he thought. He considered saying something less mean but, finding nothing, went after the white in earnest.

Stephanie watched with finicky dismay as the white quickly receded, leaving an island of yellow in the middle of his plate. Here, she thought, it's coming. Nick scooped up the entire yolk; still whole, he popped it into his mouth.

Stephanie had the odd sense of being back at the beginning of the relationship again, for the differences in their assumptions seemed so starkly outlined. She admitted to herself that her father was right about one thing—the differences between Stephanie's Rye crowd and Nick's family. Her mother, Sarah James Harrold, had been the daughter and only heir of Archibald James, wealthy stockbroker and himself a scion of one of New York's oldest families. Stephanie didn't think of herself as spoiled, but Miss Porter's and NYU weren't exactly the college of hard knocks (her father's alma mater). On the other hand, Nick's mother is a lush, his father the kind of guy who gets his kicks from knocking his sons around and spends his hours away from the container factory in front of the tube downing one cold one after another. Nick had propelled his way through high school and college by working summers in the container factory and taking an extended apprenticeship in the restaurant trade—dishwasher, busboy, waiter, finally maître d'. He made a very early decision not to be like his parents; after a particularly horrendous summer punching holes in shipping cartons, he decided to escape the production line by getting an education. At age thirteen, having been a devout, tremulous Catholic from the day he could talk, Nick had an argument with a friend who said you couldn't prove there was a god. The friend won. In church a few days later, Nick saw the light, got up and walked out in the middle of Mass and hadn't had a believer's thought since.

When they were still getting to know each other, Stephanie felt, in a way that later seemed ridiculously romantic and unfair to Nick, that he had created himself. She made him heroic, larger than life, a conception that impressed and titillated the spoiled princess in her. Nick resisted her idealization as well as he could, which only made Stephanie appreciate him more. In 1973, when she first got to know him working on the moratorium to end the war,

28

Nick's sense of himself and his sense of purpose seemed like a raging forest fire beside the pallid flames of Stephanie's upper-class friends. Nick had grown up at the front, he didn't have to commute in from the suburbs. He not only fought with police, he knew how to fight. Or used to. In the beginning, though, she had to admit she didn't take to Nick. Henry Brewer, who has that talent for the offhand that many taciturn people cultivate, had introduced them with, "I thought you might like each other." They didn't. Nick had been sounding off about Great Neck liberals; Stephanie had the wit to interrupt, "But I'm from Rye." Still, moth to flame—it was never clear who played what to whom in that dance—they drew closer. On issues at meetings they found themselves in passionate agreement. Personally, it was otherwise. He made it rough on her by insisting that her background was too safe. She had, Nick insisted with a slightly lecherous smile, "been victimized by too much protection." Stephanie had never seen herself as being overly protected until this intense, nice-looking guy held up his undistorting mirror and she saw herself from another perspective. She couldn't really argue with what she saw, though she did tell Nick that his coming on so tough was a way of capitalizing on his street credentials. Still, almost from the beginning, she believed in him. He had none of the grubby greediness of the hard-way-up school, and even then he had a sense of humor. Between ideological harangues, he always made her laugh.

"OK, OK," Nick said early the next morning. "I can't hold out any longer." His laugh wiped out a weekend of tedious argument. Stephanie felt overjoyed as she called Philadelphia to say they'd take the job—if it was offered to them. She felt absolutely certain that they'd win the housesitting sweepstakes. Eight days later, the secretary called. An older couple had been selected. She sounded genuinely sorry they'd lost. Stephanie moped for three days; she couldn't really believe her fantasy was over. On the fourth day Bradford Carroll called. There'd been a problem with the older couple, something about her teaching schedule and the timing of their arrival. Would they accept the year in Bucks County? She hugged Nick while trying to figure out where to store their three sticks of furniture. Nick suggested a bonfire.

Last Days on Cape Cod

Nick stood ankle deep in water, his jeans rolled up to his knees. He touched his newly cultivated mustache—coal black, and still quite scraggly. She liked the way it hung down over his upper lip. Nick was very thin, wiry rather than slight, with absolutely no belly and a compact, squared off behind which she loved. His black hair was long, a little dirty and even more scraggly than the mustache. His eyes matched his hair and so did his eyebrows, which were thick and set off surprisingly fair skin and delicate, small features. Nick was just the handsome side of pretty.

"We're going," he said. "We've agreed on that. But you still got to ask why were we chosen. Because Carroll thought you were cute? Because I pulled my inspired number about the stereo?"

"Don't be paranoid."

"They're the ones who're paranoid. You want to be plunked down dead center in exurban paranoia? What kind of folks are slaves to their gear? Imagine what it's like, one of us in the house all the time. I mean, you're a nice girl, we like each other a lot, sure the shots of the farmhouse looked great, but this has got to be a classic formula for paranoia. I think you just want to live in a fancy-assed house for a year."

"Not just any fancy-assed house."

"The last time the Bergers went out together was October 12, 1963, the day before they bought their Picasso."

Stephanie didn't let herself smile. "Nick, I don't have any real objections to beauty. Do you?"

Nick retreated back toward her; the tide was coming in.

"I admit I like the idea of my own trout stream. But I wish I knew more about the owners. Who knows, maybe these Bergers don't exist. Maybe they're just figments of that slick weirdo Carroll's kinky head. Maybe they just want to use us as a tax deduction. You want to be some fart's tax deduction?" Embarrassed, they both said nothing more.

A step ahead of Nick and dry legged, Stephanie recognized that the debate about the housesitting was, as these things usually are, a debate about them—policy questions about who they were, what they'd been doing and where they were heading. Up to the moment of their interview in Carroll's office, she really had been enjoying the plant store and their laidback low-profile existence on the Cod. If she bitched about the minuscule apartment, she still loved its location: at the wide end of an egg-shaped inlet where, just now, they watched a candy-striped sunset being blotted up by a hungry gray sky. Stephanie hadn't revised her opinion of her father's last phone call, when he'd asked: "What are you two doing with yourselves?" (Meaning, their career paths.) She still sloughed off her father's bullshit as part of his own problem. She didn't want any of his scrambling nine lives. Besides, she didn't think they were goofing off. She knew damned well that, when the time came, she and Nick—individually or collectively—would get the requisite act together. But on the drive back from Philadelphia Stephanie reminded herself that she was almost thirty. She'd reached the point in existence where things get serious.

The offer of a temporary new life dropped out of the sky just at the right moment. And now she felt it was time for both of them to get moving again. Perhaps she did want to lay out their differences on that gorgeous cherry table in the dining room of the Bucks County farmhouse to see if Nick was made for her and she for him.

Two weeks before their scheduled departure from Woods Hole, the manila folder arrived from Philadelphia. It contained:

1) a map, with directions from Woods Hole to Doylestown, Pennsylvania, just off the Pennsylvania Turnpike, then on through a maze of back roads, tight forks and quick rights and lefts onto country lanes till, bingo, the dreamhouse.

2) various functional instructions: how to light the water heater; how to operate washer and dryer, dishwasher and garbage disposal; where to buy air conditioner filters; "reputable" grocer's name; name and location of bank where their monthly checks might be deposited; home phones of the head gardener and maid, a doctor and dentist; a sheaf of directions on how to operate the trapshooting machine (so easy Leonardo could do it, Stephanie said).

3) Nick's favorite—a wine list which gave the floor plan of the vintages' positions in the cellar—Burgundy, red, to

the left of the door; white, to the right. They were assigned certain bottles that had "matured" as well as a number of "special treats for special occasions."

4) Stephanie's favorite—a handsome illustrated hand-printed catalogue of the Bergers' art collection. The only other copy, the instructions indicated, was in France with the Bergers. On paper, the collection looked beautiful and outrageously expensive. Nick calculated that its value was well over $25,000,000. They were bonded for $1,000,000.

5) A brief cool note from Carroll which said, "Enjoy your stay in Bucks County. You are privileged indeed to live with these beautiful objects. If you do have any questions, please do not hesitate to phone." (He listed three phone numbers.) "In any case, I will be in touch."

Their last days in Woods Hole were splendid. Everyone at the plant store wished Stephanie well. They touched a lot. They ran through a medley of their favorite Cape Cod activities: flew Indian fighter kites at Truro, trying to cut off each other's tails; they ran down the dunes, went clamming, soaked up multicolored sunsets, reminisced, spent time together. Nick kept up minimal grumblings to keep their life from getting too goopy. Perhaps they both had a sense of the squalls ahead in Big Bucks County.

Nicholas composed a poem for their departure.

As we get ready to leave the Cod
Without so much as a backward nod,
Let it be said if all goes great
That my beloved Stephanie chose our fate.
But, if Lord forbid, it don't work out so hot,
Remember that this dude resisted to the end.
(Which doesn't rhyme but does make a hell of a lot of sense.)

Nicholas insisted on going on record just one last time.

Big Bucks County

The car didn't fight the curves, it eased itself through that lush, rolling green acreage. "Like somebody memorable once said"—Nick nodded at a thousand-shade green field—"it gives a guy green indigestion." But she could tell he liked the lay of Bucks County. It was hard to resist. Farms were ruled into loamy black rectangles; soft, inviting fields of grass lay stretched like costly fabrics over the ground. Elegant horses, all legs and high clearance, luminous Black Angus and red suede prime beef and sheep like bleached snow were picturesquely arranged in the landscape. Weathered rail or tidy white board fences or honey-gray and brown fieldstone walls accented the rise and fall of the land. Every square inch had a cultivated, managed look. Stephanie felt pleasantly manipulated, gently turned on by their easy progress through the lush scene. Man's hand had been everywhere here, but the hand left no prints, no smudges. Everything—thick leafy oak and shadowy elm, cropped fruit trees, framed views, pedigreed beasts—hummed of careful breeding and whispered the soft rustling sound of money. Obviously hayricks of money had made and kept the land this way. Money insulated this place from haste and ugliness and noise and all the predictables of suburban squalor.

Stephanie realized that they did not know how the Bergers made their money. "Nick, how do you think the Bergers earn a living?"

"Deviousness. Pillage."

Although she had reservations about how this margin was come by and maintained, Stephanie could not quibble with the quality of the maintenance job. In Bucks County, she found it possible to breathe.

"Big Bucks," Nick growled cheerfully, and she could see that he loved to guide the car around the long slow curves.

Map in hand, manila folder on the seat between them, Stephanie commanded, "Turn right here."

"Ay, ay."

The turn took them off a state highway onto a country road wide enough for only one and a half cars. Pullovers had been provided every fifty yards or so: the last leg of their journey.

"It's all so goddamn neat and clean."

"Crisp, Nicholas."

"Yeah, like laundered bills."

At a blind corner, they slowed and cut back sharply to the right. The road dipped, leading down to a stone bridge over an appropriately lively stream. They were warned:

CAUTION

FLASH FLOODS

He eased the car to a stop just beyond the bridge, and they got out for a closer look and a final pause before entering the life of the Bergers. Below the bridge, the stream dropped over a rock ledge into a dense oak woods, the only mysterious place he'd seen in Bucks County. Nick found it a happy relief from all that clarity. "That's what's been missing. They've bred out all the wild and the mystery.

This little bit could have a fence around it too." They leaned over the railing, staring into the woods. The oaks were huge, gnarled, ugly, almost comic in their ferocity.

"Do you think all of Bucks County once looked this way?"

"I don't know."

"You don't?" Nick began half-jokingly. "You read all the guidebooks: Washington's Crossing State Park; Doylestown, the county seat; New Hope, artists' colony and the Delaware Canal." As he spoke, his voice acquired an edge. The anticipation was getting to him. "I thought you were our self-styled Bucks County expert?"

"Not quite yet," she replied quietly.

They stood awhile longer in silence, gazing distractedly down into the water. If they could've read their future in that incessantly provoked pool, if the stirring unquiet water had offered up a vision of the overlay of lies and betrayals through which they'd wander until left marooned on the beaches of themselves, if—

She had the feeling there was much to say, but no words came. Finally Nick got impatient: "Let's go check out paradise."

Back in the car and hastily up the hill, across a flat series of fields, through a grove of beech trees, then, Stephanie looked up from the map as they turned into a private road marked BERGER. A double row of pin oaks formed a long gallery that led them down a lazy slope. Halfway down the lane, she saw the farmhouse, which looked even more appealing in living color. Two enormous elms stood off to one side of the house, which was smaller and less imposing than Stephanie had supposed. That trick of scale endeared it to her immediately. "Nick, it's a very beautiful house."

"Not bad," he replied, sounding happy to be there. Stephanie relaxed with relief, only then realizing how tense the last part of the trip had been. She loosened her seat belt and leaned toward Nick. She gave him a long, very loaded kiss, a kiss of love and affection and for good luck. Stephanie clung to him, savoring his lips, a few hundred yards away from the smooth white gravel carpark, trying to say, "You'll love it, Nick. It's important for us to start in step here." She laid out her soul in that kiss; she wanted to supply the momentum they needed to enjoy this foreign place.

The gray fieldstone looked warm and inviting—the walls soft, touchable, a little crumbly like an aged cheddar cheese. The day was brilliantly clear, but she could picture how the luminous honey-gray rock would look on rainy days, always slightly brighter than the sky. The low front door had a dark wood lintel above and a footworn sill for its single front step. The windows of the upper story appeared smaller than those on the ground floor—downstairs there were eight-pane windows, upstairs six. The window trim was white, which helped bring out the fine, certain lines of the farmhouse. The only imposing feature was a tall brick chimney which anchored one end of the house. The slate roof that overhung the second floor suggested a gray, well-worn felt hat. Light blue clematis drifted down over the front door. Stephanie thought the farmhouse an absolute dream.

To get a feeling of how the whole place fit together, they circled the house once, then entered. From the photograph Stephanie couldn't tell how huge that fireplace was, or how the massive timber mantel had been eaten away on the underside by the heat. The still photo didn't catch the weight and beauty of those fitted stones—all lustrous honey-grays and earth-browns. She loved the inglenook, that heavy steel bread-oven door. If Nick hadn't been with her, Stephanie would've stayed in front of the fireplace all afternoon. Instead, together they took the compulsory breathless tour—stood in front of the Cézanne landscape, a vibrant Rothko, and those large Matisse cutouts, which Matisse, they later learned, made with scissors while sitting at a table when he could no longer stand up to paint. They stood sheepishly in front of the late Turner in which a burning red-yellow sun turned the sky and water—the whole world, it appeared—into a giant reflector of colored light, a kaleidoscope so vivid and subtly blended that it was impossible to tell which colors were underpaint and which overlaid. Light augmented light as it might have at the world's creation. So they stood, ignorantly and in awe, in front of that violent ecstatic act of universal lovemaking. There were dozens of paintings, more paintings than they'd ever seen outside of a museum painted by names they'd never heard of in styles they couldn't fathom with points of view and contents undreamt of. They stood and wagged ignorant heads and felt intimidated, small and ignorant.

What a relief for them to go outside and poke around the miniature palace of a guest house, walk the footpath to the skeet range which was laid out so that you shot away from the house into the soft red clay of the facing ridge. The bright red barn stood on higher ground, three stories high, with massive rough-cut beams and an intricate truss ceiling and all the farm tools hung in graduated sizes on a giant panel—a huge pegboard to hold objects ranging in size from old threshing machines, reapers, and a cider press to scythes, rakes, shovels and yokes down to oilcans, clippers, and pruning shears. Nick insisted that the lawn wasn't grass but "turf, probably a foot and a half thick. Perfect for whiffleball." This turf delighted the feet—thicker than the plushest carpet, springy, cool, alive.

They found themselves embedded, like a couple of those fireplace boulders, in someone else's meticulously detailed, completed realized dreamworld. She looked forward, with some awe and a little less fear, to coming to know the feeling and spirit, the moods and demeanor of this marvelous place. Nick felt more tentative.

Turning back toward the house, Stephanie spotted the swimming pool. She walked over to the edge for a closer inspection. "Think it's clean?" she asked.

"Looks it. But let me check my notes." Whipping out the manila envelope like a camp counselor, Nick led Stephanie to the pump house, a stone structure built into the hill's slope. The pump house was listed as the oldest building on the Bergers' property, built in 1643.

"You know, this is the real thing." It wasn't the elaborate pool toys, the striped floats or outsized inner tubes that caught Nick's eye as he stood there in the filtered half light. "These walls are two feet thick, Stephanie. And they encased that pump housing in concrete and sunk it below the floor. Know why?"

"No."

"To cut down the noise and vibration. We probably won't be able to hear it at the pool."

Outside, where they undressed, all they heard was the stream and the bobwhites and the chattering of teams of kamikaze swallows.

A Walk in the Woods

"Let's go," Nick urged as he impatiently watched Stephanie lace up her new Dunham boots. "We don't have much time." He felt a bit uneasy about leaving the house unoccupied.

She looked up and smiled.

"Come on, let's go while there's still some light."

They walked uphill past the pump house and swimming pool, entering the woods on a path that followed the stream. It had rained the night before, so the trees were wet and glistening, the ground soft. The late afternoon sun threw gold coins onto Stephanie's shoulders and into her hair. Nick thought she looked particularly beautiful.

"We haven't had a date in a long time, pal."

"It's so quiet here. And so private."

They kissed and, holding hands, walked upstream. The path narrowed, and Nick let her go on ahead.

"Isn't this the same stream we passed on our way in so long ago?"

"Yes," Nick replied.

They had walked about half a mile when they saw the skeletal shape of an enormous tree. It stood off to the right on higher ground.

"What is it?"

"An elm," she said. "A dead one."

"I can see that. What happened to it?"

"A fungus. It's spread by a beetle. They don't know how to stop it."

"God, it's ugly. It's like a black-and-white photograph, in the midst of all this color."

The stark white silhouette emphasized the tree's symmetry; the two equal boughs branched low to the ground.

"Imagine if they lost those elms on the lawn. Maybe I ought to take it down."

"Do you know how to do that?"

"No," Nick admitted. "But I remember Henry telling me he used to cut down trees all the time when he was clearing the land in Maine. Maybe when he comes down—"

"The gardener could do it."

"I want to do it myself."

Nick led her away from the stream back into the woods. After climbing over fallen logs and holding bushes out of each other's way, they came to an overgrown dirt road.

"You know where you're going, Nick?"

"I've been running along here. Know where it comes out?"

"I've haven't a clue."

"You'll see."

A quarter of a mile farther on, she saw the back of the barn. "It's a semicircle. I'm impressed."

They came out of the woods just above the barn. The light had shifted to uniform gray, without an apparent source. They stood looking down the gently sloping lawn toward the row of pin oaks until Nick spotted a figure moving around the side of the pump house.

"Hold it, Steph." He gently pulled her into the shadow of the barn. They watched as the man paused and seemed to study the sky. He walked into the pump house and reappeared a moment later carrying what looked like a cup. Moving a little haltingly, he walked over to the lilac tree. He reached up and pulled down a branch, touched a bloom, then let the branch spring back. He circled the tree, brushing the branches out of his way and peering closely at the trunk. He walked unsteadily to the side of the pump house and turned on the outside faucet. Finally he drank from the garden hose.

"I don't think he's dangerous, he's so out in the open. But let's go check it out."

"Hey!" Nick yelled as they started down the slope.

The man slowly turned and took them in with a long measuring look.

"What are you doing here?"

The man, who was at least sixty, wore an old houndstooth jacket with Budweiser bottle caps for buttons. The pencil mustache had been rolled and waxed, his scalp positively gleamed under the one-eighth inch of crewcut hair. His black paratrooper boots had been spit shined, his green fatigues scrupulously pressed. The man's nose alone bore no hint of military comportment, but it broadcast the continued humiliating treatment it had received from Clan MacGregor Scotch whiskey.

"Are you Stephanie Harrold?" the old man asked.

Surprised, Stephanie replied, "Yes."

"You Nick Young?"

Nick nodded.

"I thought one of you was supposed to be on the premises all the time?"

Stephanie answered, "Who are you?"

"Massey, Russell Massey's the name. I make the lawn here." Massey kept his head turned to the side as he spoke.

"Oh, the gardener," Nick said. "Glad to meet you."

Massey said nothing.

"I thought you were supposed to come on Friday."

"Friday ain't enough. Got too much work to do."

Nick recognized Massey's problem then. The averted head and thick speech tipped him off. "OK, Mr. Massey, we'll see you on Friday. We've got to put dinner together."

He took her arm and walked Stephanie to the farmhouse. Inside, she said, "What the hell was that about?"

"He was absolutely loaded. That's why he kept his head turned away."

"Is he going to be here all the time?"

"You heard the man. Friday ain't enough."

"I don't like him, Nick."

The Garden

"Actually," Stephanie said a few days after their run-in with the gardener, "there is something I really need. You may think I'm crazy, but a little herb garden would make this place perfect."

"I thought it was already paradise." Nick sounded only a little facetious. He basked in the June sun at the edge of the heated pool. At last glance the pool thermometer read seventy-six degrees.

"Fresh basil for pesto, thyme, rosemary, tarragon for the chicken you like, handfuls of fresh dill. It'll save us a few dollars and I'd like to leave the Bergers something. And

Nick, we could start an asparagus patch. You've always loved fresh asparagus."

"But it won't produce for two, three years."

"It'll be our gift to them. A memento of our being here."

"It would be a great idea if this goddamn lawn wasn't such a big deal. Did you see the gardener—"

"Massey."

"—fussing over edging the lawn near the flower beds? I thought he was going to kiss the roots."

"He's weird. Spooky."

"Did you see his nose when he bent over—all that ninety-proof rushing to it?" Russell Massey had a gross carbuncle for a nose and a surprisingly literate mind only very slowly erasing itself. "When I offered him a beer he said, 'Never drink on the job.' "

"I'll bet he wears the paratrooper boots to bed."

"Well, he may be a drunk but he's no dumbie. Did you hear what he asked me? If I knew anything about oenology? I thought he was talking about masturbation."

"Wine," she said.

"I got it, I got it."

"Nick," she said, returning to her original question, "we can't be expected to live in a house for a whole year without making a few improvements."

"Let's wait and see what Massey says before I start digging up his turf."

"You know he'll say no. Just think," Stephanie continued, "real, live, red, unplastic tomatoes that have dirt on them and don't come in a box. Fresh garden tomatoes!"

"Let's go find us a place to dig." Nick knew they were asking for trouble.

Starting from the pump house, they walked down the east slope, the farmhouse on their left.

"The slope's too steep," Stephanie said as they stood by the magnificent old lilac tree.

"And the elms throw too much shade this way in the morning."

They continued down the lawn alongside the edged flowerbeds of tea roses, delphinium, and carnations. In the front yard they stood on the fieldstone walk facing the farmhouse.

"Can we put it here, Nick?"

"Too late, pal. This yard's already laid out for whiffleball." Nick pointed along the stone wall that ran past the house up the west slope. "Anything that hits the stone wall is fair down the right-field line; the ridge"—he jerked his thumb over his right shoulder in the direction of the trap range. Behind him to the left lay the carpark and beyond it the pin-oak–lined drive—"works as a natural backstop, and home runs to straightaway center have to hit the roof in the air. The elms are ground-rule doubles."

"What about triples? You have to knock out a window?"

"You got it."

They circled the west side of the farmhouse. "No afternoon sun," Stephanie concluded.

They followed the stone-wall right-field foul line up the hill past the intricate rock garden and the flowering crab and pear trees. The hill kept its steep incline all the way up to the barn, which sat on level ground. Just beyond the huge red barn, at the very edge of the lawn, Nick stopped: "Here, à la Brigham Young, I'll plant."

"Isn't it a little out of the way?"

"It's a south slope and the drainage looks good; it won't be shaded by the barn. And it's the only spot that maybe won't get Massey on our asses."

The next morning clamorous birds woke Nick early. Feeling virtuous, he slipped out of bed mumbling, "Early to bed, early to rise." He left Stephanie sleeping soundly and was out at the excavation site by 7:30. Friday was Massey's scheduled working day, and Nick wanted to have the entire plot turned over before the gardener appeared.

The warm sun streaming through the slender casement woke Stephanie at eight. After preparing two cappuccinos, she walked up the hill.

"Looks great." She admired the thick black clods of earth with their dense green tops. "You want a break?" She held out a big white mug.

"Let me just finish this corner." As Nick pulled up on the pitchfork, the roots gave way grudgingly. She watched the muscles of his chest knot, his triceps tense as his biceps relaxed. Sweat plastered his black hair to his forehead.

"You look so hot."

"Feels good," he grunted.

Minutes later, as they sat at the edge of the ten-by-ten-foot patch, they heard Massey drive up.

"Nick, let's bring him up here."

"Beat him to it?"

"Yes."

"Good idea. You go get him. I'll take that break."

"We'd like to show you something, Mr. Massey."

Stephanie led Massey east around the farmhouse, skirting the pool. As soon as Massey spotted Nick up near the barn, he broke into a wide-stanced, crablike trot. At the edge of the dig, he suddenly stopped and, breathing heavily, stared down at turned-over dirt. "What did you do?"

"We're making a vegetable garden." Nick tried to sound innocent, but it wasn't easy.

"Can't believe it." Massey moaned as he bent over to pick up a handful of black soil, then let it drop slowly through his fingers. He trembled with true feeling, his emotional equivalent of the d.t.'s. "You destroyed one hundred square foot of this country's finest sod." Massey's perpetually red eyes teared. Stephanie, who'd just come up alongside them, expected him to fling himself down like Laertes.

They stood dumbly. "Knew you was trouble when you weren't here that first day. Knew it when you offered me a beer on the job."

"Oh come on, Mr. Massey," Stephanie said. "Nick was only being polite."

Massey wouldn't look at them, only down at his vanished turf. "Knew you was solid rotten when you left the pool rake out."

That had been Nick's fault. The evening before Massey came to cut the grass, Nick had conscientiously cleaned the pool. Unfortunately, he'd left the rake out overnight, and Massey had found it the next morning.

Now Massey was saying, "Spoiled nit! No business here. No business digging up my whole lawn."

Stephanie almost laughed. They'd cut a tiny ten-by-ten patch of earth, and beyond that little smudged corner acres of lawn stretched up and down the gentle hill like a fitted green vest. If she had said, "I did it," Massey would've been disappointed. This was strictly a male confrontation. Nick wore that expression he got when he felt he'd done something wrong.

This second black mark cut their relations with Russell Massey to a barely civil minimum. Stephanie didn't care much, but it bothered Nick a lot. She realized then that Nick would be lonely in Bucks County. The first day Massey cut the grass, Nick had spent more time than she would've expected with the old buzzard asking about various kinds of grass seed and the way turf was best built up and maintained. In the pre–Bucks County days, he'd never shown the slightest interest. Nick insisted that he was simply collecting information about the Bergers, which he was.

Obviously, Nick also liked company. More than she did. And now the only regular visitor with whom Nick could communicate (both maids spoke Spanish) despised him.

For Massey, the vegetable patch simply confirmed a prejudice. Massey had his doubts because Nick obviously cared about Massey's opinion. The old man wasn't used to such coddling from the lord of the manor.

William Harrold

The moment Nick spotted the automobile, he rocked tensely forward onto his toes. Behind him the stream, usually so soothing, seemed to intensify its incessant liquid babble. Stephanie stood beside him, her elbows held out away from her body; she didn't want to stain the armpits of her new blouse.

"Christ, I hope it goes all right."

"Why shouldn't it?" Nick asked impatiently.

Stephanie disagreed: "The last time— Just don't get into politics."

As the Lancia passed in and out of the dark shadows thrown by the pin oaks, it glinted on and off like an electric sign. Nick wondered if William Harrold signaled his daughter in semaphore: "Money! Power!"

Aloud he said, "He certainly didn't waste any time getting down here."

"We've been here over a month. He has to see what our place is like."

"He still wants to believe you're his little girl."

"Nick," she said shortly, "I invited him." But both knew they couldn't have kept William Harrold away.

The silver car descended the slope below, then came steadily up toward them. Seventeen thousand bucks, Nick considered. Eighteen coats of hand-rubbed lacquer. Somehow it isn't stodgy. Must be the only four-door in the world that isn't. *Road and Track* listed its top speed at 160 miles an hour.

William Harrold eased the gleaming silver car in alongside their pathetic old gray Dodge, which made the peeling paint on the hood look all the more scabrous. Even Nick felt a little embarrassed. The antenna on the Lancia retracted, the windows went up, the door locks snapped into down position, then William Harrold lifted his fingers off the control panel and disembarked from the car. He turned and locked his door. The chores done, the father charged at the daughter, stopped a foot short of Stephanie and enveloped her in his massive arms. Nick stood awkwardly by, watching William Harrold's fierce pugnacious face remit for an instant.

Mr. Harrold turned away again and fished an expensive-looking maroon leather bag out of the carpeted trunk of the car. He handed the bag to Nick as he finally said, "Hello."

"Hello," Nick replied as they started toward the house.

"Very nice Merion blue you've got here. But it's cut awfully close. Do you take care of the yard?"

"No, a gardener comes with the place."

"Massey." Stephanie almost said "Daddy." "I wrote you about Massey the gardener."

"Oh yes, bottle-cap buttons and nose to match. Is that it?"

William Harrold halted abruptly on the flagstone walk to survey the farmhouse. Nick almost climbed up his back. "What is it, late-seventeenth, early-eighteenth century?"

"Yes. That's about right."

"The kitchen addition came later."

Stephanie nodded agreement. Nick wondered if William Harrold dated the house from sight or if he'd remembered a letter of Stephanie's.

"How long did it take to get down, Daddy?"

Nick never heard that word without it stirring his deepest class feeling. "Daddy" contained everything about them that he despised and felt threatened by. He changed the subject, trying to keep calm. "Did you have a good trip?"

"On the highway I kept it at seventy-three. It's criminal driving that car in the States, especially in the East. I use the CB because I have to with this monster, though the sound quality's terrible and I've got too many good buddies out there. Do you have a set?"

"I can't get that heap over sixty."

"Unsafe at any speed." As soon as it was out, Stephanie knew she shouldn't have said it.

"You need a new car."

"Can't afford it." Nick answered for them.

William Harrold looked away, toward the pool.

"How's Mildred?"

His features hardened. "The same." William Harrold could've been a Mongol brigand. He remembered himself, "She's fine. She had a tournament today. Otherwise, she'd have come down."

A lie, Nick reckoned. Stephanie and her stepmother hated each other.

"But you wouldn't have made such good time then."

"No," William Harrold smiled. "Couldn't have done it under three hours with Mildred along."

50

The tailor had done everything possible to attenuate the blocklike form, but not even the soft shoulders and the considered fall of the fawn jacket softened the powerful body. There was nothing genteel in that swaggering walk.

Inside, William Harrold first peeked into the kitchen. "Is that a stock going?" He looked at his daughter affectionately.

"Fish stock."

"Her mother was a fine cook. How about a beer? I'd love a beer."

"Certainly," Nick said. At least he got the chance to play host. "What would you like, Beck's, Heineken, Michelob?"

"Beck's. What do they get for imported beer here?"

"Sixty-five, seventy cents a bottle."

"Only give him one, Nick. I don't want him filling up. We have a nice *Auxey-Duresse* for lunch." For the first time William Harrold looked impressed.

"Stephanie, let me in on the secret—what's for lunch?"

"Absolutely not." All her father's chumminess was getting to her.

William Harrold laid his arm on Stephanie's shoulder as she steered him into the living room. He squared off in front of the Rothko to take its measure. "Very fine. Excellent." He passed on to the Turner. "Impressive. Very impressive." To the Maillol. "Handsome. Quite handsome." He chased this final opinion with a long swig of Beck's. "Thank god there are no Impressionists."

"These cutouts are nice," he said a few feet farther on. "But I've seen better displays. It's very hard to get light in here, the ceiling's so low. They ought to have mirrors, pick up what light they've got and throw it around a bit. In the Paris Museum of Modern Art, the old one, not Beaubourg, the whole Jazz sequence is laid out horizontally, Stephanie. Each cutout is in a separate case about waist high. As you

51

walk along you feel like you're turning the pages. You see them from the same angle he saw them as he worked." Another massive slug at the Beck's; the glass was now two-thirds empty.

Nick had never felt qualified to criticize anything about the Bergers' arrangements. To him every object they owned, every decision they'd made seemed impeccable. To his surprise, Nick felt tempted to defend his patrons' taste.

"The fireplace looks modeled after early Benjamin Thompson. He published his designs as Count von Rumford; he actually was knighted by an Austrian prince for keeping the prince's toes warm." He paused for appreciative laughter, but hearing none, he continued more somberly. "The stonework's exceptional. Really the finest thing around here." William Harrold ran his fingers over the courses, impressed by the size, match and quality of the fieldstone. "Yes, it's a lovely place you've landed in."

He took a short quick sip, then tipped up the pilsner glass and drained it. Foam tipped the side of his sizable mouth. Nick thought William Harrold looked like a satyr. Must be confusing to have a guy like this for a father.

"Daddy, don't drink so quickly." She looked at Nick as though to say, I'm sorry. But you've got to get used to my calling him that. That's what I've always called him.

"Like Uncle George used to say, 'I'm thirsty as hell.' "

Father and daughter laughed together at the obscure family joke.

The trapshooting was scheduled for eleven, which would give Stephanie time to finish up her lunch preparations. She had insisted they divide the visit into strict time periods. "It's like school," Nick had mocked. "You ought to loan me your watch." But she'd known her father well enough to understand that he became most vicious when he was bored.

They stopped in front of the locked gun case. William Harrold looked in. "A Remington 870, Winchester 101—is that bored?"

"What a question to ask your host."

The satyr's face turned mock scornful. "A technical, not a personal question."

"Yes, the barrel's bored out." Nick unlocked the case.

"May I—?" Without waiting for a reply William Harrold reached in and pulled out the Orvis twenty-gauge over-and-under shotgun. "This stock looks hand built." He ran his fingers along the butt.

"Hand built," Nick agreed. "Maybe you can use it. It's too long for me."

William Harrold's arms were even shorter than Nick's. "You could cut a piece off the butt end—if you owned the piece."

"I don't," said Nick simply.

"Choose your weapon, Daddy." Actually William Harrold's aggressive reply relieved Stephanie a little. She never trusted her father when he was being charming.

As the two men crossed the springy turf, William Harrold held a second Beck's under his armpit, the pilsner glass in his hand while the shotgun, its breech open, was casually draped in the crook of his elbow. The gun pointed toward Nick.

Nick didn't feel intimidated by William Harrold's intelligence or decisiveness or even his encyclopedic knowledge of building styles and paintings and shotguns. What mystified and unsettled Nick was their ineradicable closeness, that built-in biological proximity from which he was excluded.

"I want to see that infamous garden of yours."

They swung up the slope and stopped at the sheer edge

of the garden plot, a dark rectangular stain at the edge of the green carpet. The lettuce and the scallions were just beginning to peep up.

"Did Stephanie say you were not getting along with gardener? What's his name? Irish?"

"Massey. We don't get along."

William Harrold dropped easily onto his haunches, putting down glass and bottle and resting the shotgun against his knee. He reached out over the edge to measure the depth of the grass roots. "Jesus, man. Must be eight inches thick. The garden's a nice idea, but this turf is as fine as any in Scotland. Or England. Must've taken forty years to build up this pad. I can see why your Massey's a little testy." Then William Harrold sprang up and asked, "Where's the shooting?"

The little grass that still remained in front of the concrete bunker was trampled down. "You shoot into the clay of the ridge." Nick pointed at the steep red ridge. "No worry about ricochet."

"Very sensible," William Harrold approved. "The Bergers seem like competent human beings."

Nick flipped through the labeled keys and opened the bunker's low door. He was glad he'd remembered to lock up. Inside, in the cool half-light, Mr. Harrold almost tripped over Nick's foot treadle.

"Let me get this out of your way."

"What in the world is it?"

"My foot treadle. I couldn't shoot alone, and since Stephanie doesn't like to—"

That drew a sour look from William Harrold.

"So I rigged up this treadle." Mr. Harrold, on his haunches again, ran his hand down the long aluminum pole. "I know it's a really ridiculous-looking machine. On the other hand, it works."

Extending from the handle of the trap itself was a large U-shaped piece of metal, and the U-shaped piece was attached to the long aluminum pole. The pole, which resembled a drive shaft, ran along the floor to the door. Another section of pole lay at the door. This piece, when fitted into the long pole, ran out of the door to a spot in front of the bunker, where the entire device terminated in a bicycle pedal. When Nick pushed the pedal, the pole rotated a full circle; the U-shaped piece, translating this rotation, did a full turn, which released the trap's handle and threw the clay pigeon (or pigeons—the trap could hold two) into the air. Each time the trap was sprung Nick had to go back inside the bunker to reload, crank the handle down, and cock the trap. So he could never take more than two shots. But, as he'd said to Stephanie, that was better than not shooting at all.

"Rube Goldberg would feel encouraged," William Harrold offered ambiguously. "Isn't it dangerous?"

"I stand alongside it. It can't throw directly to the side." Nick let Mr. Harrold contemplate the odds for a moment. "But to tell you the truth, I'd rather not use it now. I'll release from the inside, OK?"

William Harrold readily agreed. "OK."

It was cool and damp and quiet inside the bunker, very private. Nick felt tempted to release a pair of pigeons before William Harrold called. But he didn't. Through the pane of bulletproof glass that ran almost the entire length of the bunker, Nick could observe most of the shots. William Harrold stood easily, the shotgun resting on his hip. He snapped the gun into shooting position with an accomplished movement.

"Whenever you're ready," Nick yelled.

"Just want a practice shot. See how the baby shoots."

"A little to the right and high."

"Bird!" William Harrold called.

Nick, who'd already cocked the trap's handle, pulled the cord.

The pigeon hurtled out over William Harrold's head with a prolonged swoosh! The shotgun snapped up onto his shoulder, he sighted, the boom sounded and one pigeon was instantaneously atomized.

"Cleaned it!" Nick heard William Harrold mutter. "So much for that barrel. Can you give me two?"

"When you're ready," Nick called.

"Bird!" A short sharp strangled cry.

As Nick released again, he thought, America's great. Takes less than a generation to make a gent. That's what the U.S. gave the rest of the world—the feeling that aristocrats are made, not born. Give people enough leisure and they all can play polo and shoot trap.

"Bird!"

The almost simultaneous reports, and two more birds shattered in the air.

"Keep 'em coming, Nick."

Inside, Nick could tell how happy William Harrold felt.

The sounds Stephanie heard—the gun's rhythmic boom and the periodic command, "Bird!"—were softened by the distance. They're both armed, she thought and smiled nervously. A duel in my honor.

She measured the dry mustard into the blender, added one-third of the cup of olive-oil and peanut-oil mixture, then turned on the motor. Drop by drop she poured in the oil. Her mother's lovely face formed and dissolved in her mind.

He never discusses anything emotional with me. Now he's so out of practice he doesn't remember what emotions are. Mother was the only one who could reach him, she thought. She warned herself not to idealize her dead mother. Yet Stephanie knew that Sarah had been exceptional, that she'd forced her husband to respect her existence as partner and equal. Since then he had run roughshod over one woman after another. Replaceable parts. One of her father's recent notes to her, which Stephanie hadn't even shown Nick, actually said, "When I was in New York to see my mistress . . ."

Her mother's beauty and understanding had been absolutely revoked by death forever. The blades of the blender suddenly labored harder. The machine seemed to gulp as the mayonnaise gained body. As Stephanie added the last drops of oil, she cursed quietly, "Goddamn it, Mom. We both could use you."

Backlit at the entrance to the bunker, William Harrold looked enormously wide. "Can you quail-walk with this trap?"

"I don't know what that is."

"Simple enough. I just walk ahead four or five yards, then you release. You release when you want to, not when I call. It simulates the actual pheasant shoot. You don't know when or where the bird will rise."

"Don't see why I couldn't try. Just don't walk out too far."

When William Harrold was ready, Nick shouted, "Hold on a sec." For some reason he was having trouble getting the pigeons in the sling.

Harrold stuck his head cheerfully through the doorway. "Electric traps are really much better, you know. You can shoot as many pigeons in a row as you want."

Looking at this tough man suddenly turned child, Nick thought that he himself would never have the gaiety the rich had. Down inside somewhere he was too serious, had too great a sense of responsibility—or was it shame?—to enjoy games the way William Harrold seemed to be doing.

"Ready?"

"Anytime," came the shout.

"Boom! Boom!" sounded the over-and-under.

When the birds were all used up, Nick came out of the bunker.

"That's it. Wiped out."

William Harrold said, "Thanks." Then, "Let me ask you one thing: Who pays for these pigeons?"

"I—we do."

"I wasted them all."

"That's what they're for. You're a very good shot."

"You know, my shooting used to annoy the hell out of old Cheshire. He used to complain bitterly about my taking birds off his gun. He raised them—William, the son, still does—about five thousand a year for the three big shoots."

"Five thousand pheasants for three days' shooting?" Nick sounded incredulous.

William Harrold ignored the question. "Near the end the good duke's eyesight was so poor I couldn't help but take off the birds. It seemed only fair not to let them get away. But, god, did he get angry. He'd shake his fist in the air, squinny at me and shout, 'Harrold, you dog! If I weren't eighty-six years old—' "

"How about a swim?" The desolation of the range and the proximity of this boasting, accomplished juggernaut depressed Nick. He wanted to get back closer to Stephanie.

"Done."

When William Harrold emerged from the pump-house changing room, Nick couldn't help being impressed: The old man's in pretty good shape. Front and back William Harrold was carpeted with dense curling hair. The arms were heavily muscled. The generous belly carried the thrust of his chest in a full solid curve. His scrotum's loose weight hung clearly outlined in the close-fitting dark blue bathing suit. His lined satyr's face seemed to glow with pleasure at his own obscene vitality. Nick wondered what Stephanie felt when she looked at her father. But she prudently remained in the kitchen, putting the final touches on the vinaigrette for her green beans.

Nick entered the water with a modified racing dive, swam a brisk length, did a kick turn and poured it on coming back.

William Harrold stood above Nick at poolside, the veins on his legs prominent. "Not a bad stroke, but your right arm's too strong. Never make a top competitive swimmer. You pull to the left."

Nick lolled back. "I'm not a bad sprinter." But he remembered a long-distance race he's lost to an old high school rival. Nick had been heavily favored; friends had money down on him. The course had been unmarked, and he'd kept wandering off course—pulling to the left.

William Harrold sucked in his stomach, grappled his toes over the tile's edge, and hit the water with a flat racing dive. While he sprinted, Nick took a few desultory turns up and down the pool. He practiced his turn, clinging to the left lane to stay out of the way of the charging white whale. William Harrold's kick was unusually powerful, his arms worked in perfect unison. Not once in ten laps did he have to correct his stroke.

He's used to command, Nick considered as he side-stroked easily and watched William Harrold practice his kick against the wall. That's the captain-of-industry bit. The close-cropped hair made Nick feel he could look at his skull. Harrold was the only one knowledgeable enough to criticize the Berger's arrangements. Till he arrived Nick had either ignorantly despised a thing or naively revered it.

He realized how much power a man like Harrold had. And that made Nick wonder whether Stephanie could really respect him.

"So how did you say Mrs. Harrold is?"

Harrold's head whipped around quickly, spraying drops of water on Nick. He searched Nick's face for signs of irony. Seeing none, he replied, "Fine. Unfortunately she couldn't get away today. She would've loved to be here."

Nick offered to carry the large stoneware platter but, not to be deprived of the occasion, Stephanie bore the salmon trout out to the terrace, where her father already sat, sipping a dry martini.

He stood up to examine the fish. "Gorgeous. You poached it."

"I know how much you like it."

"I took one look at the copper fish poacher and your fish stock and crossed my fingers. And you of all people know I'm not superstitious, Stephanie. I hoped you'd have the good taste to poach a fish for your father. And a salmon, how splendid."

"Actually," Nick said, "it's a salmon trout."

"Didn't overcook it?"

Nick prepared to defend her then realized it was another family joke. "Mildred overcooks everything," Stephanie explained.

"Her roast beef is gray, her fish like beef jerky. I used to think she did it on purpose, to annoy me. Now I realize it's worse."

"Worse?"

"She likes it that way."

The white garlic mayonnaise sat in a low glass bowl beside the cool pink fish; the beans vinaigrette added a vibrant green.

60

"And where did you get this beautiful-looking French bread? Not in Doylestown, Pennsylvania?"

"Steph baked it herself."

"Julia Child, Volume II."

William Harrold ignored his daughter. "I've always wondered why some people call her 'Steph' when Stephanie's such a beautiful name."

Nick's cheeks caught fire.

"Daddy," Stephanie answered, "Nick's been calling me Steph for three years and I don't object."

William Harrold reached for the French bread, broke off the heel and sniffed it. "But how do you get this crust? It feels like the genuine article."

"That's the culinary secret. I'm not sure I should tell you." Nick had never seen her act coy before. "If you don't have a steam-injection oven like the French, you heat a brick on top of the stove for forty-five minutes. Then just drop it into a pan of cold water and leave the brick and the pan in the oven for five minutes."

"You do any cooking, Nick?" The tone sounded casual, but Nick felt the question was meant as yet another test.

"Not much." Another demerit. Nick was still mulling over that business about "Steph." What an arrogant bastard.

"How can people flock to McDonald's when, with a little effort, there's this?" He munched on the heel.

"Most of them haven't had the opportunity to eat Steph's French bread."

"You make your own opportunities, Nick."

"Daddy, let's not get into this. It never leads anywhere. OK?"

"OK, OK," her father replied sharply. "Look, don't you think the flies have gotten even thicker than the gnats? It's awfully hot out here."

"You want to eat inside?" She offered this reluctantly, disappointment in her voice.

The butter floated in the crock, a thick yellow pool; the flies did have to be beaten away with a free hand. Still Nick felt like dumping the butter all over William Harrold's linen suit. Stephanie had so much wanted to eat lunch on the terrace.

With William Harrold leading the way, his glass and plate in hand, and Stephanie moving behind him with the great stoneware platter, Nick quickly stacked the other dishes and serving platters up his arm and followed after.

Inside, it was hotter, only there weren't any flies.

"Who are these people, the Bergers?"

"Wealthy art collectors."

"That's self-evident."

"They're in France, Daddy."

"That much I know." William Harrold's impatience was showing. "But who are they?"

"Frankly, Daddy, we don't know and it doesn't seem to make any difference."

"Hell of a way to do business."

"Do you like the salmon, Mr. Harrold?" Nick didn't know how to address him.

A giant section of the pink-skinned fish hung on his fork. "Delicious. Quite a wonderful texture. Do you know where these people are living in France?"

"Something called the Dordogne?"

The fierce brigand's face relaxed as it had when he'd first seen his daughter. He looked young. "Such a beautiful area. Sarah loved the Dordogne—that honey-gray fieldstone, the old, low cottages, the geese, Sarlat—what a beautiful, quiet market town. A living piece of the Romanesque. Did you see that film *The Duellists?*"

"No."

"You know, the Conrad story?'

"No."

"Well, they set the film in the Dordogne which, strangely enough, reminds me of Bucks County. Only the Dordogne is older, much more settled and decadent. It's got the same damp, sweet air, the same highly cultivated feel. That's where the caves are—Lascaux, Les Eyzies, Pech-Merle. Some of the oldest artifacts of man are there. They'd closed Lascaux when we were last there." Stephanie detected a softness in her father's voice. "But Sarah got the French minister of the interior to let us in. Awesome experience. Your mother wept, she was so moved. Stayed at a lovely inn, the Cromagnon. Two-star restaurant it was then. Your mother—" Nick wondered how much Stephanie reminded William Harrold of his wife. "The Cromagnon made a dried salt goose, a *comfit d'oie* it's called. Your mother, who read the Michelin devoutly, ordered it because the book listed it as a *spécialité*. They brought this thing in with great pomp; on the plate was a shriveled-looking mound of leather. Greasy leather at that. Sarah probed at the thing with her fork, but that was no go. Then she tried to slice off a piece with her knife, and it almost slithered off her plate. I put my hands out to catch it just in case. Meanwhile, all these folks fluttered about pouring wine, oohing and aahing and watching over our shoulders." Stephanie was laughing so hard she was close to tears. Nick had trouble smiling. "Finally she tore a tiny bit off by trapping the thing against the edge of the plate. The cheering section hovered. She tasted it. Sarah chewed a moment then said, in German, "It's so salty and dry." I told the waiter to take it back, it was no good. The waiter and the sommelier were stunned, they rushed to the front desk and brought back the owner. Then the owner fetched the sous-chef, the sous-chef got the real chef. The place was in an uproar. All at once they were all explaining that this was the oldest recipe in France. Sarah kept saying it was salty. I tasted and said, 'Oldest recipe. It tasted like the oldest goose in France.' His daughter's laughter rewarded the much-told punchline and relaxed him. "I haven't tasted this wine in a long time. I like it very much but I always forget about it."

"Not bad," Nick caught himself saying.

"So what do you intend to do next year?"

In their pre-visit briefing, Stephanie had warned Nick that her father was at his most dangerous when he was charming. "Uh, I was thinking of trying to do some work in movies again."

"Movies? You can't be serious."

Again, Nick had been caught off guard. Stephanie would feel terrible that he hadn't truly thought out plans for next year. It suggested Nick's "tendency to slide through," something they'd begun to discuss lately. Besides, William Harrold had good reasons for being skeptical—Nick's last movie venture never got off the ground.

Harrold turned away from Nick. "What about you, Stephanie?"

"I'm not absolutely sure yet, Daddy. But I've been thinking about the future a lot these days."

"Glad to hear it."

Stephanie produced the whiskey cream mold, and William Harrold clapped quietly: "This is an excellent piece of work, Stephanie."

Nick's voice crept down into a quiet part of his chest. "It's great, great." Father's and daughter's complicity overwhelmed him.

"What did you say?"

"I thought the meal was great."

"You have any problems here at all? Anything you need or I can help you with?"

"Nothing. Thanks, Daddy."

"Good. I've had some thoughts about your generation; I'd like to impart them before I eat a bite more of this delicious dessert." He sipped his espresso; the smile turned oily, hard. "Your generation is the most spoiled in the history of all mankind. This is obvious because at no time in the history of our world has there been such widespread affluence and such extraordinary privilege as that which has prevailed in the United States since the end of World War II. I think that this affluence is an enormous burden to bear, that few were prepared for it and no one truly understands the psychological effect of such circumstances on desire and expectation. Part of the problem with you people is that you—most of you anyway, though not you Stephanie—were deprived of breast milk. Think of it, the only mammals since the beginning of mammals not to suckle at the mother's breast. What a chain to break, what a collection of moronic lemmings all those potentially lactating women who listened to their doctors and their overnice husbands and sprinted out to buy Carnation milk and formula." Stephanie wanted to object, but her father rolled on: "The affluence you publicly despise is an inalienable part of you. You've also had the misfortune to grow up with an absurdly absolute sense of right and wrong. Life to you is like the Westerns you packed into like cattle on Saturday afternoons, where good and evil came color coded: heroes in white hats, villains in black. Most indulgently and most pathetically you are a generation which believes it's too good for power. You—in the past only a few crazed monks did this—you have voluntarily renounced involvement. You haven't stopped patting yourself on the back since Vietnam, and so you believe you're too good for war, for business, for politics, for the helping professions—now let me finish, Stephanie—and for government. Each and every one of you fools want to be artists because only that seems extrasocial and pure, only that expresses who you are—or some such moronic tripe—and this depresses me most because intelligence and energy and fortitude—fortitude makes artists at least as much as talent—is sprinkled among you no more or less liberally than it was among my generation. Some of the best or most talented of you— that's really the same thing—have lain down and rolled over and played dead in the name of some abstract, non-existent moral principle of 'noncorruption.' Better drop out and be functionally impotent forever than get the slightest bit tainted. This, in my opinion, is the true cause of America's decline."

Stephanie's hazel eyes seemed to dissolve and re-form as she held back the heavy tears. William Harrold took another sip of espresso, dived a spoon into the whiskey cream. Nick, who couldn't take his eyes off the wide, fierce face, took up the slack. "Some of what you say is on target, Mr. Harrold. We are victims of affluence but—"

"Frankly, I didn't intend to start a discussion group."

"No, but I'd like—"

"Not now. Perhaps some other time. Now I want to discuss something with my daughter—alone."

"Daddy," she wailed, "you're in my house. How can you behave like this?"

"It's not the least bit difficult." With that William Harrold stood up, took his coffee cup and refilled it from the Sienese pitcher. He went toward the door. "Besides, it's not your house."

"I don't think you're being fair," Nick called after him.

The screen door banged shut.

Stephanie began to cry. "Let me get this over with. Don't start anything else."

Stunned, Nick mumbled: "Sure, sure, Steph—anie." In his heart Nick wanted to kill William Harrold.

Stephanie caught up to her father halfway up the hill. "Daddy, you behaved terribly, abominably. I could hate you for this!"

"Either hate me or don't. But make up your mind, and don't give me that liberal crap. You sound like your stepmother, Stephanie. For now, I'm not interested in discussing your relationship with that young man. You know what I think of him and what he's after."

"You made that perfectly clear. I think he reminds you of yourself when you were his age."

"When I was half his age I was earning fifteen dollars a week in the garment district while working myself through law school at night. At his age I was a partner in your grandfather's firm."

William Harrold stopped at the excavation site and stared down into their ten-by-ten-foot piece of trespass. She stopped beside him, feeling like an orphan. How could her father torture her like this? What sort of man was he?

"I'm pleased with your decision to spend time here to sort out your future. I've always held out great expectations for you. I even enjoyed the more imaginative of your student excesses; they showed energy. But now you seem becalmed, and I can only attribute it to this fellow."

She shook her head, near furious tears.

"Stephanie, you're not getting any younger."

"Daddy," she cried.

"I have nothing more to say. I think this will say the rest." He reached into the inside pocket of his fawn jacket and pulled out a sealed envelope. The letterhead looked familiarly official: Krutch, Smeed and Bigelow. His lawyers, Stephanie's executors. "Please do not open this until after I leave. And please open it alone."

Without thinking, Stephanie folded the letter and put it into a pocket.

William Harrold looked down at the black dirt and said, "Pity." He walked back down the hill to the pump house, where he took his bathing suit off the drying line, stuffed it into a plastic bag, and put it into the maroon leather bag. Stephanie stood at the doorway. When he finished, they walked down the hill and up the front walk to the carpark. There he turned to look at her.

"Thank you for the excellent lunch, Stephanie. It really was impressive. I'm going to head back to the city now."

She wanted to cry out, What, to see your mistress? You dirty bastard. You're so despicable. But she only managed, "I thought you were staying overnight."

"No. I just wanted to see this place and how you were coming along. And deliver that letter into your hand."

William Harrold started forward to kiss Stephanie on the cheek, but she turned away.

"Good-bye, Stephanie."

She said nothing, only stood there dumbly as he backed the car around. As the Lancia started down the hill, Nick came out to her.

"Sometimes I think he's crazy," she said bitterly.

"I'm sorry he put you through this, Steph."

"But he attacked you."

"Love, it's rougher on you than it is on me."

"Nick, I would've liked to tell him to fuck off forever but I couldn't. Something about my mother, the last link to her. I don't know, I can't quite bring myself to hate him." She said it as if it were a moral failing.

"It's OK, love, it's OK," Nick murmured as he pulled her closer.

In bed alone the next morning, Stephanie opened the envelope. As usual, Nick had gone out early.

According to the revised provisions of your mother's will, as one of the trustees I am directed to distribute to you

68

upon your attaining the age of thirty (30) years, the net income in convenient periodic installments; to wit, the sum of $11,400 (eleven thousand four hundred dollars) in quarterly installments, which represents the interest on the principal of $190,000 (one hundred and ninety thousand dollars)

Provided that:

I) Such trustees shall have discretion as to the payments of such income upon the following conditions:

A) That you conduct yourself in a manner acceptable to such trustees;

B) that you shall enter into a marriage deemed suitable by such trustees.

Only such income not so distributed shall be accumulated, reinvested and become part of the principal.

So that's it; that's why the bastard drove all the way down here. Five years for this! The offending letter told her that she'd wasted five years. So gross, Stephanie thought, so deeply callous and insulting. That her father would so brutally circumvent her dead mother's intentions. Such a disgustingly overt bribe. Between the lines the letter read, very clearly: "Dump Nick."

She read on:

"Upon your attaining the age of thirty-five (35) years, and remaining unmarried, the trustees shall reexamine the terms of the trust."

Slimy flunkeys, Stephanie railed. After five more years those bastards can keep my money if they don't approve! In her rage she accidentally knocked a glass of water off the night table. It broke. As she cleaned up the glass, she fumed, "Executors, my ass. '. . . a manner acceptable,' '. . . marriage deemed suitable'! —Daddy's hand is all over it! It's positively medieval."

The seething stage passed, leaving Stephanie filled with a dull, outraged ache as she searched through the bedroom closet and found the shoebox which contained her legal documents. The last agreement had come into force on her twenty-fifth birthday, a year before she met Nick. Unequivocally, it said she would come into her money at thirty. Of course she could fight her father in court, but that would cost money and, besides, her father controlled the executors. The ugly irony was that the measure designed to keep Nick's hands off the money was actually unnecessary; if anything, Nick was too scrupulous about not taking it. Her money, he insisted, was only to be spent for her clothes, her travel, her kitchen gear. While admiring Nick's staunchness, she did get impatient with that continual distinction between his and hers; Stephanie preferred the pronoun "we."

I'd much rather not have the money. I wish they'd just take it away forever so I wouldn't have to think about it again. This time Stephanie knew she really meant it.

That afternoon, each time she felt she'd put the letter behind her, her father's lecture and the infuriating, perverse legal phrases would flash through Stephanie's mind. Why did Mother put Daddy's lawyers in charge of the money? I can't believe that Mother was careless, and she must've understood what sort of man Daddy was and how arbitrary he could be. No, she must've wanted to be sure the Jameses knew where she stood. William Harrold didn't like the idea or the fact of Nick, didn't approve at all of Nick's being poor, and hated his being a Catholic, even a lapsed one. But William Harrold had long ago explained to his daughter that she ought to thank him: He was only insuring that the charge that had been constantly leveled at him wouldn't be leveled at Nick.

"But, Daddy," Stephanie had answered, "we're not married."

William Harrold had continued undeterred: "Only after I became a partner in Abbot, Mortar, and Glebe, did I ask your mother to become my wife." Yes, William Harrold often intoned, he'd worked himself up the ladder the hard way. He could have added that he found it hard to resist stepping on the fingers of any guy who still lingered below, particularly the guy living with his daughter.

If her father hadn't visited the day before, Stephanie would have told Nick about the executors' letter. But she didn't want to insult Nick more, didn't want to increase his hatred of her father, and didn't want to make him believe he made her life harder. In most important things, he didn't make it harder. Besides, she thought with a mixture of guilt and relief, he wouldn't ask her. He knew very well that around her twenty-ninth birthday she'd receive an indication from the executors about the disposition of her money. So her holding out was merely a time-buying expedient, since she would have to tell Nick sooner or later.

The Dordogne, France

"When Madame de Fayal arrives, my dear, please do your best to be congenial." My husband Peter turned his soft arrogant smile on me—the smile that once had wilted me. As though I couldn't perform this bloodless rite in my sleep, as though I hadn't performed the same laborious sequence of polished hypocrisies a thousand times before. We stood like glazed China dolls, all lacquered surface.

He held me by the elbow, squeezing slightly for emphasis. Even his grip felt tentative. Oh, Peter was once such a different man. How did this all come to pass? How does one finally embrace the intolerable, the unthinkable? Imperceptibly, day by day, distances widen until, finally, contempt replaces disinterest.

"Command performance?" I whispered. I loathed the underhandedness, I swear I did. The way we lived disgusted me. In our eight years together my role as mistress, co-host, tour director had become a part of me; first a costume I hoped would fit, then my skin, armor, and finally an armor which fused to my skin and which I couldn't shed.

In the beginning how much fantasy one brings to the excitement of presenting oneself to another being. How dashing Peter had seemed, how mature and knowledgeable. My teacher. We did the detective work together—the muddy landscape with that underpainting by Hals he sensed lay there; that prize hangs in the Stedelijk. A year later, the unattributed Veronese; that time, it was I who had recognized the potent billowing fecundity of the master's hand. How alive we seemed then; now inertness shrouds it all.

Peter had put on weight, but was still vaguely handsome. His tanned, broad face looked healthy; only his color seemed too ruddy, and those strange white peaks, like tiny whitecaps, spaced along his jawline. To others, I imagined he appeared to be an athletic man who had been seriously ill. Which indeed Peter had. I'd "almost lost him," as they say. Lost. Found. Hardly the proper terms. He wore that navy suit—Peter owned fifty suits. As always, it was perfectly pressed. I remembered a dry-cleaning store in Paris where Peter berated the proprietor for one half hour for pressing the pleats incorrectly. Always the demand for perfection from those who served him—or rather, us—in restaurants and planes, with maids, mechanics, dealers, drivers. My humiliation, being so constant and total, had its exquisite edge. On how many occasions did I stand silently, like a child humiliated by a parent's insensitivity in front of potential allies. How few times did I call a halt. Why? At first, a desire to be a part of Peter's exquisite universe. At the last, a desire to disguise my contempt. In the middle, a long period of pitched battles.

We waited for our guest in the forecourt of the rented château. We had rented it fully furnished and fully staffed from an international agency that took care of all the details. The château was brick, spacious but not ostentatiously large, and perfectly symmetrical with its slender, high double windows and three chimneys aligned with mathematical precision. The château matched us perfectly—a neoclassical set, frontal, severe, and chillingly empty.

Side by side we watched as the black Mercedes made its ponderous way up the circular drive, crunching white gravel as it came. We rose and stood formally at ease until the limousine stopped. Peter gestured to the chauffeur that he needn't get out, then moved with a listing tentative roll toward the car. He opened the back door and gallantly helped the thick, overdressed, overjeweled woman out of the car. Bony shins appeared first, followed by the compressed knee and thigh, giving a glimpse of old-style girdle beyond. No mystery there.

Madame Martine de Fayal delicately shook hands with Peter, then offered me the tip of her faceted fingers. I inclined my head very slightly toward her, marking the cobwebbed lines around the mouth, the dry sunken skin around the eyes.

If I hadn't known from the dossier she was fifty-eight, I would've guessed seventy.

We had a dossier on all our potential customers.

Martine Françoise de Fayal. Born 1919 in Köln of Marcel Gillette and Eva Hesseltine. Married Philippe de Motherlant Haas de Fayal, 1955, after working as his private secretary for twelve years. Tentative grasp of husband's amorous affairs and viselike grasp of husband's business affairs, which include holdings in De Beers Group, ITT, Ciba, and Belgium Real Estate Corp.
Education: Collège D'Enseignment Secondaire
Address: St. Denis, St. Moritz; Paris, 24 Victor Hugo, 16e.
Notes: Excellent nineteenth-century and Impressionist collection, including Seurat, Degas (bronzes), Monet, Manet. Bought sketches for Van G's "Potato Eaters" from Cortland (divestment), 1969. Wants to enlarge sculpture and ceramics collection.

"Such a pleasure to see you again, Madame de Fayal." Peter smiled oleaginously as they walked in arm in arm. I brought up the rear, contemplating the formidable human expanse.

The entrance hall was tiled with large marble black-and-white diamonds, which made me feel like a bishop moving on a chessboard. Soon, I thought, checkmate. I pulled back from my thought. My mind had become a long-playing record with a single groove, returning only bitterness. Once I had liked, even respected myself.

The maid had set out an elaborately excessive tea and, playing gracious hostess, I poured. Madame de Fayal gushed about the *pâtisserie*.

"Fauchon," I replied, suppressing the impulse to tell her to watch her waistline. "Peter had it flown down this morning."

"You shouldn't have, Peter, dear."

Though he'd heard her remark, Peter tipped his bad ear forward. "As we say in English—sweets for the sweet."

I almost gagged on my tart—plump stawberries over raspberry puree—a field of red on red. Martine de Fayal darted yellowing fangs into the layered golden crust and gobs of sculptured meringue.

At my back I felt the art radiating its insistent beauty like heat. I didn't even have to glance into the gilt mirror to visualize the scene—oils crowded on the wall, antique pottery lining the alcove, portfolios stacked in the airtight, temperature-controlled cabinet with a select, seductive few lying on tables about the room. Over the years, this beauty had become a constant accusation. Our very presence offended it; we were trivialized by these manifestations of the artists' struggle to overcome the constraints of subject matter, form, their historical time and, most of all, themselves.

They chatted. I intervened only when Peter reached for the sugar bowl. "Only one lump, dear." I smiled. To her I said, "You know his heart."

Madame de Fayal replied, "Il a un coeur de lion."

"But not the most reliable lion."

Peter ignored my comment, took two lumps. "Madame de Fayal, it is wise to flatter me before we do business."

On the tea table, next to the Fauchon delicacies and the silver tray and server, lay the hand-printed catalogue of our collection. Martine de Fayal oohed and aahed her way through a number of pages. "So Monsieur, Madame Berger"—she had the habit of raising her eyebrows inquisitively, which left two fleeting circumflex marks on the withered face—"you have been in France for—"

"We have only been here since May. And because of the difficulties of shipping our collection—"

"A number of pieces still have not arrived. Amanda feels lonely without her beauties close by."

"But many are left in America, no?"

"A great many—almost all—remain in Bucks County. Only a few of our most precious gems have come over with us."

"Ah, but in America you have no problems of *sureté*, no terrorists, no?"

Peter looked at me. "Yes, they are very well protected."

"It is such a pleasure to be here among a little portion of your beauties." The room did have its attractions. Above the chaise on which they sat was a huge Turkestan rug. The red of the rug matched my blouse. In the mirror I could see the violent play of a black and white Franz Kline, next to it a jolly cornball Dufy landscape (perfect for the soft-core pictorial taste), and next to that a fluently sensual drawing of Mme. Matisse which had all of the master's gay authority. Greek, Roman, Mesopotamian, Sumerian, and pre-Columbian sculpture and pottery filled available niches —huge heads with blank eyes, small, sinuous bodies, a hand reaching out for something, two slender inexorably feminine amphorae. And the Han bronzes.

The woman locked on the bronzes. "Are these your famous horses? I've never seen them before."

"Indeed they are."

She rose from the chaise. With the fat person's vulnerability, she steered across the room. How desperately awkward her movements compared with the animals' eternal, passionate equipoise. Again, glib, ugly thoughts crowded in on me. I rode a slowly descending elevator which dropped in measured stages toward the pit.

Madame de Fayal stood before the horses, hesitant about touching them.

With his tentative, rocking gait Peter pursued her to the mantel.

"Our high-stepping, foam-drenched Celestials. They enchant all those who have eyes." He laid a loving hand on one horse, his own eyes alight with a sweet, sad feeling. The decayed boy lived in that look and wrenched a tiny fissure in my heart. I quickly shut out emotion: All our meaning as a couple had resided in the excellence and beauty of the collection. In turning virtue and magnificence into a commodity, Peter had debased our coinage. His need—no, to be honest, our need—for money had led to these demeaning charades, ingratiating softshoe routines to pump dollars into our coffers. But there was worse, much worse.

"Our mutual friend, Mrs. Stepney Coyle, told me how she admired these animals." Madame de Fayal's words contained a warning; Peter was never slow on the pickup. Two weeks earlier we had sold Mrs. Coyle a lush Bonnard—in "absolute secrecy." Of course the secrecy ploy worked wonderfully as bait. The rich fend off ennui only by constant titillation.

"I'm pleased Mrs. Coyle admired them." The host remained as gracious as ever, but he directed a charged glance my way which Martine de Fayal intercepted and happily interpreted as genteel distress. Ah, the bargain-hunting impulse. "I have a few drawings I'd like you to see," said Peter, apparently trying to change the subject. They moved to a large cherry table, on which Peter had placed a leather portfolio. Together they examined an allegorical scene by Fragonard, a Samuel Palmer etching of a dark, brooding, twisted oak forest, a rearing horse by Delacroix, and a magnificent Goya of a waving sea of upward-thrusting arms.

Madame de Fayal resumed her gushings: "It's like a field of wheat, like the sea."

"Like a lot of suffering people," I added.

"Of course, Amanda," Peter intoned in that way that nullified rather than confirmed my remark.

They turned back to the Delacroix horse. She drew in her breath sharply. "That is beautiful. *Magnifique.*"

"I thought you'd appreciate his lines."

Madame de Fayal eyed Peter and noisily exhaled that hot breath. "Your husband is such an exemplary salesman, Amanda."

Before her arrival I had proposed, quite seriously, to leave Peter alone with her. Peter had declined, primarily because of his health, I suspect. He'd added indelicately that Madame de Fayal would get even more worked up with me in the room. Grudgingly, I agreed to this role of pimp and chaperone. But I'd said—and meant it—that my tolerance was wearing thin.

They leaned over to inspect a Dürer drawing of a hare, a Constable sketch of a farmhouse dog and road with the sky a whole world of its own, a drawing by Thomas Lawrence of a self-satisfied woman seated in a chair in a magnificent garden that she clearly owned. Etching gave way to watercolor, watercolor to drawing and lithograph. The light source moved, lines receded and pressed forward, lavishing colors and textures on the greedy eyes of Martine de Fayal. Bodies began to replace objects, flesh tones graded toward florid, vibrant pinks; a sex flush lubricated the space between a woman's breasts, a laboring mouth gaped open with pleasure, an arm was flung out in a gesture of total abandon. These rhythms pressed like hands upon the woman's flesh, entering, striking deeper and deeper. Peter moved her eyes about at will, drawing them like a magnet down to the wet curling hair, to the arching back, the straining erect nipple. I almost expected to see her rub back and forth against the edge of the table.

Peter produced a Rubens drawing of his young second wife. He let the woman contemplate the billowing flesh before speaking in a silky, detached tone: "His young wife's hips are thrown forward into a position that's anatomically impossible. The cloak not only hides the anatomical anomaly but also what the artist knows will be revealed only to him." The diction of the Marxist art critic and the hot explicit flesh of the Rubens worked on Madame de Fayal; she eyed Peter lasciviously, overtly. Peter returned the warmth. I stared into the gilt mirror, seeing them reversed. It felt both awful and titillating. Peter liked mirrors for what he called their "visual imperialism. They multiply my possessions without devaluing them."

"This is a prize, Peter," Madame de Fayal finally gasped. "Strikingly beautiful. Philippe and I cannot live without it."

"Then I cannot hesitate to meet your need." They exchanged tense, expectant smiles, lust's currency. "Now before I show you its pedigree, you must see that Etruscan figure we spoke of."

Having conquered once, Peter struck again, this time on his surest ground. Peter Berger was an authority on sculpture, an expert on metals and alloys and casting, consultant to many of the world's finest collections. He'd once been a promising young sculptor, but gave it up because of the pay scale and because, he said, "I could not match the beauty around me."

The torso, carved in flawless, cream-white marble, stood nineteen inches high. The body appeared to be that of a young man. Some unknown tension angled the chest forward, twisted the torso and raised the figure's right shoulder, tensing muscles on that side of the breast while leaving the left side relaxed. This imparted an unusual spiraling momentum to the figure, and one leaned forward with the body, asking for completion of the action. The marble broke off at the hollow of the groin. A sensuous object, difficult to resist for a woman in heat. Especially when Peter offered her the torso for the painfully reasonable price of $10,000.

"Done."

While Peter dredged up the title and sale validation, our

guest calmed herself. Her girdle must have been a warren of odors. "Then what makes you part with such beauty?" Her smile didn't conceal her flush of victory.

"Since my illness"—Peter glanced up from the papers—"I really can't do justice to all of our pieces. I don't have the same energy for the collection now."

I added, "Our accountant has advised us to part with a few of our treasures. In America the taxes are becoming as odious as yours."

"Indeed," the woman replied coolly. "Unfortunately we all are victims."

Peter's color was now edging on vermilion, so I asked him if he wished to lie down for a moment. "Excitement is not good for him, you know." Peter protested, but when both Madame de Fayal and I urged him to rest, he smiled weakly and agreed. He exited after gallantly kissing Martine de Fayal's hand and saying, "Of course, I count on your utmost discretion."

"Of course," replied the lying bitch.

Oh, to see Peter walk away with that heavy, tentative roll —as though each step might be his last, a step without spring. He walked like a terrified man.

"He doesn't look well," she said as we stood in the driveway impatiently awaiting the chauffeur. Neither I or Madame de Fayal had any desire to spend another minute together. "His color is too high. He's put on weight."

"Peter would like to exercise more, but the doctor won't let him swim or play tennis. He does walk one mile a day. The pacemaker—"

"The extra weight does not disfigure your husband. He is still an extremely attractive man." She might have been a horse trader appraising a stud. Madame de Fayal then looked me up and down appraisingly, as though I were an object and she was estimating the price Peter had paid for me.

"I'm glad you think so," I replied.

Fortunately her chauffeur was opening the sedan's back door.

"*Au revoir.*"

"*Adieu*, Madame de Fayal. I trust you'll enjoy your new treasures." Why did I despise her so? Not because of Peter, certainly. I despised our similarities much more than our differences.

I pulled myself together, ready to go face Peter's momentary elation—a successful sale, money to support our lavish habits. I knew I'd spend the night listening to his crying. He'd clutch at me for comfort; I'd pour water and dispense the heart pills. My husband's most serious illness was his fear of death.

The Phone Call

Nick woke up thinking about mornings on the Cape. The silence depressed him. How much better it would be, he thought, to have a few friends around. He felt anxious to get out of the house.

"Let me do the shopping."

"I'd rather you didn't, Nick. I've had it with pink floral toilet paper."

"You don't sufficiently appreciate the fact that I'm the fastest supermarket shopper in Bucks County. Cheapest, too. I never deviate from the grocery list." Nick's only drawback was the minor error: the bruised melon, a cracked egg dribbling over its paper partition, a lemon with skin like rhinoceros hide, or the dread instant chocolate pudding.

Stephanie drove off, which left him alone in the garden forking over the little corner reserved for the asparagus patch, thinking, Everything about this place is precious, priceless. In the beginning Nick actually had to stand in front of the paintings and work to be impressed. But he hated the churchy mood they asked for. Nick hadn't submitted himself to that mood since the day of his thirteenth birthday when he decided that everything he'd believed about God until then was total horseshit; he had walked out halfway through Mass and never set foot inside a Catholic or any other church again until his younger brother Ted got married. In front of those swirls and bars of color, he felt the same pressure, same shame, same lack of worthiness he'd felt in church for not having enough faith. The beauty in the Bergers' house shrank Nick down, made him feel as though he were an insensitive clod.

After William Harrold's visit, it had taken weeks for Nick to feel at home again even outdoors. The trapshooting range seemed changed; he would've liked to have it exorcised. Nick would go for a run through the woods, and he'd see that broad, fierce, scowling face chiding him about "Steph." Again and again Nick replayed William Harrold's speech. Nick admitted that, like the rest of his generation, he was relatively spoiled. Nick's family had been poor, but nobody starved to death. On the other hand, Nick had worn the same pair of khaki pants through two years of junior high school while everyone else was buying rainbows of chinos. Not much to complain about when stacked up against real problems, but something a kid takes to heart. Much worse, William Harrold had been diabolically on target about Nick's inertia. Nick's energy seemed dried up. Too many times he'd told himself: I can't do that—work for that political candidate or get involved with this community group—because I don't believe in it. Without thinking, he'd painted himself into a corner that left almost no room for meaningful activity. He felt estranged, inert—he who had fought cops in the streets and been designated an official outside agitator at Columbia.

Lost in his serious thoughts, stooped over and sweating, he turned over the turf in Stephanie's asparagus patch and shook out the clods of earth. The grass had a pad of roots ten inches thick; fat brown earthworms tunneled through the matted turf. Holding the sod in his hand, Nick could see Massey's point.

Bucks County had come up with the crisp low-humidity day he figured he was entitled to after a week of life in a vegetable steamer. Nick talked to himself aloud, cheerfully, "I dig some of that art. I ain't no Philistine." He laughed aloud, thinking of that little stone fertility goddess from the Minoan Palace on Crete which felt so smooth and cool to handle, and that big pencil-and-pastel drawing of a female nude by Matisse. The drawing had dark solid outlines—the woman was standing, her back half-turned to the viewer— and her back and full behind had soft pink fleshy color but just in a few places. Matisse had left the rest of her body the color of the paper itself, a warm brown. The pink tones seemed to be exactly in those spots where the light would hit her back, and that light lay as softly on her shoulder as a hand. What a way to earn a living. Do the guys who draw female nudes stay turned on all the time, or are they like what people say about gynecologists, all business? Or does the artist commute between the two poles, as it were? Nick enjoyed his joke.

As he dug, Nick's claustrophobia eased off. After all, he'd

overcome the local ogre's objections and was reclaiming land for his beloved while opening up avenues for future gluttony. He avoided the issue of whether his present work was mission or trespass.

He was so into the rhythms of the old fork and shake that he didn't hear the phone until its second or third ring: Don't think it was more than three, but can't be sure it was only a deuce.

Through that pause between rings he stood perfectly still, trying to figure out what the ringing phone meant to him. "The sixth or seventh ring, Carroll said. Get it before the seventh!" That got him moving down the hill. How many? he wondered as 3/4 buzzed at him. He knew he didn't have to answer it by the seventh ring, that he was "allowed" to call Carroll back; it didn't have to be Carroll, it could be anybody, even a wrong number, yet he found himself legging it downhill so that Carroll, if it was Carroll, wouldn't have anything to hold over him. "I mean, we're slaves to the place anyway," Nick hollered in explanation to the rhythm of his pumping legs.

Sprinting down the slope he felt the complete ass, a serf running to answer his master's beck. The pause held for several strides—he kidded himself he'd gained ground—then 4/5 blasted at him, the volume way up now.

With 5/6 he was closing on the exquisite stone farmhouse, cursing Stephanie for having shut both the screen door and the inner one. He leaped a rose bed and a low hedge, skidded a half step and regained his footing. He hurled the front door open, then picked a barely-in-control path through that treasury of a living room. As he dogtrotted toward the window seat, he felt impelled to knock all the expensive artwork off the shelves, to rip paintings from the walls. But no time for pleasant diversions, not while the phone renewed its merry tinkle. 7/8, too late. He picked up

84

the receiver, totally out of breath. While he panted at his end, the other end was perfectly still.

Nick was about to put down the receiver when the caller at the other end cleared his throat and out came Carroll's suede-lined voice: "You sound a trifle out of breath."

He could swear Carroll was trying not to laugh. Nick would've gladly eaten out the agent's heart.

"You know, Nicholas, that was the eighth ring."

"I can count."

"I really don't want to be overly literal, particularly at the start. At the start I assume you may need a little extra leeway. And I certainly didn't intend my call to inconvenience either you or Miss Harrold." The voice sounded X-rated as it fondled "Miss Harrold."

"It was a minor inconvenience," Nick replied in lordly terms. He thought, I'm having trouble breathing.

"As I say, personally, I'm of course sorry to disturb. Professionally, you understand, I have to be scrupulous about the terms of our agreement, even if they do create occasional minor disruption."

What kind of kick is he getting out of this? Nick wondered. If it just was between Carroll and me, I'd tell him to fuck off. Which might end our tenure. Nick swallowed his pride and said nothing.

A pause followed. It had passed the pregnant stage and was about to gestate when Carroll broke it: "Well, as usual, a pleasure talking to you. Give my regards to your charming . . . eh"—Carroll hesitated again—"companion."

"Good-bye, Mr. Carroll."

"Good-bye."

Nick went at the vegetable garden with a vengeance. For two hours the air stayed filled with a solid arc of Bucks County earth, his own green-brown rainbow. Nick turned over a ton of that dirt, shook out every single hairy clod of grass, and personally relocated dozens of surfeited earthworms, all in the attempt to wear out his fury. Secretly, Nick was happy that he and not Stephanie received that phone call. Forking over the earth, he kept licking his wound, storing up humiliations for Stephanie's return.

He didn't let her have it right away. He bided his time while sullenly helping to unload the groceries. She talked about how much everything had gone up. She had counted the items as they went through the checkout, estimated a dollar an item and still she was under the total by about four dollars. Nick rested the final bag on the kitchen counter, and Stephanie kept putting stuff away. Then he pounced.

"You know what I was up to while you were out galavanting around?"

"I'd hardly call this galavanting." She shook a roll of paper towels at him.

"I had a short wind sprint from your garden to answer the phone."

"What?" Stephanie looked tired.

"Remember Carroll told us we had to answer the phone by the seventh ring?"

Her dimples flattened out. "He said he wanted us in the vicinity of the house. If we were busy, we could always call him right back."

"I wasn't about to give him the satisfaction."

"What satisfaction? What are you talking about?"

"Saying we were out of the house. I mean, Christ, we're chained to the goddamn place day and night, we ought to get credit for it."

"Nick, that's crazy. You get mad at Carroll because you run to answer a phone call you didn't have to answer in the first place."

Nailed, Nick thought. Sometimes it was perfectly clear who was the more logical one. "I thought I explained to you what the question was about. We sit here for a month and a half without hardly ever being out of the house together. I want credit for that." Feeble answer, Nick admitted to himself. But how could he tell her that Carroll was a mortal enemy who represented all that he hated about the perfectly arranged, perfectly smug, perfectly laundered place. "If you stop to think about it, I admit it doesn't look smart to run two hundred yards downhill to answer a phone. You had to be there."

"No, Nick, you had to be there."

Sitting in the living room after a fine French meal, Nick mentally kicked himself again: What an asshole I am sometimes. It's not her fault that I ran to answer Carroll's phone call. For cover, Nick held a slim volume of Walter Benjamin in front of his face. Stephanie thumbed through the Bergers' catalogue, a square format book with a light-blue cover. The photographs, about which Nick did know something, were rather high contrast black and white, severe; the lighting was expert and dramatic, the prints themselves excellent.

"Did you know that those bronze horses," she pointed, "are Eastern Han Dynasty, Nick? That makes them over two thousand years old."

"As old as good old Jesus Christ himself."

Stephanie went over to the pair of horses on the glass shelf next to the fireplace and gestured toward them with a flourish. "The catalogue quotes a contemporary Chinese warlord who calls them 'Blood-sweating horses, Celestial horses.' They were ceremonially buried with the rich nobles as emblems of their power. Look at them."

Nick got up and stood beside her. Even standing on the

shelf, he thought, they look in motion—nostrils flared, necks arched.

"All fire and majesty."

"You love them, don't you?" Nick asked.

Stephanie had pulled back her hair, which exposed her fine clear forehead and gave him an uninterrupted view of her face. It struck Nick again how many different faces a good-looking woman has. This was the homey attractive face—not her dress-up sophisticated look but the face he'd enjoy living with forever.

She stroked the horse's mane. "They're terrific, aren't they?"

Suddenly, from his punk mood, Nick saw a way to make their life in Bucks County more pleasant. "We'll be here for a year, right?"

"Most likely."

"You think it would make sense to get to know more about this stuff? I mean, I don't know anything at all and maybe I could warm up to it more—"

Stephanie brightened.

"Maybe each night we could learn about one or two of these beautiful babies. We could start with the catalogue, then maybe try to find other articles. They've got so many reference books around." One twelve-by-eight-foot wall held expensive-looking, oversized art books.

"A study group?"

"Strictly informal, pal. Pass/fail, nothing too heavy or academic. If you can't keep up with the pace, we could arrange remedial lessons."

"I'll give you remedial, buster."

A Friendly Visit

A cool July morning lured Stephanie out for one of her rare walks. Strange, she thought as she moved past the pool and on up toward the pond. Already we've gravitated to our own spots. Nick roams around outside— swimming, playing Huck Finn in the woods or fishing, taking pictures, fiddling with those damned rifles. (She waited with clenched teeth each time she heard the trap whirr and the shotgun boom away). Outdoors, Nick; inside, me. I get acquainted with the smell of the house, its creakings and shiftings, turnings and spacings. The fireplace. I play with the Pavia espresso machine—that throaty whirr turning into its steamy gargle. Now, that's a sound I can get behind. Every surface of Amanda Berger's kitchen was exquisite to look at, pleasurable to touch. Skilled fingers had been there before Stephanie's—men who lathed and grinded, workmen who polished and varnished, craftsmen who sanded and waxed and hand rubbed.

The kitchen was a set for her own personal choreography. She never had to lengthen or shorten her step moving from sink to fridge to the freestanding island of pale-ash cutting board to that boil-water-in-seconds, six-burner Vulcan range which Nick called "the Hudson of stoves." Usually cabinets were too high for Stephanie, but Mrs. Berger's cabinets were all at her eye level. For the first time in her life she could actually see what was on the second shelf.

Everything is so perfectly arranged, she admitted. Still she found herself taking the path along the stream so that she could pass the blighted elm that Nick and Massey had feuded about. Nick had won that round—he and not Massey was going to cut down that elm.

The only bothersome cloud on the young couple's horizon was the lingering memory of her father's visit, and that unspeakable letter from her executors. Nick had said, "Your father actually locked his car door. Here on the property. A real trusting sort of guy, isn't he?" Stephanie would've liked to hate her father. But she couldn't. Nor could she walk away from him as Nick had walked away from his family. But then, she thought, Nick had always been emotionally tougher than she.

A month and a half had passed since her father had handed her the letter, and still she hadn't said anything to Nick. And now her birthday was only a month away.

Stephanie gingerly stepped down the slippery path, took a long step over a tree trunk, then cut back up away from the bank toward the huge elm. The poor dying tree saddened her—the huge graceful boughs bare, the few remaining leaves all dry and curled up, the withering scaling bark turned that odd, dull grey.

Stephanie had walked a mile from the house when, suddenly, an unexpected noise startled her. She thought immediately of art thieves: They're casing the place! Turning around slowly, she saw two fully clothed teenagers lying side by side on the far bank of the stream, among the rhododendron. They didn't see her. He had his hand on her breast, his leg was raised tentatively over hers, and they moved in dreamy slow motion, as though they had no idea what to do next. It looked so utterly familiar and soft-core, Stephanie felt vaguely amused.

As the girl came up for air, she looked in Stephanie's direction—a startled expression, she pulled back slightly and poked the boy; quickly both turned Stephanie's way.

Stephanie could almost feel their hearts stop. For an instant, the couple looked horrified. Then, realizing that she wasn't all that much older than they were, the boy tried to smile and the girl looked relieved. Her assumption annoyed Stephanie, who would have liked to be recognized as the lady of the manor. She spoke harshly and quite automatically: "What are you doing here?"

The fright disappeared, and they seemed embarrassed for Stephanie. Slowly the girl stood up and brushed a leaf from her skirt.

"I'm sorry," Stephanie said. "I'm not used to seeing people on the property."

They looked at her as though she were mad, clasped each other's hands and quickly walked away along the stream.

When she told Nick what had happened, they both realized, again, how strange it was that they hadn't seen anyone their own age since they'd moved to Bucks County. She was developing almost a hermit's protectiveness about the place. A few days earlier Stephanie had told him that she had begun to feel invaded on Tuesdays, the day the Spanish maids came. She'd always felt invaded on Fridays, Massey's day at the farmhouse. When Nick suggested that they invite Henry Brewer down for the next weekend, Stephanie agreed it was a fine idea.

Nick and Henry Brewer had been buddies at The New School and co-workers in various manifestations of radical politics later. It was Henry who had introduced Stephanie and Nick with a simple "I thought you might like each other." Henry had drifted to the Cape shortly after they'd moved there in '74. In his way, Henry Brewer was the most American person either of them had ever known—eight generations of Yankee blood had produced a man who combined the pioneer's independence with Ben Franklin's mechanical ingenuity with the New England farmer's taciturn nature. Henry owned land in northern Vermont which he'd cleared himself; he'd crewed on boats that sailed around the world; he'd spent time in Bali and Borneo. Henry, who was one of their favorite people, was quieter than most of their friends, too quiet sometimes for his own good. Yet neither Stephanie nor Nick ever found his calm, potent presence boring. Stephanie thought Henry was one of the handsomest men she'd ever seen. Tall and thin, Henry had gray eyes, a soft full mouth, straight nose and the most beautiful skin imaginable for a man—rosy, clear, impossibly healthy looking. These days, he wore a full beard, a shade darker than his auburn hair.

Their first invited guests—William Harrold had really been self-invited and Massey and the maids didn't count—arrived on Friday. As expected, Henry came with Cindy, a woman with whom Stephanie had never been very friendly. To Stephanie, Cindy seemed all too typical of Henry's women—very pretty, not particularly interesting, a little too seductive, and hot in pursuit of the distantly bemused Renaissance woodsman. Henry came out of his well-traveled Plymouth station wagon with a bottle of Johnnie Walker Black (Nick's favorite) under his left arm and an intriguing collection of short lengths of wire dangling from his right hand. The piece turned out to be a mobile and, like Henry, it was simple and elegant—a series of progressively longer pieces of wire which were bent at right angles about an inch from the top and then looped and hooked at the end. Henry had made it, he said, by fooling around with some wire and a needle-nose pliers; as though the way the pieces hooked together, the way the long shaggy chain hung and moved and turned slowly around its spine in a sensuous S curve would have occurred to any reasonable person with some wire and a needle-nose pliers.

"This is for you guys."

"I love it; it's beautiful." Stephanie kissed Henry and smiled hello to Cindy.

They went inside and after a brief search decided to hang the mobile in the space between Cezanne's favorite mountain and a stark, haunting Milton Avery. As Stephanie had guessed, the mobile held its own among its illustrious neighbors.

Nick stood back from it and announced in his best network anchorman tone: "And this little item, Brewer revealed, was made by 'just messin' around with some steel wire.' An intimate peek, folks, into the well-guarded secrets of the artistic process."

They all laughed. Stephanie was delighted to add a piece of their own to the Berger collection, and it made the collection seem a bit less mystically highbrow.

They toured the private museum, each paying homage to various walls and the glass shelves on which the pottery was displayed. Upstairs, in the long narrow closet where the Bergers stored their paintings, large panels swung out as though from a giant book. Attached to the front and back of each panel, which reminded Henry of the blackboards in high school, a large painting was mounted. They flipped through these precious packs which held Matisse, Picasso, Braque, Klee, Bonnard, back in time to Constable, Sir Thomas Lawrence, Turner and many more beauties that none of them were familiar with.

It didn't take them long to get visually overloaded. But Stephanie wasn't anxious to leave the gallery, for it seemed to deserve much more of their time. The massiveness of her ignorance about the art to which they had such privileged access astounded, even embarrassed her.

They showed off their bedroom, which had two walls covered with mirrors and a bed the size of a football field. Stephanie said, "A bit tacky, huh? A little too much conspicuous consumption."

"What's the matter, you don't like watching?" Stephanie didn't find Nick's joke amusing.

Cindy cooed, "Looks fantastic to me."

Nick had the good sense to change the subject: "Let's go get that elm, Henry."

Stephanie felt reasonably civil toward Cindy in the kitchen, where they repaired to fix dinner. Certainly, Cindy would never be her best friend, but she wasn't a mean person, and Stephanie did appreciate the difficulty of her position with Henry, who was about as elusive as a greased eel.

The chain saw was far enough away not to grate on the hostess's slightly tender nerves, Nick had promised to "summon the womenfolk" just before the great moment, so Stephanie knew she'd be relieved eventually. Cindy seemed to relax a little as Stephanie started dinner.

"Can I do anything?" she asked tentatively.

Stephanie thought, She probably never cooks. "Sure, Cindy, you can peel the asparagus."

"Peel asparagus?"

"It's easy." Stephanie showed Cindy how to take off the little bumps with the vegetable peeler.

"My doctor says Henry's a very independent person." Cindy looked down as she scratched at a stalk.

"A great friend, but I'd guess a difficult lover. I think he likes being elusive."

94

"That's interesting." She said it as though it were a revelation.

"I love your house and adore your kitchen."

"I'm glad you like it."

Cindy squeezed past Stephanie to the end of the counter and pointed to the Cuisinart. "Do you use it?"

"Sure, you want to see how it works?"

Stephanie pulled out the Cuisinart and made the next day's celeriac salad, which Nick craved. Cindy was impressed. When Stephanie kept the hollandaise from separating, Cindy appeared amazed. "How did you do it?" Which made Stephanie feel like the Home Ec. teacher.

"Can I have a glass of water?"

"The ice is in the freezer."

Opening the compartment, Cindy said, "It's so huge." Stephanie nodded. "And it even has an ice maker."

"They're not very efficient in terms of energy."

"What?"

"Nothing."

"You seem to have everything here."

"Everything."

As she kneaded the dough for the French bread, Stephanie listened with only one ear to Cindy's chatter about the household gadgets, her "doctor," clothes, Henry, and the problems of staying thin. (From Stephanie's point of view, Cindy was perversely thin.) It was almost relaxing to have this pretty, empty-headed thing nattering away about salads and soybeans. Meanwhile, Cindy sampled the batter for the seven-layer chocolate cake and nibbled steadily at the chocolate chip cookies, sometimes wrestling a chip free of the cookie and eating it naked. She must have licked two thousand calories off her ring finger. And though Stephanie knew the visitor didn't intend it, when Cindy slipped around the counter to get her batter fix she kept getting in

Stephanie's way; so the cook placed the visitor on a stool, slid the batter closer to her and said, "Go for it, kid." Cindy slowed down then.

The congestion in the kitchen made Stephanie aware of how much she enjoyed their solitude. How quickly she'd grown dependent on it. She imagined their old cramped apartment, then her eye wandered out of the window and ran up the sloping lawn to the pond, framed by the dense swaying maples and oaks beyond. Am I becoming a misanthrope who has to control all the variables? Or is it simply Cindy? What's so bad about Cindy anyway? It must be a relief to be a little frivolous. Still Stephanie resented the intrusion. How restful and safe—yes, safe—to stay in the farmhouse for weeks at a time. Stephanie smiled; she caught herself thinking that her version of the kept woman wasn't all that far removed from the ideal the little kumquat at her side proposed for her slender self.

The chain saw stopped, and a minute later Henry called from the top of the hill, "It's about ready to go." Cindy and Stephanie hurried across the lawn and up toward the stream. Stephanie had flour on her blouse, Cindy was all eyelashes and swingy, ash-blond hair.

Stephanie thought, It's like entering a Miller High Life ad—the two good-looking men stripped to the waist, in jeans and boots, a red flannel shirt tossed carelessly across a fallen log, the yellow chain saw resting on the ground under a forty-foot elm. Henry stood under the stripped tree, knee deep in wood chips. About sixty feet away, at the base of a huge oak, Nick manned a ratchet device called the "come-along." A wire ran from the anchoring oak to the diseased elm, drawing a taut silver thread across the lush, leafy background. The elm was wedge cut, so it was supposed to fall away from them in Nick's direction.

96

Each time Henry slammed the wedge with his sledge-hammer, the tree jumped forward, and Nick hauled in on the come-along. It was awesome, mesmerizing to watch the giant naked tree gently sway in a circle above their heads.

"It's ready," Henry yelled. A subdued cracking noise, then a sharper louder crack that grew louder still—

Nick straightened up to get a better grip on the crank of the come-along. Slowly the elm shifted back in the other direction. The silver wire went slack and dipped to the ground. The tree had almost come into the perpendicular when Henry yelled, "Tighten up! Tighten up!" He leaped away from the rise and started toward Stephanie and Cindy, shooing them as he ran.

Splintering, cracking sounds as the forty-foot monster came off its base, quivering and flexing like a giant diving board. Stephanie stood frozen in place, watching it lean back toward her. Meanwhile, Nick frantically cranked at the come-along. The silver wire snapped taut, the anchoring oak shivered and groaned, shedding leaves and snapping small branches. The elm quivered back up into an erect position, then slowly tilted away from them.

With a tremendous leafy rustling sound, a SWOOSH that tickled their eardrums, the elm thundered down. A great crash and billowing clouds of dust, the tree bounced five feet off the forest floor, then settled into the alley Henry had aimed it for. They found themselves covered with a light brown dust. Stephanie smelled of leaves.

"Was that as close as I thought?" she asked when she could breathe again.

"No, Nick had it under control."

Nick looked pale and shaky when he joined them. "I thought it was taut, Henry. But when it started to go, there was a lot of slack left."

"You did good."

Standing over the fallen tree, they commiserated about the Dutch elm disease.

"If the goverment were cool, they'd spend money on research about things like the elm blight."

"Instead of sending people to the moon."

"Yeah, if they were cool."

Nobody felt cool at the moment, except perhaps the unflappable Henry. To work off the near-miss shakes, Stephanie asked if she could use the chain saw. That left Nick with Princess Cindy, who immediately started playing helpless ignorance of the great outdoors. Stephanie soon forgot about Cindy as she cut up the elm into fire-sized logs.

Stephanie and Henry quit cutting halfway through the elm when the saw overheated. They shed their sweaty clothes at poolside; Cindy served the beer. Naked, they sat sipping and let the sweat dry. Then a very pleasant array of flesh hit the water. The men and Cindy indulged in mild aquatic horesplay followed by a few tokes of Henry's homegrown. Nick then showed the visitors how the valves in the Bergers' big inner tubes were covered, which took care of the single flaw in innertubes, the old valve-in-the-side problem.

The dope produced in Stephanie its all too frequent mild paranoia: Her heart beat faster, her feet and hands turned ice cold. She wanted to talk to Henry about his "finding" himself in an est course, but she had trouble moving her tongue for anything longer than one syllable.

Suddenly Nick got ultra-serious: "I really almost fucked up with that tree. I got so into the sway it was like I wasn't there." He sat up and looked at each of them: "I almost wiped you all out. The tree started to move your way but I couldn't do a goddamn thing. I was paralyzed. It was like I wanted to see how far I could let it go. I mean, I didn't think that but—"

"But we were right under it."

"I know, Steph. That was what was so fucked up and freaky. I felt paralyzed and kind of curious. I could see it tipping your way, I knew what I was supposed to do, but I couldn't do anything about it. I've never been so terrified in my life. Not even after my motorcycle accident. It was like this perverse experiment. To see how far—"

"You're crazy," she said furiously. "It's absolutely crazy, homicidal. I don't know how you could even play around with something like that." Stephanie felt her body shaking from fear and anger.

"I do," said Henry.

On that note, conversation died, and the four of them sank back to soak up the sun's rays. Stephanie lay on her stomach for fifteen minutes or so, trying to penetrate the mysterious brinkmanship of the male mind. As she turned over to start on her back, she saw Nick's penis gradually rise out of its relaxed, bunched curve. It twitched a little, stretched and expanded and finally leapt straight up into the air. For a moment Nick didn't seem to realize what was happening, but then he sat up quickly and started to roll onto his stomach. He rolled Cindy's way just as she sat up. She saw it, blushed, then a pleased dirty smirk crept over her face. Clearly she thought Nick's hard-on was for her. Whoever it was aimed at, Nick's dick converted that little routine about the bedroom mirrors into hard, unadulterated fact. Through it all, Henry didn't notice a thing.

At dinner when Stephanie brought in the crepes stuffed with chicken and mushrooms, Cindy said, "that looks absolutely delicious, but I'm on this low-carbohydrate diet. Would you be upset if I just had a little salad?" Nick almost gagged on his artichoke. Stephanie had the self-possession to say, "OK, but would you please make it yourself? I want to eat while the crepes are warm. The lettuce and tomato and parsley are in the kitchen."

She left and Stephanie sat down. Nick shook a clenched fist in the kitchen's direction, Henry shrugged his shoulders as though saying, "She's an ass; she can't help it." But Cindy's slenderizing routine put Stephanie off her feed. She didn't have much to say after that.

To pick up the slack, Henry, who rarely volunteered anything, said, "Sure is pretty around here."

The wasp-waisted Cindy, who had returned with her scant portion of greens, went breathy again: "This is the most beautiful place I've ever seen. I could live here forever."

Stephanie thought, Fortunately you won't get the chance, while Nick answered, "Well, it does have a few drawbacks. For one thing, the isolation. The only people we ever see except for each other are the gardener and the maids. I miss being able to jump into the car and take off for a couple of days. We only get those few hours two days a week and can't get more than thirty-five miles away. Makes me feel like I'm on a leash."

Cindy: "But it's such a beautiful leash."

"Ever have to go to movies single file at noon? You know what it's like to watch a Bond movie at noon?"

Henry laughed. Stephanie didn't; she'd heard that routine before. Other people were essential to Nick in a way that they weren't for her.

Nick went on explaining to Henry, "The Bergers have all their bets covered. Every single detail of the operation is thought out and in place.

"Like the concrete housing for the pump."

"The valves for the inner tubes, the way the trap range is laid out. It's nice, but it doesn't give a guy much flex. I can't identify with it—I mean, it's not personal because anybody else could take our place. The maids even go around sticking down thumbtacks to make sure the furniture's put back

100

in the 'right' place. They put markers down when they dust the pottery on the shelves." Nick pointed to the open shelves by the fireplace.

Cindy's mouth gaped open: "Really?"

Stephanie said, "He's exaggerating."

"But that's what it feels like. Even the things I like, like that charming snake lady I showed you, that—"

Cindy interrupted: "You sound intimidated." In her pantheon, that was supposed to be a sin.

"No," Nick replied reasonably, though Stephanie noted the remark hit his pride. "Just a little uncomfortable. You ever feel uncomfortable in a museum? It's like that, you don't feel you can shift the pictures around to suit you."

Henry's presence had forced Nick to spell out his feelings about the place, which he didn't often do with her because —with both of them, really—there was a tendency to get lazy or assume that one's point of view is understood. Nick's objections to their new life made sense for him. At the same time, Stephanie felt herself sinking deeper and deeper into the luxuriant Bucks County turf.

Henry and Cindy stayed all day Sunday. At supper, Nick asked them to stay over "at the resort. Hard morning planned for you two—little swimming, we could knock off a few clay pigeons, catch us a trout or two . . ."

"Sounds tempting." Henry looked at Cindy all decked out in her leather gaucho pants and a blouse tied just above her diaphragm.

"We'd love to, it's been so lovely," she said. "But I've got a doctor's appointment tomorrow morning at nine."

Stephanie could guess what Cindy's "doctor" was like. She could almost see the sleek, white modern office, so reassuringly hip. At the same time Stephanie felt annoyed that, at thirty-two, Henry still behaved like a disengaged Lothario. What bullshit roles these guys play. But then there isn't a shortage of women who'll play their opposite number.

A few days after Henry and Cindy's visit, she got up at dawn, made scones, and gave the Pavia espresso machine an early workout. Nick wandered down at nine.

"I miss it."

"What?"she asked.

"The Cape, the beaches, dunes, ocean, the wind, even the sand."

Stephanie nodded, meaning, I miss it too. But they sat sipping cappuccino on the brick veranda, looking past one of the giant vase-shaped elms toward the pond. If she moved her head three inches to the right she could see the great red eminence of the barn, with its weathered siding of a hundred shades and textures. The oaks along the drive shimmered unrealistically in the morning sun. Nick had on his snug black undershorts (to keep the sunburn off his tender parts). She had on nothing.

"Having Henry here—I miss him already, Steph. Miss a lot of people."

I shouldn't take it as an insult, she thought. I know exactly what he means. But she said, "You miss Cindy too?"

"I miss jumping in the car and driving around, those beautiful sunsets."

"They have sunsets in Bucks County, too."

"Half the time I feel like a squatter here. It's such a different scene. We're supposed to feel privileged to be here, pal. That's part of their message to us."

"Do you have to be so paranoid?"

"I feel I'm in the middle of an ongoing indoctrination. We're supposed to learn how to live right here. They're brainwashing us." She looked skeptical. "Oh, it's subtle, Steph. They're tricky. Did you notice that there are only

photographs of Amanda Berger in the house? Not one picture of Peter Berger."

"Yes." She did notice and even mentioned it to Cindy.
Amanda's photographs decorated four rooms. She looked
very handsome, soft and alluring, with luxuriant raven hair
and painfully white skin.

"Who knows, maybe Amanda's the beauty and Peter's
the beast."

"Like the story says, the beast didn't make out so badly."

The Secateurs

The Friday after Henry's visit, Massey charged at
Nick again: "Someone bunged up my secateurs. See
these blades?"

"Your what?" Nick asked. Massey constantly presented
Nick with difficult vocabulary words in an attempt to show
up the college boy.

"My shears, you nit, my shears. These." He held out the
shears with the crossed blades.

"Look, Massey, I never touched them. I'd be crazy to
touch them. So don't give me a hard time, OK?" He was
sipping a second mug of coffee on the terrace; Massey's
supercharged monster lawnmower had ripped him out of
bed at eight. Even Stephanie, who could sleep through
alarm clock blasts and repeated telephone attacks, had staggered down at 8:30.

Massey stumbled away muttering, "One of you did it, I know it."

Nick yelled after him, "She didn't touch them either. She knows better."

By the time Stephanie got back from town, where she'd gone to escape Massey's lawnmower, Nick had a splitting headache. "Massey claims his secateurs—"

"Huh?"

"—His pruning shears are messed up."

"Is that his new one? What was that word he sprung on you last week?"

"The legal one? Gravamen."

"A welcome addition to anyone's vocabulary."

"Did you touch the shears?"

"I never use any of his tools," she said with a quick flash of indignation.

"That's what I told him. But how do you suppose they got messed up?"

Stephanie looked extremely serious: "Cindy! Cindy probably did it."

They laughed together.

Two days later, as Nick walked by the study window, he noticed something unusual about the window frame—paint had been chipped off and a little groove had been worn into the wood around the base of the lock, as if someone had tried to jimmy it. Or had it always been that way—signs of an innocent inside job, like when you lock yourself out of the house and just as you are about to break and enter your partner shows up with the keys? Nick investigated further. Was it possible Massey's shears had been used for the job? That would have meant taking them out of the barn, digging around the frame, then sticking them back in place on the pegboard. Unlikely, Nick concluded. But for the next few days he played that game with himself of trying to picture how that window frame had looked when they first arrived in Bucks County. The pictures in his head didn't resolve: He kept seeing the frame untouched, then seeing it with chipped paint and that little telltale groove.

The Limited Getaway

Nick said, "In two hours." He held up two fingers. "*Dos hora, Inez. Una o'clock.* Don't leave until we get back. *Comprenda?*"

The smiling Spanish maid nodded her head up and down.

"She didn't understand a thing I said."

"It's OK, Nick, she can handle it."

As they pulled out of the carpark, Nick said, "The pin oaks get fuller every day. Look at them." She did. "I can't wait to show you the color shots I took. I think you'll like them."

They didn't speak again until the road dipped and dropped them down into the gnarled woods where they'd stopped just before entering the Bergers' world.

"You know, I sometimes stop here on my way into town." Nick didn't respond. He was wondering if something would happen while they were away. "Why don't we learn Spanish?" she asked brightly.

"Haven't you got enough academic discipline with our art classes?"

"I noticed you just skimmed the Kenneth Clark this week."

"You going to report me to the principal?"

The July heat poured in through the open car windows. The heavy afternoon air lay on them like damp sheets.

Nick turned left, then right, then right again onto a one-and-a-half-track lane. Stephanie wasn't surprised that he already knew his way around.

"I haven't shown you that mulberry tree, have I?"

As they came up over a hill Stephanie saw the tree, which seemed to bury the road in green branches.

"It's a landmark," as they drove under. "They can't cut it down."

"That's the last thing Shakespeare did."

"What?"

"Planted a mulberry tree in his yard. A few days later he died after a drinking match with his buddies."

"I can think of one better way to go."

"Your mulberry's huge, but it must be much younger than the one he planted."

"I wonder if his tree's still there?"

"I doubt it. But I bet the tourist board has already planted a replacement."

"For sure," Nick replied.

Alongside them, a chestnut mare, her foal following after, raced the car.

"The horse looks even more beautiful against that white railing. Nick, I'd like to do a book about different kinds of fences."

He smiled, realizing how happy she was here. He was equally glad he didn't resent her happiness. On a recent trip to Doylestown, Nick had walked into an antiques store

106

and found a print of different old cast-iron door hinges. He still wasn't sure why he bought it for her; but Stephanie loved it.

Lush pastureland abruptly turned into patchy woods; they drove through a scraggly settlement strung out along the road. One front yard was littered with rusting cars and a battered refrigerator, its door hanging by one hinge. A vicious-looking dog barked and strained against its chain as two dirty children listlessly threw twigs at it. Nick thought, How much I'd hate people looking in the windows as they drove by. The shabby row of houses reminded him of how insulated and arrogant the rich were.

Stephanie hardly registered the presence of the settlement. She was thinking of her evening ritual, how just before sunset she'd go out to water the herbs and the still invisible asparagus.

Driving along those gently curving roads usually soothed Nick. Now he kept looking at the odometer to see how far they'd come. At twenty-five miles, the leash grew taut.

Stephanie noticed Nick's growing impatience. "Why don't you find one of your nice fields?"

"Next one that looks good," he replied. But he continued driving too fast and kept missing likely places to pull over.

Two miles later, Stephanie said, "I'm going to get carsick if you keep slowing down then speeding up."

Nick slowed down and, cruising at twenty-five miles per hour, finally pulled over by a hayfield.

They walked into the shimmering field of gold. The tops of the hay brushed right against her crotch. "Perfect height," she laughed as the beautiful swaying field kept parting before them.

"Do you like it here?" she asked when they lay down.

"I do, I do. The metronome's still going in my head, but I like it very much."

"It's funny having so much time together. We've never had this kind of time before."

"I like it."

"Me too. But sometimes you get lonely, don't you, Nick?"

"Once in a while. But don't take it personally."

They lay there, very peaceful. Later, Nick looked up at the sun. "I hate to say this, but we've got to head back."

"Can't we just call the maids and ask them to stay a little longer?"

"They're supposed to leave by one. Besides"—he said this as unseriously as he could—"how the hell could we talk to them on the phone?"

Stephanie laughed. "I forgot, I totally forgot."

As they pulled into the Bergers' drive, Nick realized that the maids' car was gone. He roared down the driveway.

They jumped out of the car and ran into the house. A quick glance at the living room assured them nothing was missing. Nick said, "You run upstairs. I'll check the cellar."

A few minutes later they met in the living room. "Nothing missing from the cellar."

"It's OK upstairs."

"Why in hell didn't they stay! I wonder if Carroll called."

Stephanie said, "I have no idea."

"Let's have a beer, Steph. I'm hot as hell."

They were on the terrace, sipping beer, when they heard footsteps coming toward them. Nick jumped to his feet immediately, stationing himself between Stephanie and the sound of the steps.

Russell Massey appeared around the corner of the farmhouse. "Where have you been?" he asked like a drill sergeant of his recruits. Nick could see he was drunk.

"Today's the maids' day, not yours. We went for our drive."

"You were out too long."

"Look, Massey, I'm not going to apologize to you. We left here at 11 and were back at 12:50. That's under two hours."

Stephanie intervened: "Weren't the maids here when you arrived?"

"I didn't see a soul."

"I don't believe that," she said. "They wouldn't have left unless you told them they could."

Massey spun around and walked away with his slightly overstated precision.

Nick said a little too loudly, "We ought to get a breatholator."

More quietly, Stephanie said, "I don't trust him, Nick."

"I'm not crazy about him either. But what are you going to do? He comes with the place."

"He must've told the maids to go."

"Unfortunately, it's a little difficult for us to ask them."

"Inez will just nod her head and flash you that toothy smile."

"There's a little too much gum for me."

"Carmela—"

"She's catatonic."

"Look, just don't let that old bastard get to you. That's just what he wants."

"Easier said than done."

The Minoan Goddess

"Not a major goddess," Nick liked to insist, "a comfortable down-home deity, good for small aches and constipation as well as temporary infertility." The catalogue described the figurine with more apparent respect—a Minoan fertility goddess from about 1500 B.C. Smooth and slender and barely an inch thick, she stood ten inches high, with high rounded breasts and a flat, wide face. What remained of her face gave the impression of a full mouth, and her eyebrows were thin, perfect arcs. After two millennia the aura of her femininity still clung indisputably to her —those breasts, that mouth. Her presence cheered and warmed Nick; he liked to handle her. The scale of the figure, the vanished paint and the partly eradicated features made it possible for him to see her as a whole— the missing detail freed Nick's mind and let him concentrate on the figure's soft suggestiveness. The catalogue didn't proclaim it, but the Minoan figure was one of the collection's rarest prizes.

The Bergers had installed the goddess on a red velvet pad on the grand piano. Quite stoned one night, Nick had moved her to the open shelf beside the fireplace. (Stephanie called it his first act of actually moving in.) There he could see her from the armchair without giving up the view of the fireplace. In spite of her costliness, the Minoan goddess made him feel at home in that jungle of five-digit price tags.

Nick held the figurine upright in his left hand as he made his way toward the steady beat of Stephanie's "Tap, tap, tap." He wasn't going to wait until she finished chopping the parsley because he'd just noticed how the faintly painted lines that outlined the side seam of the goddess's costume had been indented a little to emphasize the round breasts and her pinched waist. Nick thought, Steph will be happy I feel called upon to say a few art-critical words. So the art classes are taking hold. Just then his toe caught on the tile that made the level change from living room to kitchen. He stuck out his right arm to catch himself, and the goddess slipped and pitched forward. He grabbed for her and slid his leg out to try to break the fall; he got a hand under the figure, juggled her for one split second then watched as the goddess fell headfirst down to the tile floor.

An instant after she hit, the figure seemed to hold together. Next came the dry rippling crackle, and the earth-colored lady dissolved into the earth-colored tile; she sheared apart, eight fragments slithering in different directions across the kitchen floor.

He'd broken 3,500 years of history, destroyed an object that people touch with the reverence they once reserved for saints' relics. He had said all along that this was what he wanted to do with the whole stuffy, dictatorial farmhouse; he wanted to smash up the place so badly that sometimes he had to actively restrain himself from crashing into the glass shelves. Yet of all things, he thought bitterly, the goddess was the one thing he loved.

Stephanie just stood there leaning over the counter, the chopping knife in her hand. Two fragments of the goddess rested inches from her boot. She did not move, did not say a word. The reasonable half of Nick's brain said, That's right. It makes sense for her to lie low. The other part demanded that she provide him with the one thing that did not exist—a way out.

"Stephanie," he wailed, "what are we going to do?"

"I don't know." She exhaled that very quietly, knowing how crazy he could get if she said the wrong thing.

"Do you know how much it was worth?" They both knew exactly what the Bergers' catalogue said: $25,000 (Est.).

One inexcusably stupid misstep.

Like an infant, Nick wanted to bury his head and make it all go away, to be free of the Bergers and their booby-trapped collection forever. His stomach seemed to pry itself loose of its lining and fall into a blind, bottomless cavity; his heart constricted. He had only himself to blame. Yet what did he owe these people whose life-style he despised, whose house was set up, he believed, as a showcase for greed?

He ranted on: "They were crazy to leave this stuff lying around. Something like this was bound to happen." Countless times before he'd deftly negotiated that four-inch rise from living room to kitchen.

Like the tar baby, Stephanie just lay low and kept her peace. Yet he resented her keeping quiet as much as he would have resented her uttering a word. Her presence itself crowded him, accused him.

On the floor lay a fortune in eight jagged pieces. He counted each of them as she picked them up so gently it seemed she didn't trust him to do it. Inspiration struck him when the pile of fragments lay on the cutting board: "Let's put it back together. We could glue it, Steph. They have these extraordinary glues now. I mean on the tube you see 350-pound guys hanging from girders on their heads. Better, we could go to Philadelphia to the art museum and get a restorer to do it. They can work wonders."

Stephanie's hazel eyes fixed on Nick as though they were trying to hold him up. The eyes, as kind and supportive as they were, also asked for noble behavior.

He changed the subject slightly: "We're insured."

"Yes." She answered that.

"Then they don't stand to lose anything."

"No money." She hesitated, then said, "The figure can't be replaced."

"I know that," he shouted. "But they've got hundreds of other fucking figures." Stephanie stood her ground and just waited.

Finally, she said, "They'll have to know about this." Which translated: Don't give me any bullshit. You know you'll have to write to tell them.

Under stress, you first wish for a miracle—anything to relieve the uncertainty and guilt. When the miracle doesn't come, you want unlimited amounts of sympathy. Nick expected, no, demanded that Stephanie find that narrow, unlit, high-altitude catwalk that led to his pain, a path which he himself had trouble locating. If she couldn't find it or if she slipped—not entirely unlikely—he could accuse her of not loving him enough. Which would divert attention from the real question of what to do about the goddess lying in eight pieces on the floor. Love makes excessive demands on occasion.

Nick went on the offensive: "What do you think they've got insurance on us for? Why all that bonding?"

"For something like this."

"You think they'd miss this goddamn piece?" She looked at him with dissatisfaction, her mouth curled up tightly, reminding Nick that he was the one who loved the goddess.

"Oh, Nick, I don't know. I'm just terribly sorry this happened." Her hazel eyes offered him as much sympathy as he could soak up. No secret escape routes hid there. She presented a guarantee that infuriated Nick and assured him at the same time: it was tough, but Stephanie never lied about the important issues.

He moved to the counter and very tentatively touched two pieces of the figurine. They brushed together with a dry crackle, like static.

"Do you think we can put it together?"

She said, "I don't know."

"I don't want to pay these overprivileged assholes a cent."

"I know."

Stephanie pulled him against her full body. Tears made her eyes look enormous.

A Rough Day, Rough Night

Unwilling to admit she was right, Nick acted the pigheaded thug and argued with Stephanie all afternoon. He kept saying he wouldn't write to the Bergers. Stephanie insisted he had no choice. He said that if he wrote they'd get booted out of their newly curdled paradise. She answered. "We have to take that chance." He said if they did get the boot, she'd believe he'd broken the figure on purpose. Stephanie laughed and replied, "That's total crap. It's the one thing around here you loved."

"You always hurt the one you love."

"Goddamn it, Nick, you know what you've got to do and

114

there's no point in dragging both of us through it again and again." She turned back to the Bergers' catalogue.

Nick couldn't argue with that, but he did muster another fifteen minutes of brooding before skulking off to the trout pond. In his huff, he hooked then lost what looked like a two-pound rainbow.

While he cast and reeled in with his perfectly balanced Orvis rod supplied by Mr. P. Berger, he thought about his stupid, wasteful misstep and the need for the combined confession and apology. Eating humble pie didn't excite Nick's appetite. He considered the owners of the shattered goddess. There was one color photograph of Amanda that actually turned Nick on—she had a slight smile on her face and was leaning toward the camera. She wore a soft furry black sweater—her breasts' firm weight was cupped by that black fur, her white skin and black hair, a lush, positively edible mouth. He couldn't pass that shot without getting an erotic charge. Sometimes he could only bear to look at it out of the corner of his eye. What had she been before? A show girl? Probably not. Her face didn't have that hard, vacant expression. Student? If so, a very popular one. What was she now? Kept woman? Connoisseur? Nick remembered somebody once saying it was always harder on the poorer one of a couple. True or False? He wasn't sure. To know that you had to know the couple. Even about Stephanie and himself, Nick couldn't always be certain for whom it was rougher. Usually he supposed that she was under more pressure, since her old man kept continually loosening and tightening the fiscal thumbscrews. The executors should write any day now, he thought, which explains why she's so damned tense. Nick didn't want Stephanie caught in a rundown between William Harrold and himself, partly because he'd witnessed how it confused and exhausted her, and partly because he didn't like being favored as the lesser of two evils. Also, William Harrold was a formidable opponent. And all this crap about not going out of the house, playing mistress of the manor when she chased those high school kids out of the bushes, resenting the maids—being alone all the time—none of this is healthy for her. Nick found support here for his own ambivalence about Bucks County. And Stephanie had even thanked him for inviting Henry down. But trying to ease her out of the kitchen, Stephanie's home base, hadn't worked as well, and Nick blamed himself for putting it badly. A few evenings before he'd congratulated Stephanie on her spinach quiche: "This is delicious. Wonderful." He paused, looking for words. "But how about tomorrow, instead of you slaving in here all day, I'll grill us a couple of simple, plain old American hamburgers?"

"You don't like my cooking?" she asked.

"It's not that. I love it—" Nick had tried to explain, but he only dug himself in deeper. Fortunately, just yesterday morning in Doylestown, he'd stumbled on a big picture book about kitchens, which he figured would smooth over the gap between gourmets and hamburgers, tarragon cream sauces and plebian taste.

As he whipped the rod's cork handle back and forward again, then watched the tapered line cut its parabolic curve through the air, Nick thought, How important all this shit seemed before I did in that goddess.

While Nick fished, Stephanie thought, Three more weeks to my birthday. She suddenly remembered that the executors' letter was dated. She walked coolly to the closet, dredged out the shoe box, located the incriminating dated letter and envelope, and carefully shredded the evidence. It was neither Stephanie's style nor desire to lie; she didn't enjoy living with her unsavory little secret. But she couldn't tell Nick yet. He didn't need another burden just a few hours after he'd destroyed the goddess. She'd hold out until her birthday. By then, Stephanie hoped, she'd think of some explanation. Or some acceptable excuse.

Nick was always a light sleeper. The watchdog in him was inbred so deeply that any creak or flutter served to vault him out of a deep sleep into bolt upright position. That night he couldn't get to sleep at all and spent the midnight hour jumping in and out of bed, disturbing the beauty who was trying to sleep. About one o'clock he went downstairs to the living room and lay down on the sofa. Too jumpy to pick up a book, Nick kept trying to squirm out of writing the letter to the Bergers. By 2:30 A.M. he hadn't gotten any further than he'd been at 2:30 P.M. His eyes burned, his heart beat 6/8 time, his stomach felt lined with metal filings while his conscience kept running barefoot Hindustani glissandos over blazing coals. Around three, he finally nodded off. But he slept only a few minutes before a sound startled him. A sound like footsteps.

For a split second he couldn't figure out where he was. He expected to see the old bedroom in Woods Hole but found himself surrounded by strange old furniture with bare beams above and vividly colored rectangles dangling from the walls. As his head cleared, he heard the footsteps again, but this time Nick was certain of what he heard: a burglar or prowler or worse right outside the window. Quick revision of his opinion of the Bergers—they had reason for suburban paranoia.

Too punchy to think about protecting himself, Nick staggered to the door, loudly opened the screen and took a step outside. Before his eyes could adjust to the darkness, he saw a shadow bolt past the pool and continue up the hill at a run. Quickly Nick stepped back inside, his fingers searched for the switch, then the lights blazed on—the low lights along the front walk, the eerie green/blue lights in the pool, and that blinding spotlight over the front door.

Not a soul in sight. Maybe it was an animal, Nick lied to himself, knowing the shadow he'd seen wasn't made by any four-legged creature. Wide awake now, he went back inside and got the six-volt flashlight.

Turning himself into a lighthouse, he threw the beam along the stone wall and started up the hill after the fleeing shadow. He wasn't afraid, which was strange because he was so vulnerable out there; all those vectors pointing his way at the source of the bright light—the perfect target.

He lit up the pump house, flashed his beam on the swimming pool, moved over toward the barn and made the barn's shadow swing away from the pond then back again. The low hedge he'd jumped running down Carroll's phone call, the garden patch itself—familiar things turned menacing, nothing but dark edges and deep, lurking shadow. Every dark place might hide a maniac. Carroll had insisted that their job wasn't dangerous, but footsteps under a window in the middle of the night and a fleeing shadow didn't sound like a nursery game to Nicholas, and he had doubts about the agent's trustworthiness in any case. Besides, it was his and Stephanie's ass, not Carroll's.

The crickets chirped away, the cicadas banged their knees together like mad. Under his bare feet the turf felt cold and jagged, as though Massey had been out there sharpening it. Nick moved onto tiptoe, realizing he was drenched with sweat. "Cool," he commanded. "Stay cool." He felt somebody watching him, lurking in the dark just beyond the range of the six-volt. He didn't want to appear afraid so he took long firm strides; but it was all bluff.

With the farmhouse at his back, Nick moved uphill toward the pump house. No human sound. Just nature there. He stood absolutely quiet; nothing. Suddenly Nick began running up toward the pond. He started around the pond at top speed, his flashlight bouncing rays into the dense woods. As he ran he felt fearlessness return: He remembered standing his ground in the municipal parking lot as the big dude ran toward him; biding his time until the guy was almost within reach, then starting a punch from his toes. The smooth click of impact, the large body crumpling. As he sprinted around the pond Nick remembered standing up and crossing the room toward his high school math teacher, Mr. Power, the bully. He saw the cornered expression on Power's face. I never hesitated in those days.

The split-rail fence came up in front of him suddenly, he veered left; the flashlight sent weird wavy ground shadows running into the woods. Trunks of oaks and maples swirled by him, the bark dark rivulets. He knew the lay of the grounds well, better, Nick figured, than the person who kept him company; the flashlight was in excellent shape. So Nick completed the turn around the pond, running hard, and burst back onto the lawn just above the pool. He had to convince his tormentor that he really wanted to find him. Maybe that would discourage him. Nick got light-headed from running in the dark behind that bouncing beam. He ran up and down across the lawn and began to feel like a little kid in a dream—he was in a big field all alone, and nothing looked familiar.

Dripping sweat, he stopped in front of the house. He stood outside, outlined in front of the lights until he cooled off, then went in, turned off all the lights and waited. Pressed up against the door so that he wouldn't move at all, he waited another fifteen minutes, straining to hear. He felt convinced someone was out there, had been out there all along. But he heard nothing.

As the clock struck four, he climbed the narrow wooden stairs to the upper floor. Stephanie lay sleeping, her red nightgown showing the top of her breasts and soft cleavage. Of course he should have awakened her and said, "I think I just saw a prowler outside." But she looked so peaceful and untroubled, lost in a pleasant dream. And he felt utterly exhausted. So he told himself, It'll keep until morning. He crawled into the sack and nudged her gently. Stephanie turned toward him, and her red nightgown parted more invitingly.

The Letter

The moment the car disappeared into the row of oaks, Nick stepped off on patrol. For two hours he policed the grounds for signs of the late night intruder. Up and down, high and low, in bushes and behind every rock, he searched for one telltale mark. Without proof, what could Nick say to her: I think I saw somebody sneaking around outside last night? That seemed stupid; worse, cruel. He still didn't believe he'd dreamed up the previous night's drama, but it had been late, he had been exhausted and strung out. Nick admitted he might have been mistaken. And, if not, if somebody had been lurking out there, odds were that he or she or they would make a return appearance one of these nights.

He was satisfied to let it go. He had that little matter of a smashed $25,000 goddess on his mind, and he also had to figure out his literary approach to the confession of a capital crime.

He warmed up to write the dread confession by swimming two miles and knocking off thirty clay pigeons. He liked shooting while Massey was cutting the grass, first because it drowned out the noise and second because Massey had said to him last Friday. "You use up all them birds?"

"Yes. Why?"

"I have to file my expenses with Mr. Carroll."

"Massey, don't give me any of your crap. I pay for them, not you."

"But the bunker shouldn't ever be empty."

"Listen, I'm here now, not Mr. Berger."

Massey glared at Nick as though saying, I know where you come from, boy. Then he stomped away.

After lunch Nick shouted into the kitchen, "I need pencil and paper, madame."

He sat down at Amanda Berger's Block-Front, Slant-Top Escritoire (catalogue, p. 50). Stephanie came up with supplies and took the liberty of patting Nick on the shoulder. He gave her a searing glance—his Don't-condescend-to-me look—then settled in. He lasted a good two minutes, if that. He was up off the chair for a blanket—"Seat's too hard." For the next three hours he must have leaped out of the chair a dozen times to get coffee or take a leak or sharpen pencils. He'd lined up eight stiletto-tipped Number 2's at his right hand, plus an assortment of black Flairs, one red Flair for special underlining, and a handful of black Bics. When his hand got tired of writing with one pen, Nick switched to another type and kept going. Not that there was all that much going.

Under his breath Nick cursed the Bergers. He argued with Stephanie and chewed at his nails until she threatened to dunk them in iodine. Nick was a good counter-puncher, and he wrote that way, with short bursts of energy-concentrate that felt so intense that he liked to run out from under

121

them. That's why he jumped and paced and did exercises, saying, occasionally, "All this builds character."

The first draft looked like a berserk switchboard, all these lines running over the page from one batch of scribbled notes to another, then off to remote terminals in the margins.

"I don't owe these bastards anything."

"You owe them the decency—"

"That's their word, pal."

"Living here—"

"You make me feel like I'm in finishing school, Steph. No, finishing camp. They needed somebody to housesit, remember that. They're not doing us any favor." He blew up: "You're trying to lay your middle-class guilt trip on me, and I won't buy it." She seemed so outrageously bourgeois to him. Was she on their side? Four years before, just after they'd started going out, they had a long, running argument about stealing—Nick had given her the then current leftist rhetoric about passing on the price to those who could better afford it, and she'd blasted away at how self-indulgent and small stealing was. Nick didn't remember who won, though in the long run obviously she did because he cut out most of the light-fingered exercises soon after they began living together. Stephanie had the infuriating habit of demanding the best from Nick, which told him, always, how important she was to him. He never felt good when he disappointed her. And sometimes—many times—that was an awful drag.

The first draft. Amazing how much can ride on a phrase, a word. They'd start talking about something he'd said to the Bergers and suddenly, out of the blue, Nick found himself involved in profound assessments and counterassessments of his character. Like the tip of an iceberg, but with every facet of that surface capable of indicating exactly what was going on below.

The second rewrite came more easily. He announced the end by hollering, "Copy!" and Stephanie appeared for the final editing session.

At 9:30 they reached their official, agreed-upon version. He couldn't say for sure how much of it he wrote; a lot of Stephanie had worked its way into the text too.

July 28, 1977

Dear Mr. and Mrs. Berger,

Our first letter to you described a happier occasion. We wanted to thank you for the privilege of living in your beautiful home among all your precious and beautiful artworks. I write this letter in great pain, with a feeling of anguish. (She said this sounded awkward. They argued until he said it hurt him as much as he said it hurt. She let it go at that.) Let me get to the point: Yesterday I was carrying the Minoan household goddess (#324 in your catalogue) toward the kitchen; I wanted to dust it off. (Steph went along with his lie. Nick didn't want to tell the Bergers he was showing off the painted lines on the body). I carried it carefully, for I admire all the pieces in your collection and treat them carefully but particularly this one. It has been one of my favorites since we came here.

As I carried the figure, I tripped on that low step between the living room floor and the kitchen. The goddess slipped out of my hand and broke on the tiles.

I cannot tell you how upset and guilty and miserable I felt then and feel now, writing to you. I only wish it was in my power to restore that beautiful figure. It is not. I understand that she is irreplaceable. For that I am sorry beyond words. I know that your collection is insured, so that the monetary value of the piece may be recovered. But I also will do everything in my power to locate a similar figure and to get it for you. If there's any difference in price, I will of course make it up to you.

I'm very upset and also embarrassed and ashamed that my carelessness caused this horrible accident. I hope that I can make it up to you. I will do my best to make certain that such an accident never happens again while we're here, that is, if you would like us to remain in the farmhouse. However, if you would like us to leave, please inform us of your wishes. I anxiously await your reply.

> With sincerest and deepest
> apologies,
> Yours,
>
> Nicholas Young

When Nick's literary trial was finished, Stephanie typed the letter. She also told him how much she admired what he'd done. That amused Nick. "Backhanded compliment if I ever heard one. You wrote at least a third of it." They mailed their collaborative effort to Carroll, following the mystifying injunction about not communicating directly with the Bergers.

Stephanie guessed that Nick's mood might improve after they sent off the letter, but she was wrong. The next morning he seemed very touchy, and even yelled at her for burning the toast: "Christ, you always do it. You know how much I hate burned shit."

"I'll eat that toast," she grumbled as she slipped two more pieces into the toaster-oven. "You might think I did it on purpose."

Stephanie attributed Nick's testiness to his uncertainty about whether they'd be expelled from Bucks County. If that happened, Nick would feel that he'd given William Harrold more ammunition. She didn't know that Nick had another more compelling question on his mind.

Nick insisted Stephanie take the afternoon off to see *Modern Times*, which was playing at the Community College in Doylestown. Again, as soon as the old gray Dodge disappeared, he set off. For an intense hour Nick's eye skimmed the familiar turf; he tracked up the hill, around the pond, searched in the woods, looking for a bootprint or something that had been dropped inadvertently. Though he found nothing, he felt like he was waking up; a long-estranged physical alertness slipped on him. Nick never doubted that the intruder was a man. Always his enemies had been bullying men: first his own father, then William Harrold, and even old Powers, the high school math teacher who had gotten him thrown out of New Bedford High one week before his graduation.

That June day had been almost as hot, and Nick had been dozing at his desk, trying not to listen. But Powers kept going after Sylvester Stokowicz. "I told you how to do this equation; I led you through it step by step." Mounting anger flushed the teacher's gray face. "What is wrong with you, you Polack moron?" The math teacher's pointer flashed downward, catching Stock's outstretched knuckles with a POP!

Silence. Then Nick's voice: "Why don't you stop picking on him, Mr. Powers?" The rows of aligned heads wheeled around at Nick, who sat in the back row. A book dropped onto a desk. Someone coughed. "Calling him names isn't going to help."

The gray bulk of the teacher shifted menacingly. Behind Powers, rows of figures and letters marched along the blackboard.

"You don't think it's fair, Young?" A sadist's smile played on the big man's face.

"No, I don't." Suddenly Nick couldn't take it any longer. A whole year of sitting there while this stupid, prejudiced bully pushed him and everyone else around. A year of un-protested boredom playing straight man for this fucker's viciousness. He found himself measuring the large body.

"Well, I'll ask you politely to shut your smirky wise-ass

face, Young, before I shut it for you." The street fighter's snarl replaced the thin veneer of gentility. Powers actively slapped the pointer in his palm.

Nick was already on his feet and moving up the aisle toward the front of the room.

"Sit down, Young."

Nick had reached the open space in front of the dais. As he took the step up Powers came toward him and whipped his pointer like a baseball bat. Nick threw up his forearm, blocking the shot, and the pointer snapped in two. Nick saw the face grow flabby, the eyes lose focus as bully turned coward. Nick stepped in close and brought his right fist up into the shiny black coat. The fist burrowed into the cushion of soft flesh, his knuckles scraped across the gold watch chain. Nick didn't swing again, only watched as Powers flailed to catch his balance and backed three steps into the blackboard. The teacher hung there for support, his knuckles dangling in the chalk tray.

Nick turned and walked slowly back to his seat. He sat there while his classmates gawked at him and shook their heads in wonder, while his friend Billy whispered, "You're a crazy motherfucker, Young. A real crazy." Nick sat there until the vice-principal charged into the room accompanied by a cop and Nick's football coach, and they dragged him unresisting down the hall to the principal's office, his coach almost in tears as he repeated, "They won't let you graduate. They won't let you graduate." And all the way down the hall Nick kept thinking, Stupid to hit him. Real dumb.

Punching out Powers had been stupid, a no-win situation. He'd laid his ass on the line and for his noble antiauthoritarian action he'd been barraged by shriekings at home and the chance to pay his own way through a third-rate prep school in order to graduate. Stephanie had helped

126

edge Nick away from this self-destruction, helped domesticate his self-consuming anger. But in the process he'd misplaced the energizing power of his anger. Actually, it was even subtler, since Nick's anger even worked for him when it had been politically engaged. Then the sixties ended, and Nick started to drift. If now he could learn to take only the well-calculated risks, perhaps he could shake off his sloth. An odd way to get started, he thought, but the intruder offered Nick the chance to play amateur detective while proving once and for all that he could protect William Harrold's daughter. Besides, he argued with himself, she just isn't used to physical fear. For evidence, Nick found himself considering something that had occurred two years before.

In the middle of the night Nick had heard Stephanie murmur, "Dammit." That had been enough to wake him. He'd lain there half-awake as she pushed the shoes she'd tripped over out of the way and made her way to the bathroom. Wide awake then, he'd slipped out of bed and silently crept down the hall, trying not to make a sound. At the doorway he'd paused, gathered himself for the move, then taken that single step up and into the bathroom as he shouted, "Boo!"

Stephanie jumped off the toilet seat, whacking her elbow on the sink. She sank back down onto the seat clutching her elbow; her face started to dissolve, then the tears came. "You scared me. You really scared me," she sobbed. "Why did you do that?"

Nick had no answer. "It was stupid. I really didn't mean to do it. I'm sorry. It was stupid, crazy."

When she was finally quiet, Nick had stepped back into the hall. Then, feeling absolutely crazy, unable to let it go, he'd stuck his head back in again and quickly but not too loudly said, "Agggh!"

Deep spasms took hold of her body and shook her. Her

sleepy face looked like it might crack. "Nick . . . why . . . did you . . .?"

"I'm sorry, darling. I don't know. I'm so so sorry." He took her head in his hands, and they stayed there in the bathroom for a very long time. Then he helped her back to bed, lighting the way ahead of them, cradling her body as though she were an invalid.

"I promise I'll never do that again," he said to Stephanie when they were back in bed. "God, I don't know why I had to do it to you." Nick began crying then. For the first time in their life together, he cried.

Remembering that night now and how frightened she'd been, Nick knew he couldn't tell Stephanie about the footsteps and noises. She loves this place so much, he thought. I can't spoil it for her. At this point, he couldn't really be sure if the noises were real or in his imagination. He told himself he'd wait and see what developed. Remember, he counseled himself uncertainly, Carroll said if there were burglars they were after the art; they wouldn't hurt us.

Stephanie

Money is supposed to liberate you, she thought, to allow you to live in the present. Stephanie was tired of the endless deferring, the waiting for the payoff that never came, the unremitting tedium of living in the interim. She blamed her father for not having taught her anything about the potentialities and responsibilities of money. Responsibilities, she thought with self disgust. That's Daddy's word.

With her birthday only a few days away, Nick already exuded the excitement with which he always prefaced a major event. Each night he asked if she wanted her present, and each night, characteristically, she said no, she'd wait until August eighth.

Only Nick's rules and his sense of delicacy kept him from asking, "What have you heard from the executors?" She was enormously grateful for Nick's restraint, particularly since he'd been in such a volatile, unsettled mood since he'd broken the figurine.

Stephanie still hoped that her father's and her own position could be reconciled, for which fantasy Nick, if he'd known about the executors' letter, would've labeled her "a dirty liberal."

The Lawnmower

Stephanie's forearm ached, but the egg whites were just beginning to form peaks, so she kept whipping them. Just then Massey and Nick started screaming at each other. She abandoned the incomplete chocolate Bavarian pie and ran out of the house with the whisk still in her hand. By then Massey was waving at the red lawnmower like the flagman at Indianapolis.

"Not me, you young buck. You're the one who drained it!"

Nick realized that it wasn't either Massey or himself who'd forgotten to check the oil. Massey was more right though—the intruder had probably drained off the oil and the motor had almost burned out! Oh Christ, Nick thought as Stephanie came running toward them, now she'll want to know what it's all about.

"Never been so insulted in my life." Massey wore his old houndstooth jacket with the Bud bottle caps for buttons. As usual, Massey was a little fried, and now his varicose nose looked like grated beets. "He says I been fiddling with my own machine. That make sense?"

To himself Nick reasoned: Best move would be to bold-faced lie and say, "Oh yeah, I remember, I drained it because the oil was filthy." But he couldn't stand the idea of Massey's showing him up. "I didn't say that, Steph. I said there's no oil in it, the engine's overheated, and that maybe he forgot to fill it."

"Not me," the old man replied. "Never forget."

"Well, it wasn't this boy." Nick thumped himself in the chest. "Who was it, Massey? Little green men? Leprechauns?"

Massey glared at Nick as though he wanted to kill him.

"Why don't you two forget it," Stephanie said, "and start arguing about who's going to put in the oil?"

The grass barely looked long enough to clip with Massey's mustache scissors, but the Bergers employed a compulsive gardener. Like clockwork, every Friday at 8:15 A.M. he cranked up the big mower and ripped the young couple out of bed. Nick had tried to talk Massey into letting them

130

catch a few seconds' additional sleep, but he muttered something about lazy nits and sticking to his schedule. "Got other work to do, you know. Not like some people."

Stephanie changed the subject: "Mr. Massey, could you spare a little mulch for the herb garden? Nick, why don't you go knock off a few clay pigeons?" Stephanie had never promoted Nick's shooting, so Nick accepted the peacemaking concession. Soon he heard the oiled lawnmower whining in the distance while he boomed away with the over-and-under shotgun.

Nick tried to forget the lawnmower incident, tried to conceive of it as an example of Massey's Bud-soaked consciousness. Only late that same night he heard the sounds again: a rustle, what might have been bushes being parted then—clearly—boots on gravel. Stephanie, who lay half-awake beside him, muttered sleepily. "Did you hear something outside?"

"Just a raccoon, love. Lot of them up near the pond."

She flipped over and pulled the sheet up around her shoulder. Nick sat up stiffly, pretending to read and listening intently for the next half hour. But, after the sound of the boots, he heard nothing that sounded unusual.

Surprisingly, Nick slept well that night, and the next morning he woke up first. He took a quick shower and went outside to check the grounds for clues. Sure enough, he found three large bootprints in the soft earth at the edge of the rosebeds. They looked huge to him, a spaceman's tracks. So suburban paranoia is for real. A wave of new respect for the Bergers. He almost felt as though he had a job to do for them. As he stood staring at the prints, Stephanie's voice jumped from behind him: "What you up to Nicky?" He took a half step back, feeling he'd been caught red-handed.

Nick thought quickly: "Who would've thought a month

ago I'd be out here at dawn taking snorts of the roses?" The morning hung hazy and thick, the rose smell was spread like honey all over the garden.

Only half-awake, she smiled. Dimples.

Keeping his back to her, he crept up closer to the prints. She laid her big white coffee mug down on the glass table, then came up from behind, put her arms around him and leaned her head on his shoulder. Nick pretended that her weight pushed him foward and, angling his body toward the flowerbed, he took another step. With his lead foot, he gently rubbed out two big bootprints. But he couldn't get to the third one. It lay there just out of reach, looking like a dinosaur track.

She came around to his side, leaned down right over that huge, unmistakable bootprint, and sniffed the dew-covered flowers, then straightened up and turned back to the table. "It's a little foggy this morning, but I think it'll burn off."

He could have turned to her then and said, "Stephanie, my pal, my love, we've got ourselves a major problem. Take a look at this!" But habit kept Nick from doing the sensible, sensitive, fair thing—the he-man tough guy began to screen fair maiden from brutal truth. Condescension crept into his equation too: She's got enough on her mind now. Further, Nick wanted that secret for himself because, for the first time, it gave him a mission. Until now, on this manicured ground, Nick felt he couldn't gain equal footing. In front of the paintings and sculpture, though he no longer felt like a dolt and even liked some of the art, he often felt uncomfortable; the catalogue's inflated prices and the critics' exalted rhetoric didn't help. The intruder suddenly gave Nick his first real purchase: He could pretend he was protecting Stephanie from the unknown threat and, as a fallback, accuse her of being too soft and too middle class to stand up to the threat.

132

Late that afternoon, when Stephanie went upstairs to shower, Nick took a few photographs of the footprint in the rosebeds, and then he wiped it out. On Monday, when Massey came by to pick up a pair of large pruning shears for a job at a neighbor's house, Nick ran over to the barn. "Could you please come on over here with me? I want to ask you something, Mr. Massey." The "Mr." cost Nick effort.

"Yeah, what you want?" Massey's facial skin looked like old currency, with delicate blue and red threads running in all directions across his cheeks.

Nick led him to the damp ground at the edge of the pond.

"What kind of fern is this?"

"You simple nit, that's a maiden hair. About as common as they come." Massey stomped away down the hill, but not before Nick had the bootprint that he wanted. Nick was disappointed. The intruder's feet were a lot larger than Massey's.

The night before Stephanie's birthday, Nick headed out to the trap range to relax. His mind was overloaded with mysterious footprints and the issue of the $25,000 goddess and the further question of whether they'd be given the bum's rush out of Bucks County. They hadn't heard from the Bergers yet, which wasn't surprising since the Bergers lived in France. But both kept half-expecting an outraged phone call from Carroll.

Nick came up over the ridge and below, on the ground around the trap, were dozen of clay pigeons all laid out in neat, parallel stacks on the ground. As Nick picked up the top pigeon the black and white clay disk fell apart in his hand. He tried to pick up the next one, and it too fell into pieces. The third pigeon did the same, and the next. He picked up the rest of the first pile and found himself juggling fragments. Uncertainly, he started on the second stack. Each disc was broken. Frantically, Nick began to sort through the stack, throwing fragments over his shoulder, then in a rage he waded into the other piles, kicking at the pigeons and sending clay fragments spinning out in all directions. Not a single pigeon—Nick figured there were at least four hundred of them—was intact. The door to the concrete bunker was open, the padlock smashed and hanging limply down. Inside, Nick found that his treadle had not been disturbed and that the trap itself was in perfect working order. Such a crazed joke, Nick thought as he looked around in dismay. He felt like a spotlit target; he felt totally alone.

To calm himself, he picked up every single piece of clay. All the broken pigeons he could reassemble he put back into their boxes and threw the remaining fragments into a trash bin. Then he headed back to the farmhouse, fully resolved to explain everything to Stephanie. She's got to know, he told himself. Only fair. I mean, she's living in the middle of this craziness, too. Besides, you can't go around hiding this stuff and playing he-man hero or you'll go batshit. You're already going batshit. And when she does find out, which she will someday, then she'll feel betrayed, mad as hell, very righteously pissed off. Yet the more Nick thought about it, the nuttier the joke became. He stopped at the front door. "Suppose this guy is a nut?" He didn't want to pursue that option, because it made his not telling her seem dangerous.

He walked into the kitchen not certain about how to proceed. Stephanie stood over the cutting board, humming as she trussed up what Nick now recognized as a Cornish game hen. She looked totally content, happy as a clam at high tide. Once again he thought, Not here, not now.

He felt strongly about keeping the bad news outside the house.

"Come out for a walk," he said aloud. He didn't want to bring the evidence into the farmhouse. Carroll had insisted that the robbers would not go into an occupied house, and Nick didn't want to break the spell and encourage any further intrusion. The skeet range was close enough.

"Not now." Without looking up Stephanie smiled, then pulled the string through the hen's pebbly skin. He felt they couldn't talk about it in the kitchen.

"Come on. We can go swimming afterwards.

She turned her hazel eyes on him. "I've got to finish this and get it in the oven or we won't eat till 9:30, and you know how much you like that. You go on. I'll be out later."

"You always say that." It came out harsher than Nick meant it.

Her head jerked up. Stephanie looked him over carefully, then chalked up his obvious anxiety to the broken goddess. "Later," she said softly. "I've got to finish the hen."

He took the Nikon and moped back to the skeet range, where he took a number of shots of the broken pigeons. And just behind the bunker that held the trap, Nick found a bootprint—the same one he'd found in the rosebeds. He photographed that too, thinking that it might someday serve as evidence. Then he asked himself: evidence for what?

The Birthday

On her birthday Stephanie received a letter from her father. It was typewritten on the brokerage house's stationery, contained a check for fifty dollars and the following message:

Aug. 6th

Happy birthday, daughter. Welcome to the many and various delights of middle age. Enclosed is the usual birthday dividend.

Mildred and I are well and look forward to those three weeks in Spain. She sends birthday greetings.

I trust all continues to please you on that lovely estate.

With love and affection,
Dad

Stephanie did not show the note to Nick, but she did say that her father indicated she'd be hearing from her executors any day now.

Nick gave Stephanie the book about kitchens, a ten-inch-square format coffee table book which was well laid out and had reasonably good color reproductions. His inscription read:

"To the best I know. To more and better everything, from soup to nuts."

She told herself harshly: He works so hard to satisfy me and I'm so unfair to him. He'll understand what Daddy and his flunkies are trying to do to us. No, that's not the question. I don't want to say anything to him because I'm so profoundly embarrassed. Stephanie vowed she'd tell Nick as soon as she could work up the nerve. Her fear of not being able to tell him, her sadness about her father, her happiness with Nick's present—she started to cry.

Nick comforted her. After a while he said, "Happy?"

Unable to speak, she nodded.

Nick wanted to believe that people were not put on earth to make each other suffer. He didn't, therefore, believe that people were put on earth for any purpose, or that there was a god. The only god he could imagine was a demon joker, maniacally ironic and ingeniously sadistic. But, given the uphill nature of existence, Nick did not think it made sense to make things harder on others, especially those others whom you loved. In moments of uncertainty, fear and paranoia, when his self-confidence was shaken, Nick found himself behaving badly. He had so much ego and self-esteem tied up in his concept of good behavior he became impossible to live with when giving himself failing marks.

Stephanie had turned 29 on August 8th; the next night Nick crept downstairs and into the night. He left the lights off. He told himself to keep perfectly calm: he didn't want to get worked up the way he had that first time, running around in the dark like a madman. This time he'd be systematic and cover the grounds in two big loops on either side of the house. He started the first loop at the front door, crept uphill to the pump house, swung around it and up to the pool, then continued up the hill to the trout pond. At the edge of the woods he stopped, leaned against an oak, took aim and quickly sprayed the woods with his flashlight's beam. As the beam snaked in among the dense laurel and rhododendron, it threw jagged peaks of eerie shadow into the deep background. A tree trunk swung menacingly to the side, a bush shivered then froze. The layered depths seemed to snatch up his light. He took a half-step back, felt a hand grab his thigh; he jumped forward and reached back, grabbing a low-lying branch. To his right a twig snapped; he spun around as something small sped away. Goddamn it, he coached himself, keep cool. He snapped the beam up into the trees, ran it along the thick overhanging limbs. He thought the beam picked up some light overhead and retraced its route to find the source. Suddenly he froze. A pair of enormous quizzical yellow eyes blazed unblinkingly into the light. A harsh squawk and an awkward flapping, then the owl moved heavily off into the woods. It took Nick a moment to realize he was still holding his breath. He exhaled noisily and looked nervously about. No witnesses.

Smiling grimly and sweating, Nick turned and descended the hill till he stood between the two majestic elms. Not a sound except for the cicadas and a cooing wood dove. He moved on into the front yard and kneeled down behind the stone wall. He waited a few minutes but saw nothing, heard nothing. Forward to the carpark where, feeling ridiculous yet jumpy, he shined the light into the car. Despair mounting, he impatiently swept the hay field with the beam. Nothing there. Or was everything there, lurking just beyond the reach of the light? Heading back toward the front yard he suddenly heard the familiar sequence of sounds— footsteps, a scraping, someone running away. Instantly, he took off up the hill toward the sound. He was running so quickly he didn't see the hunched form until he was upon it. His heart pumping alarms, he tried to swerve and threw up his arms and suddenly his head was enveloped by small round dangling balls and a maze of branches—the crab apple.

Standing by the innocent tree holding his scratched arm, Nick thought: He's out there, I know he's out there. But there was absolutely no sound. Even the cicadas seemed to hold their breath. Fear took hold of Nick and shook his exhausted body. It had been years since he'd been so afraid.

From now on, he thought, nighttime is spooktime. All the things that are perfectly ordinary during the day—the crab apple, the rose bushes, the stone wall—will turn enemies every night. And every night I'll be out here, trying to run down whoever it is.

Determined to complete his search, Nick headed up the hill toward the barn. He remembered a story about the Australian Maoris who used to make night reconnaissance patrols stark naked: One of them would slip up silently on a sentry and could only tell if he was a friend or enemy when he'd actually laid hands on the man's body. Nick ran, he slipped from dense tree to thick bush, he played his light over the ground and lurked in the shadow, but he found nothing, nobody. Once he'd read that the cuckoo, a parasite bird that lays its eggs in another bird's nest, is so ashamed that it hides itself from sight when spying on its abandoned chick. Nick felt like the crazed hunter of the cuckoo bird, chasing the source of the sounds and coming back, each night, empty-handed and exhausted. He knew he'd kill his prey if he ever cornered him or her or them or it.

Pictures of a Reluctant Exhibitionist

Even if her own bad faith hadn't already overloaded her sensibility, Stephanie would not have been equipped for Nick's emotional tailspin. Overnight their tone, which had meant so much to both of them, changed. Nick suddenly had no tolerance for what she said or did. Each time she used the word "Daddy," which was fairly often because William Harrold was on her mind, Nick insisted that the term encapsulated all the arrogance and insensitivity of privilege. He nagged her unmercifully—had she mailed the telephone bill? Picked up a new filter for the swimming pool? He wouldn't stop running down "Plan Number 1," his name for Stephanie's attempt to keep track of how they spent money. They had $400 a month and, though they never went out together, somehow were managing to live beyond their means. Sensibly, she'd bought a ledger to keep accounts. Nick bitched about having to save sales slips and bet that the ledger wouldn't have an entry after the first month. (He was right.) They argued about everything—taking the garbage to the dump, washing the dishes, even sharpening the knives, which was the silliest discussion they'd ever had.

One night as they sat together reading Arnheim, Nick suddenly muttered, "Pomp, pomp." He laid down *Visual*

Thinking, rubbed his eyes and said, "I can't read this heavy shit anymore."

She looked at his nails, which were chewed down to the quick. Two nights before she'd found bloodstains on his pillow. "What's wrong, Nick?"

Her earnest eyes touched him. Hesitating, he looked away from her. The furniture and paintings told Nick he'd always be a stranger here. After three months he still walked around the living room on tiptoe. They'd moved to the one place guaranteed to keep them as far apart as possible. He exploded: "I think this shit is BORING!"

"You don't have to yell, I can hear you."

About noon every day Nick walked down the line of pin oaks to the mailbox at the end of the drive. As usual, he left in a state of excitement and came back depressed and furious, carrying the handful of circulars and envelopes with initials printed on the outside from the hundreds of organizations the Bergers supported. That morning the letter hadn't arrived either.

"Why don't you call Philadelphia?" she suggested softly. "Maybe Carroll's heard something from them."

Nick glared at her. "He'll just fob me off with bullshit about waiting for a reply. If he had the answer he wanted, he'd let us know right away."

Later, as Stephanie paddled in the inner tube, waves of what seemed like revelations swept over her: She understood how upset he was about not hearing from the Bergers. But that didn't explain why Nick let his sense of style stand in the way of their having a reasonably civilized time in Bucks County. For the first time in their relationship Nick's "background" actually seemed a handicap, not a heroic opportunity. He suddenly seemed like one of those see-through models in the natural history museums--brutally obvious and totally without mystery, with all his insecurities and limitations on display. She felt rotten about feeling this way, but Nick had become very difficult for her to reach. And so very hard on her. It was as though she'd been branded an enemy. She knew she couldn't stand much more of it.

When Stephanie got back to the house, she found Nick sitting in the living room arranging a series of photographs on the floor. Since they'd come to Bucks County, Nick had used his camera exclusively outdoors, photographing all that newly discovered nature. He considered this his way of getting acquainted. He'd done a striking color sequence of the tea roses and black and white studies of reeds and pond grass that had the delicacy and movement of Japanese brush paintings.

Now he presented her with a series of the pin oaks along the driveway. Stephanie was impressed. "Nick, this is better than Park's Catalogue. Better than anything you've done before."

He nodded, half-pleased. "I was going to take some shots of their pottery—before I smashed it."

Stephanie intervened: "Why not take pictures of me?" She put on a not very practiced approximation of a sexy pout.

"What? Dirty pictures?" Nick spoke a little mockingly, as though he doubted she was capable of it.

"Why not?"

One of the three TV networks had shown *Blow-Up* a few days before Nick had smashed the goddess, and Stephanie, who'd never much liked any act that smacked of sadism, had mentally rerun that sequence of Verushka working under David Hemmings's camera. She remembered those arching and stretching and writhing shots of that long sinewy body.

With less enthusiasm than she expected, Nick set up the

142

ancient view camera on the patio. She laid a wine-red blanket on the grass and added two striped pillows from the wicker couch to lie on or in or around, if the mood took her.

Nick seemed uncertain of her reasons: "Just do what you want to, Stephanie."

Modestly she started to take off her T-shirt. Standing there, her chest bare, she felt awkward, silly.

"You sure look like you're having a great time." Nick looked more impatient than interested.

He disappeared under the black hood of the camera. She put both hands under her breasts and lifted them up slightly, feeling absolutely absurd. Why am I doing this? she asked herself. To get Nick out of a foul mood? Or am I challenging him? Or me? She'd always hated sex under any sort of compulsion.

"Hold it. Touch your nipples, Steph."

She laughed nervously and hated the sound. Using her palm, she lightly stroked her nipple. She wasn't certain she wanted it to get hard. Half-heartedly, she toyed with herself for a moment.

"You sure you want to get into this?" Nick emerged from the hood, and again she felt him imposing that intolerable distance between them. She resented Nick for driving her to use such extreme measures to reach him; she wasn't at all sure she really wanted to do this and felt angry at her own bad faith.

"Yes I do. Just give me a little time." Her mind picked that moment to supply Stephanie with a vivid image of Nick's poolside hard-on: For Cindy or me? Their joke about the mirrors in our bedroom—as though they shared a secret from which I was excluded.

"What do you want, Nick?" she said aggressively. "What will turn you on?"

"Whatever turns you on. Looking ain't bad."

"Tell me what you want."

"Why are you making this into such a big deal?"

She felt the tears start in her eyes: "It is a big deal."

"I'm sorry." Nick wanted to let it go at that, but Stephanie felt determined to look into his head and see the pictures hidden there. Seductively, so breathy it sounded funny yet half-hot, she said, "What turns you on, Nicky?"

"I told you," he answered a little more responsively, "I'd like to see you play with your nipples."

The day was warm but not too humid, the sun lay on her like warm butter, oiling her as it slowly seeped into her pores. She poked at her nipples. "I'm not sure this is going to work."

"Look, love, this was your idea. I think it's a fine idea, and I also think you aren't sure you want to do this. Either you do or you don't. You know how much I hate soft-core bullshit."

The remark annoyed her, but it contained just enough understanding to get Stephanie started. There she was, half-naked on the ground. Blushing like a girl and feeling like a hooker, she stroked her nipple until it came up hard. The shutter leered and blinked at her. In *Blow-Up*, David Hemmings kept moving over and around her, smiling, scowling, urging, commanding; the Hasselblad became his cock, moving, clicking, throbbing, zeroing in. Again Nick disappeared under his hood; she saw only his legs and his fingers squeezing the rubber bulb.

She stretched out and opened her legs into traditional centerfold position. Silly, yet she felt a growing tension in the pit of her stomach. She turned her back to the camera, twisted her torso and lifted her breasts toward him.

"Hold it," she heard Nick say.

Stephanie almost giggled, but not quite.

"Take off your jeans."

She did, and her panties. Then she placed her hand very lightly on her pussy.

"Dynamite." There was genuine tension in Nick's voice. "Open your legs a little wider." The voice came out of the black hood. "Could you open yourself up and play with yourself?"

His asking—the "could you"—brought her down. She sat up and clenched her arms around her knees, suddenly modest.

Nick looked absolutely disgusted. "Let's forget it. I'll go take shots of marsh grass. The light's perfect now." He tried to sound dispassionate, but annoyance thinned his voice. Then his anger broke out: "Or maybe we should have a little costume party, dress you up in black stockings and high heels, break out the once popular garter belt. That'd look nice and hot. You could rub up against the fireplace or put on that white bathrobe of Amanda's and let the camera adore your beautiful tits. Later we can really get kinky and drape you over the armchair and get one of those long candles."

"That's not funny."

"OK, let's stop. I'll go do the marsh grass."

"I don't want to stop."

"What do you want, Steph? Tell me that."

"I don't know, but you could try to be a little more understanding. This isn't easy you know."

Nick frowned. Stephanie always knew he had a dirtier mind than she, and she vaguely had attributed it to his not being raised in her sterile environment. Nick knew hookers when he was growing up; he'd first gotten laid at thirteen. But he had insisted from the beginning that she had great potential, and once she got going Stephanie did enjoy herself. She was just a slow starter.

They'd been together long enough so that Stephanie

145

thought they ought to have had a precise idea of each other's sexual needs and those boundaries that one didn't cross. And here they were out on the boundaries, a dangerous place to be when generally annoyed at your partner and playing cat and mouse with what was in his head.

"I'd like you to masturbate for the camera, Steph."

"So that's what you wanted?"

"Entrapment," he charged correctly. And smiled. "Guaranteed to turn me on. Turn you on too. I love when you play with yourself in bed."

"But here, in cold blood."

"If you don't want to, don't."

"If that's what you want."

"God, I can't stand it. Why are we going round and round with this crap?" He started to lift the camera body off the tripod, but she stopped that by putting two fingers in her mouth, moistening them, and placing her fingers at the lips of her vagina. Lightly she stroked herself, moving in leisurely, small circles. She pulled the hair up out of the way and stroked. The camera clicked and clicked. Stephanie spread her legs a little farther apart and moved her fingers to the base of the clitoris, staying with the same rhythm but increasing the pressure. Her fingers made a kneading circular motion as they traveled up and down the length of the clit. She got wet. She leaned back and picked up the tempo.

"Good and dirty, Steph. Good and very dirty." The voice filtered through the strange black hood.

"I'm going to join you," Nick said. The distance between them excited her. They couldn't touch, Nick's head and shoulders were covered, but she could see the lower part of his body. The camera kept clicking while his hand moved to his crotch, zipped open the fly. His cock came out already hard. His fingers took hold of it and began to slide up

146

and down, up and down. How sexy to see Nick half-dressed and playing with himself while she lay a few yards away.

Her legs began to tense. Nick leaned over, his body tensing too. Her fingers kneaded the top of her clit, the muscles of her pelvis began to draw in, squeezing tighter, tighter. Sinews of pleasure raced through Stephanie's body.

"That feels good, Steph, good."

Bent half over, Nick pushed back the hood, forgetting about the photographs. Mouth open and his eyes on her greedy pressing fingers, Nick was going faster now. Close herself, she arched her behind off the blanket and brought her heels together, squeezing. She kept digging at the itch when, suddenly, the itch turned sore; she'd dried out. Stephanie took an instant to wet her finger. Just then she thought of Nick at poolside and was sure his hard-on had been for Cindy. The tension dropped. She kept at herself but she couldn't finish. So she faked it. She told herself she was too dry, too sore, too sensitized, but really she was too angry with him, and she faked it. Which Stephanie hadn't done—hadn't needed to do—for over a year.

She watched Nick come, spurting sperm into the air like a fountain. Then he walked over and lay down beside Stephanie.

"Whew! Feels better."

"Better."

"Thanks, Steph. Took awhile to get started, but then—"

He had a soft almost whimsical expression on his face, a smile of appreciation and gratitude for her complicity in the show, the artwork.

"You're welcome."

He laid a gentle hand on her stomach. "These past few days, I haven't meant to behave like such a turd." Nick stroked her hair and snuggled closer.

After a while, she said, "Remember that day at the pool

with Henry and Cindy, when you got a hard-on? Just who was that for?"

Nick sat up. "You, of course, dumbie."

"You sure?"

"One hundred percent sure. Nobody else but you."

She said: "Set the scene: It was hot, all that Native Tan and sun-ripened flesh. She honestly didn't turn you on?"

"Nope, it was for you, pal. Though I got to admit she had nice nipples." Stephanie didn't reply. "That was supposed to be a joke." Nick searched her face but she just lay there looking up into the perfect blue noncommittal sky. His face got in the way of her sun. "Steph, I don't even like Cindy."

"Just enough to get it up for her."

"Bum rap. It could've been for her, but it wasn't. And even if it was, which it wasn't, you can't blame a guy for an involuntary reflex."

Her turn to be mad, play mad, sulk, not talk and be wooed. Out on the perimeters of two people's sexual needs, the going can get rough.

The night was so stifling that Stephanie awoke around 4 A.M. Nick was not in bed. She got up and started toward the stairs calling his name softly. The steep old risers cracked and groaned under Stephanie's feet as she picked her way down into the darkness. "Nick, Nick," she called again softly, afraid of being heard by someone other than Nick.

Stephanie always woke up slowly, so it took her a long time to find the light switch, and by then she was sweating from fear. Nothing in the room, nobody. She crept to the front door, where she turned on the garden lights. Then she stepped outside, yelling loudly, "Nick, Nick!"

She thought she heard footsteps running away from the house, but Nick appeared a moment later from the direction of the skeet range.

"Where were you?"

"I couldn't sleep," he said. "Had to get some air." His voice sounded tight. In the spotlight Nick gleamed; he was covered with sweat. "Trying to tire myself out doing windsprints."

"You mean that 2 A.M. wide-awake business you used to pull on the Cape?"

"That was only for a while—last August. Once I get on this crazy schedule, it's really hard to break."

"How much sleep did you get last night?"

"I don't know, three—four hours."

"Good thing we're not busy."

Stephanie lay on her back by the pool, a washcloth carefully folded over her nipples to protect them from sunburn.

"Goddamn son of a bitch." Suddenly Nick burst out of the woods, screaming like a wounded beast. He sprinted across the concrete apron, took a low running dive and hit the water with a resounding slap. He'd finished his second furious lap before she bent over the edge of the pool.

"Nick, Nick," she yelled, "What is it?"

He took two strokes back up the pool, then stopped and came back to the edge. "Nothing really." He draped his arm over the pool's tiled edge. "I just like hearing noise sometimes. It gets so spooky quiet around here."

"How safe she thinks she is." Nick saw Stephanie as totally vulnerable, a bright little painter bobbing up and down at the end of a short rope, not knowing she was moored to a threatening, unknown, nocturnal form.

Finally Nick did call Carroll. Carroll said, "I'm sorry, I haven't heard from them yet. I'll let you know as soon as I do."

As soon as Nick hung up, he started shouting, "Those bastards leave us dangling slowly in the wind. Two and a half weeks to reply and nothing. If that fair? Is that well-mannered?"

Nick moved toward the fireplace, then leaned against the mantel. His right hand hovered inches from the open glass shelves crowded with pre-Columbian and Sumerian pottery.

"Those fuckers actually get off on torturing the 'staff.' You can't get more perverse."

Nick's right hand fanned the air near the shelves.

"Nick—"

"They don't give a shit what their 'inferiors' must be going through. Couldn't care less what it's doing to us." He turned around toward her. "The arrogance of those bastards. It's so unfair."

Stephanie was scared. She'd been a fool, she realized, with her absurd belief that they'd flower in Bucks County. The exquisite farmhouse, the question of her money, Nick's uncontrollable, mostly unaccountable anger, all this kept driving them apart, showing them the ugliest parts in each other's being, the ways in which they basically did not agree. Their tide had gone way out.

"This time," Nick said as they pulled out of the Bergers' driveway onto the road, "Just drop me off at that inn just outside Doylestown. You can drive around by yourself and pick me up in an hour and a half."

"Don't be such a grump."

"I'm tired of it, Steph. As soon as I get the feel of these beautiful open roads, I know it's time to go back."

They drove slowly through the hazy, hot August countryside.

"Did I tell you what happened the other day?" she asked.

"Which other day?"

"I was weeding in the herb garden and suddenly I got the feeling someone was watching me."

150

"Not a crewcut little old drunk with small beady red eyes? Not a creepy little ferret bastard?"

"He makes me so uncomfortable."

"When was it, Steph? You remember?"

"Tuesday. You went shopping that day."

"What was he doing hanging around then?"

"He told me he was edging the lawn."

"The edges of those flowerbeds would make a neurosurgeon proud."

"He thinks he owns the place."

"At the very least he knows we don't."

They drove aimlessly, trying to feel liberated, on holiday. When Stephanie pointed out a beautiful stone bridge, Nick replied, "I feel like we're on a choke-leash."

Time hung so heavily over them that they were back at the farmhouse a half-hour ahead of schedule.

Plan Number Two

"Plan Number Two," as Nick termed it, was their six-week-old concession to civility which involved dressing up for Saturday night dinner. She figured that, since they never had a chance to go out together, they'd need a weekly boost, some sense of occasion. And Stephanie honestly thought that Nick would relax on the exquisite set that seemed to actively demand at least one calm, adult, pleasant, candlelit evening per week.

151

That afternoon she called Nick a little early—the light was just dimming down toward gray—to give him sufficient lead time. When he didn't come, she called a few more times. Meanwhile, the chain saw whined on incessantly. Almost an hour later Nick came in.

"I didn't realize how late it was."

"I called and called."

"I couldn't hear, Steph. Had the earplugs in." He pulled the wax stopples from his pocket as though producing evidence.

Nick's jeans and boots were stiff from their coat of dried mud, which made his bottom half looked bloated. Sweat and sawdust had formed a paste which clung to his eyebrows, hair and mustache. He looked like he was wearing a fierce yellow mask.

"It's Saturday night." Stephanie didn't bother to say that the chicken with fresh rosemary was almost done, the petit pois were bubbling along just short of perfection, that the French bread she'd made from scratch was the best so far.

"So?"

"I thought we said we'd dress for dinner every Saturday, you know, Plan Number Two."

Nick kneeled down next to "City Square," his favorite Giacometti, and started to unlace a boot. The sunroom was scented with onions and rosemary. Cursing softly to himself, Nick yanked off his filthy boots without bothering to lace them down far enough. This annoyed Stephanie.

"It's not a big deal or anything." Her voice had migrated high up into her adenoids, her face felt flushed. "I just thought it would be nice for a change."

"Change! We did it last Saturday, and the one before."

"You want to shower?" She tried to be as agreeable as possible, she didn't want the mood to evaporate before they started, but guarding the tone of the evening was like holding water in the hands. "I can keep dinner hot."

Boots off, his crusty jeans followed, then he padded barefoot and bare assed across the terra-cotta tile of the kitchen. Nick's T-shirt just touched the top of his round, dimpled buttocks. If she looked at a thousand men's asses, Stephanie thought, she'd never find one that equaled Nick's. His body had lines, not bulges or buckles or knots or boles. She followed, thinking of herself as an African maiden, ready to lower the flame under her chicken.

Nick halted at the cutting board. "Honey, I'm tired. I haven't slept well for three weeks."

"I know, I know."

"I've been sawing all afternoon. I want to get enough wood cut for the winter. If we're here for winter."

She changed the subject: "All I want tonight is to have a good meal in a relatively civilized fashion. I want to drink at least a bottle and a half of the two white Burgundies we've been allotted for August, week of the eighteenth." He smiled weakly. "And most of all—more than anything else in the world, Nick—I want you to have a good time."

"OK. Plan Number Two." Nick tried to smile but it cost him a lot of effort. How she longed to see that old easy smile eat up his face.

Nick went up to shower and finally reappeared scrubbed and shiny in clean khaki slacks and a tight-fitting French T-shirt. She thought: he looks too good to be in a shitty mood. In the months they'd lived in Bucks County, his mustache had filled out, which made him look older, more substantial.

"I spotted a brown thrasher in those poplars today. I knew him without looking in the book."

"Add him to your life list, Nicholas Tory Peterson," she said with genuine pleasure. His look faltered as he considered whether she meant it ironically or not. "You're getting good," she continued, trying to put the right shading on the remark.

"Better." Clear indication he preferred to drop the subject. No other one came to mind—except the broken goddess and the executors' forbidden letter.

They ate in silence. Nick seemed to gobble the artichoke whole. Chicken, peas, French bread and whipped butter appeared and started to go quickly. Nick, who'd already downed a large Scotch, was working even faster on the Burgundy.

"Did you have fun cutting up the elm?" In the handsome Colonial space her words sounded bloodless, sallow. With so much more important business on her mind, she filled in the blanks with idiotic trivia—which seemed an insult to their relationship, to their significance.

Nick looked as though she'd said something very dumb. Restraining himself, he replied, "The novelty wears off pretty quick. It was hot, a lot of sawdust, you saw."

Candles, silverware, white linen did not create a festive occasion. She wondered why the hell she'd persisted with Saturday night's ceremonial? Because she wanted it, that's why. Stephanie determined to enjoy the food and wine. Yet how could she with the true confession rising in her gorge? And how much longer could she go on like Atlas, holding up their world?

Finally Stephanie said, "Is that letter still bothering you?"

"I'm more bothered about breaking the goddamn thing in the first place."

"But there's nothing we can do about it."

"I know that." No anger there, just a spooky quiet resignation, with less energy than anything Nick had ever said. "Honey, I'm depressed, distracted. I hate being such a heavy." He'd said the same thing fifty, a hundred times

154

before, and again it seemed to Stephanie he was about to shake off his depression and offer an explanation that would make things right again. But he stopped.

As the meal continued, she watched Nick pick at his food and chug down wine. A part of Stephanie sat at a great distance from him. It took effort, but finally she asked herself: Where did all this accumulated misunderstanding come from? Only from the fear of offending him. The confession moved to the tip of her tongue and got stuck there. I can't let him find out himself. She took a deep breath.

"Nick," she said aloud, "they're screwing around with my money."

His fork stopped inches from his mouth, and he looked at her.

"When my father was here he gave me a letter from my executors." Nick laid his fork down carefully. "Basically, they won't let me have the money until I'm at least thirty-five, if then. Or unless I marry someone they approve of."

"Those bastards." Nick amended his statement. "That bastard. Your father is such a prick. You poor baby."

"What are we going to do?"

"Well," Nick answered malevolently, "you have two clear options: Lose the bread or dump the liability."

"Oh, Nick, please don't make it any harder. I'm embarrassed enough as it is. I wanted to tell you sooner but it was so dumb and demeaning. I'm truly sorry."

Nick was in no position to accuse Stephanie of holding out on him. Instead he raged at William Harrold, feeling as though the fierce, broad brigand's face was pressed up against his own: "How can he treat you like this? He is your father, isn't he?" He watched that hit home. For three years Nick had been absolutely scrupulous about the money. Her money, he'd insisted, was only to be spent for her clothes, her travel, her kitchen gear. Till her twenty-ninth birthday, Nick had battled fairly evenly with William Harrold. Now he felt at the ultimate disadvantage—William Harrold could hold out forever, and nothing he could do could demonstrate his sincerity. Nick turned his despair on Stephanie. "He wants to buy you. It's so goddamn insulting. And you"—Nick almost said "bitch" —"sit on the letter for three months and don't say a word. God, that pisses me off."

"I'm sorry."

"What, were you afraid to tell me? Listen, baby, I don't need his money. I'll work if I have to. I always have."

"What are you going to do, Nick? Tend bar? I don't want you in another nowhere job."

"Instead you'd sell us out! Shit!" Nick drained the wineglass again, sloppily refilled, took a quantum slug. "While we hung around here on our subsidy you could check out just how I looked in a fancyassed world." Was it possible Stephanie's father had made her suspect he was after her money? Worse, how could he be perfectly sure himself?

"That's totally beside the point!" Nick had twisted it all by his own paranoid inventions. She wanted to be accused of the crime she committed, but instead the envy and resentment that she didn't want to acknowledge in Nick stood between them like the picked-over carcass on the stoneware platter. How could she quiet Nick's fears, tell him that he'd already passed all tests for her? Although in a dark subterranean cavity, Stephanie supposed she had wanted to see how far Nick would come her way or, rather, William Harrold's way. But the question of style was such a small part of their coming to Bucks County, such a small and insignificant part of everything. Would she have to spend the rest of her days nursing his injured sensibility? The idea frightened and repelled her.

The tension that had grown between them in the past

few weeks pounded in her head like a huge tom-tom. She wanted to de-escalate, but it was obviously too late. Had they waited three years to really bring their differences out into the open? Were they now at war?

Nick was about to dab his sweaty forehead with a greasy napkin; Stephanie couldn't help intervening: "It's greasy."

"So what?" He smeared his forehead, then emptied his glass again. "Am I supposed to play the martyr now and give you up? Crawl back down the ladder?"

"Nick," she said, "I'm not on my father's side." He'd wiped his damp forehead once too often; it bore grease marks in the form of a rough cross, like an Ash Wednesday penitent's. "The insult is at least as great to me as it is to you, can't you see that?"

"Your old man and me, we're fighting a war for you, baby."

Nick was lost in the aura of his wineglass again. She felt like telling him to skip the elegant long-stemmed middleman entirely and go straight at the bottle. But she clung to civility—at least for the moment. He drank again; she couldn't stand it: "Why don't you slow down, Nick?"

"Slow down?" His speech was getting slushy. "I'd like to finish off every one of our 'allotted' bottles. After all, if they kick us out, we'll be missing out on all the other tasty goodies." He laughed grossly, his mouth wide open.

William Harrold's dictum came back to her: what he said about upbringing, style, or, as Nick insisted so obsessively these days, CLASS. We're so different, she concluded. I can't take this blind, unreasoning rage, the battle psychology, his struggle against the benefits—yes, the inevitability —of comfort. There is no grace, no ease, no normalcy in that position, which makes it an unlivable situation. Even just our being here humiliates and embarrasses and alienates him. A paid vacation in Bucks County hits him smack

157

dab in the middle of his inflexible concept of male honor. She'd had it. As she sat at the steamy, pathetically elegant table, for the first time in four years she could imagine not loving Nick. The thought terrified Stephanie.

To calm herself she got up to get more water, and as she passed the sideboard Nick suddenly bellowed "Shit!" and sat bolt upright. His chair skittered backward on the polished boards, his arm shot out for balance, and his hand tipped the head of one of the paired horses on the sideboard. The horse wobbled. As Nick reached back behind him to steady it, she lunged across the sideboard. He got hold of a hind leg, she grabbed a foreleg, and their momentum pulled them in opposite directions. A brittle cracking sound, and the poised right foreleg of that magnificent creature came away in Stephanie's hand. She stood with the verdigris bronze in her fist, staring blankly, stupidly at the fragment.

A sense of total absurdity overtook her. With exaggerated formality, she thought, I have just destroyed an irreplaceable object. She sank to the floor holding the leg up in the air. She panted, "I don't believe it. This can't be true, Nick. I did it. I just destroyed—"

"We did it together, Stephanie. You pulled one way and I pulled the other." He explained the act as patiently as a grade school teacher.

"I—" She could barely speak.

"No, both. Believe me."

"What do we do now? We cannot let them know."

"I don't know. Let me think."

Another look at the mutilated horse and Stephanie burst into tears. She couldn't stand it any more.

Nick sat down, suddenly sober, and put his arm around her. "It's not destroyed, Steph. We can get it fixed. Really, the break's not that bad."

158

Nothing he could say could actually help, but Stephanie felt somewhat relieved that he tried. She realized then that, all along, he had needed her to be with him. Not that either of them had known that, not that he wanted her to break the horse or anything that vaguely approached that. But suddenly Stephanie had joined Nick in that place where he had lived alone for the past three weeks.

Nick spoke moderately: "Things do break, love. We can't be expected to treat this stuff with kid gloves twenty-four hours a day. I mean, these things do happen. The Bergers themselves have probably broken things."

She turned to him, childlike: "Why does this stuff have such power over us, Nick? Why is it changing our lives?"

"Because I don't know how to deal with it, Steph. All it does is make me feel stupid and angry and uptight. It tyrannizes me so much sometimes I've got to control myself to keep from smashing it. But do you realize how much power we have over these things?"

What a temptation, Stephanie thought. Up to that moment her entire life had been safe. The accidental breaking of the horse removed the net.

She got up and walked over to the tall graceful Greek amphora that stood next to the open glass shelves. So much skill and time and loving artistry had been concentrated in that subtle feminine shape. Yet you could demolish it in a second. What a extraordinary power to do violence to beauty, what an ultimate liberating deliverance.

As she lifted up the amphora, Nick intercepted her. He took it out of her hands and gently placed it back on the shelf. Then he took Stephanie's hand and walked her over to the kitchen counter. "I've wanted to do this for a long time." He lifted the lazy Susan off the counter and put it on the floor. In a perverse way, Stephanie loved the lazy Susan; it was the only ugly thing in the Bergers' house. Nick lifted the Turner landscape from the wall and placed it on top of the awkward little platform. Then he spun the painting till those swirling colors became a revolving blur. Paint pulsated in strobelike flashes of red, green, blue and that extraordinarily intense red-yellow of the sun. Nick spun the base faster and the colors seemed to intensify. Stephanie was tempted to look away, the paint became so bright. But she watched the colored confection revolve, emanating rays, throwing off its blurred coursing rainbow until her head started to spin.

"Nick," she announced, "I'm tired of that Avery. Let's get that Balthus you think's so sexy and switch them."

"Hey," he said, "I never would've thought of that."

Upstairs in the storage closet they flipped their way to the painting of the young girl sitting on the knees of a hairy middle-aged man. "Christ, it's so dirty. He's playing her like a violin."

Stephanie smiled a warm smile of complicity.

"There," she said when the Balthus hung in place. "Let's move the Rothko closer to the fireplace."

Nick loved hefting the big canvases around the room. Each one was so light. "Steph, they feel like sails, these things." He continued, "And those cutouts, how about if we put them across from the sofa where we can see them?"

"Wonderful." She was happier than she'd been in a long time.

Carrying the first Matisse to its new home, Nick said, "I feel like Pip, Steph, pulling down the curtains in—what's-her-name's room?"

Stephanie laughed: "Miss Havisham."

They rearranged the pottery on the glass shelves, placed a small Greek bronze of a youth's head on the fireplace mantel and stood a large Celtic vase on the hearthstone. She carried a small Courbet watercolor into the kitchen and hung it above the sink. Nick delicately ran his fingers along the seams of the Matisse cutouts. For the first time in three months, they made themselves at home.

Then she went over to the Maillol nude. The drawing was done in charcoal and pencil. Seen from the side, the woman was kneeling, with her left knee slightly lower than her right. Maillol had turned all those angles in leg and thighs, all those chances for distortion into an elegant, sensual texture. Stephanie stepped out of her skirt and stripped off her panties, then fitted herself up against the life-size drawing. Smaller and thinner in the torso, she had her fullness in buttock and thigh.

Slowly Stephanie unbuttoned her blouse. From a distance Nick devoured her with his eyes.

They made love on the Chinese rug, all blues and greens.

The Morning After

Barely awake, she moved her head up to the fleshier part of his shoulder seeking the softest possible spot. Her head throbbed unmercifully. They were in the living room, she realized; they had slept all night on the rug, on the hard wood floor.

Nick lay on his back, right knee hooked over hers. His mouth, gurgling like a miniature volcano, gave off rhythmic eruptions of stale booze and advanced morning

161

mouth. Usually he avoided the friendly, overnight type of sustained body contact; too much touching without getting aroused, he feared, might lessen the intensity of their sex. Besides, he felt claustrophobic when she leaned against him all night. Now, Stephanie lay pinned there, enduring the updrafts for the sake of the feel of his flesh.

She slipped partly out from under Nick, trying not to wake him. In slow motion he rolled onto his side. Her body felt stiff and a bit sore.

Nick bent himself into a modified question mark and Stephanie slipped free. Still she rested there. The morning had broken soft and foggy, with muted, still colors. She felt warm lying on that Chinese rug, yet fear and uncertainty made her shiver. The light burned in through the beautifully proportioned windowpanes until each small glass rectangle seemed a bright searching eye. Soon the light would track down her crime, pinpoint the broken foreleg of the Chinese horse.

Stephanie lay there thinking, first about her parents. She thought about how couples had the opportunity to make up their own rules as they went along and about how, in spite of her father's assumption that he knew what was best for everyone around him, her mother had managed to create a reasonable amount of room for herself without devaluing the marriage. Sarah Harrold also made sure that her daughter was given sufficient room. After Sarah's death, as William Harrold bulled ahead into Stephanie's life, Stephanie realized just how forcefully, tactfully, lovingly Sarah had managed things. One of the reasons Stephanie had been attracted to Nick was because she sensed that together they needn't do blindly everything that others did; that they could make up sufficiently flexible rules so that between them they could produce a positive equilibrium; that, like her mother, they had enough good will, imagination and courage to be good to one another. Until they came to

Bucks County, Stephanie had been proud of their tone. Of course their behavior wasn't impeccable: they ought to have been less cynical here, less snobbish about people there, more politically and less rhetorically active at times. But in the three years they'd been together, they'd done nothing that she felt really ashamed of. Until last night, when they'd come close. Too close. Which frightened her, for it questioned her notion of who they were.

These thoughts were beating alarms in her aching head when the telephone added its shrill aggressive trill. Nick muttered a curse and stabbed at the air with his hand while Stephanie, nude and sore, got up and limped slowly toward the clamorous instrument.

"Good morning, Miss Harrold," came the polished tones of Bradford Carroll. "I trust I didn't wake you."

"Oh, no," Stephanie lied, trying discreetly to clear out the frog that clogged her throat. "I was just admiring the view from the sitting room."

That brought Nick up onto an elbow.

"Exquisite, isn't it?"

"Yes." Nick shaded his eyes. Stephanie squinted, surprised by the amount of light the little casement window let in.

"Uh, I've heard from the Bergers about the Minoan figurine. Because of that and another matter I'd prefer not to discuss over the phone, I'm driving out this morning from Bryn Mawr. I should clear up my business here by eleven at the latest." Stephanie shook her head to let Nick know things were totally out of control. Her stomach felt like an old, worn-out sponge: tattered, full of holes, without any absorbency. "That means I ought to be at the farmhouse at about 12:30."

"Will you lunch with us?" The phrase, which could've been her mother's, just came out.

Nick's eyes rolled back into his head.

At the other end there was a considerable pause. "Why, no." Carroll's tone softened. "I'll grab a bite in town. But thank you very much for your thoughtfulness."

"Yes, of course. We'll see you around 12:30 then."

As Carroll hung up, Stephanie realized she hadn't asked if they would be allowed to stay on at the house. Phone in hand, she gave Nick a look which asked, tentatively, Please don't blow up. Nick's first impulse was to say, "Good god, how dumb can you be? You mean to say you didn't ask him?" With effort he restrained himself; considering further, Nick realized how easy it might have been not to ask the only question on both their minds: Carroll could be impossibly breezy; he always ran on.

"Two hours, Nick!" The phone still dangled in Stephanie's hand. She put it down just in case Carroll had picked up his end again. "He'll be here by 12:30." Nick's face looked ravaged, with a chalky residue that clung to his skin. "There's something else Carroll wants to talk about, said he couldn't say anything on the phone."

"Oh Christ," said Nick, despairing. Then, in the face of the absurdity of their position, he brightened: "Little discussion of our investment portfolio, perhaps."

"Nick, please, no jokes. I feel too shitty for jokes. But I would give you a kiss if you'd go brush your teeth."

"Colgate," he growled affectionately. "It's hard to take Colgate too early in the morning. Do you think we ought to glue the leg?"

"We're better off putting the horses away for now. If Carroll asks, we'll just say the Bergers had them stored. Or took them to France."

"He won't ask."

Stephanie thought: Already, before they knew the Bergers' response to their smashing of the Minoan figure, they'd broken another precious item. Still the bronze

164

wasn't smashed, its foreleg was only snapped off, which meant it could be restored. That would obviously cost a pretty massive penny, but Stephanie considered whatever it cost a minuscule price. Later, she concluded, they would confess everything to the Bergers. But not now. She couldn't hand the Bergers a second example of their criminal carelessness. Not two in the same month.

Naked, Nick came over to her. Deliberately, he took her hands. "We'll take the horse to a good museum restorer. I know they'll do the job perfectly. Just like new. I've been reading about the work. A little book called *Protecting Museum Investments.*"

Stephanie thought: Sometimes he's so hopelessly optimistic. She felt hundreds of years old.

"Think of the restoration as our gift to the Bergers. They'll probably like it even more than the asparagus."

Time was running out. Nick pulled her to him and they locked together, bodies seeking emotional comfort. "Steph, you smell memorable. Memorable." He nuzzled his mouth into the responsive ridge at the back of her shoulder, chewing lightly at the muscle. Last night's thick perfume rose off them, suggesting torrid pleasures to her.

"Cut it out," Stephanie said and gently pushed him away.

"I got hot," he admitted with a smile. "What can I say?"

"I'll have to shower before Carroll gets here."

Yet they parted hesitantly. "OK, you clean up in the kitchen. I'll get started in the living room."

It would've made a nice film sequence—Nick hoisting up the majestic Turner seascape and lowering it into position on the fireplace wall, his spearing their clothing from the floor and fanning garments out over the down sofa, plumping up the cushions, ferrying the lazy Susan back to the kitchen counter. As he slipped by her to the sink, she tucked in her behind; she leaned forward slightly as he reached around her to set down a dirty glass. Behind that narrow kitchen island a drawer would glide open for Nick, a counter door would close just ahead of her path. Stephanie had always considered the kitchen to be her space, but they shared the turf on equal footing now.

They moved by one another that morning like disembodied spirits, taking great pleasure in the domestic dance.

Upstairs, later, Stephanie sipped on a mild Bloody Mary thinking how pleasant the morning had been. The ups and downs of their relationship touched her. She was glad for their resiliency. In the mirror she watched her smile broaden, though from the inside "broaden" wasn't right. "Deepen" would've been the more appropriate description. In spite of all the pressure—they might have to leave Bucks County that afternoon!—she felt relieved, felt good, felt as she had not felt in two months, together with Nick. Yesterday she couldn't have been less certain about their "us."

When she emerged from a very long shower, Nick helped wrap her in the chocolate brown bath towel. Usually he avoided steamy bathrooms, but today was different. "I have a confession to make. I've been holding out on you," he said in a rush. "Carroll was right. This house is being watched."

"Watched?"

"I don't want to frighten you."

"Frighten me? What are you talking about?" A single lock of Nick's hair drooped limply down onto his brow.

"Part of my being so grumpy and such a rat was from trying to deal with this guy—or guys—by myself."

"Nick," Stephanie said with great control, "please start at the beginning."

But he couldn't start there: "It was crazy—remember all that running around at night? My not being in bed when

166

you woke up?" She wrapped the towel around her more tightly. That lock of hair was now pasted to Nick's forehead. Sweat kept beading along his upper lip. "You remember that morning I was outside, you came up from behind and caught me leaning down over the rosebed?" Stephanie remembered.

"I found a man's footprints there. That was the first time. I was trying to cover them up."

"Maybe Massey—"

"Massey hadn't been around for three days, the footprints were fresh. Besides, I checked his boot tread and it didn't match."

The idea of the intruder began to penetrate: "Massey's lawnmower?"

"Yes."

"The shears?"

"Those too."

In the foot race between fear, anger and relief, fear got there first. Perhaps, Stephanie thought, a madman's walking around here at night, a homicidal maniac. But Carroll said we'd be safe as long as one of us was in the house. She felt cheated by Nick, duped by Carroll and frustrated by her own passivity, which insisted that she too had been an accomplice—all those questions she hadn't asked Carroll, her desire to come to Bucks County at all costs, their shared image of her as princess, someone to be protected. Then the wave of anger crested, and months of rage spewed out at him: "I thought our relationship was supposed to be about trust. Trust, Nick. You know the word?"

"Don't make me feel worse."

In her rage, the towel slipped off her. As Nick bent down to pick it up, he noticed her tightly clenched fists. "Why didn't you tell me?" she cried, feeling the strange omnipotence that comes from being absolutely correct.

"I've been feeling awful about not telling you, Steph, you've seen that. That's why I've been such an asshole." His hair gripped his head like a stringy, greasy skullcap. "That first night I just wasn't sure somebody was out there —I told myself it was probably an animal and half believed it because I wanted to believe it. When I came upstairs, tired, strung out, not sure, you were sleeping. I wanted to wake you but I just couldn't see getting you up in the middle of the night to pass on news like that: 'Wake up, dear, I think there may be a maniac intruder running around in our rosebeds.' Next morning, when I went out to look, I couldn't find any clues. It seemed convenient to believe nobody was there."

"Convenient?"

"Then, when I finally had the footprint, by then it seemed too late. After that, lying was easy."

"You've always been a lousy liar." The mood to wound was upon her. How much he cared about her opinion; how desperately he wanted to appear perfect to her.

"Look, I know this is terrible. I can't defend it. I guess I wanted to think of myself as your bodyguard. Maybe I thought that a lot of what I meant to you was tied up with my being tough. I don't know. I also was afraid that if we ran away from here your father would think I wasn't strong enough for you." She started to interrupt but he stopped her. "I know it was crazy, but that's what was going through my head. I just kept hoping the whole thing would go away."

"To think of the misunderstanding you could've spared us, Nick. What idiocy." Almost a month wasted, she thought, because of some macho horseshit!

"I know, I've thought about it a thousand times. I had no idea how much a secret could come between us."

Anger made her perspire. She opened her mouth and

took in drafts of the supersaturated air. "Didn't you think I could handle it? The frail vessel? Believe me, Nick, I'm tough enough." The bastard, she thought. Was this a trait he'd inherited from his wife-beating father?

"Steph, I don't blame you for being pissed off."

"Blame me!" she exploded. "Blame me. As long as we live together, I never want to be left out again. The idea of being excluded from something that involves us both, it's so condescending—it makes me puke."

"Look, I feel awful; couldn't feel worse." He offered absolutely no resistance. Emotionally, morally, Nick went limp. Which made Stephanie want to press her advantage.

"Did you tell Carroll what's going on around here?"

"No. Not yet."

"That was real dumb."

"I didn't want to talk on the phone. Today we'll tell him."

Stephanie started to hang up the towel.

"You've got time," he said. "Dry your hair. I'll go down and straighten up whatever else needs it."

"Aren't you going to shower?" The solicitousness slipped out involuntarily.

"I'm not prettying up for that high-gloss asshole."

Nick hesitated an instant, not knowing if the phrase had offended her. Her distant noncommital look gave him no clue. "I'm awfully sorry, Steph. It was stupid. Worse than stupid. I love you." Then he walked out of the clouds of steam.

Audio and Visual

Stephanie had just laid down the hair dryer when Carroll's Mercedes rolled down the drive. A glance in the mirror, one more quick shaping of her hair, and Stephanie headed to the bedroom, where she slipped into the gray sundress. For once—a final look—she liked her hair. Which was lucky, since she didn't want to leave the two of them alone together. Stephanie hurried downstairs and out the back door.

They were coming toward the farmhouse, Nick pointing animatedly toward the woods. Carroll wore a brown tweed jacket flecked with green, cocoa-colored slacks and tan boots as soft as melted butter. The shine on his boots seemed deep enough to wade in. The contrast made Stephanie smile—Nick in his ubiquitous jeans and old T-shirt.

"Hello, Stephanie." Carroll bowed his head ever so slightly. "Such a positively exquisite day you've provided for me." His voice surrounded her.

"Yes, it is nice," Nick responded flatly. He stood to the side, obviously uncomfortable.

"I always find it so exhilarating to visit the estate."

If he means to kick us out, Stephanie thought, I can't imagine a crueler opening. Aloud she said, "Come sit on the veranda. I'll get some iced tea. You must be tired after the drive."

170

"Actually I feel—uh—revitalized. I love to drive that machine." He cast a loving look at the discreetly gleaming silver convertible. "The way it hugs the corners on these country lanes. Although I would enjoy sitting for a moment. I have to speak to you about a few things."

Through the kitchen window Stephanie saw them playing a protracted game of, "After you, Alphonse. No, after you, Gaston." about who was to sit on the chaise lounge. She thought, He talks too slowly. I always know how a statement will end. Often Stephanie found herself waiting impatiently for Carroll to finish his current sentence and get on to the next.

When she returned with the tea, Carroll was finally settling into the chaise. Very carefully, he lifted the crease of his trousers so that it would fall evenly down the length of his outstretched leg. The crease obligingly fell straight. Then he brushed a spot of earth off his gleaming boot. Nick's stringy hair looked glued to his head.

"What an exquisite spot for morning coffee and sun." Carroll's eyes seemed to loosen the tie on Stephanie's sundress. Underneath she wore panties, nothing else. "You know Amanda and Peter laid out this verandah to maximize both the sun and the privacy. And what wonderful *iced* tea," Carroll ran on. "What is it I taste, my dear, lemon and mint?"

Inwardly, Nick groaned, What'd you expect, garlic and onions? Yet Nick believed that the two of them spoke the same language, that he himself was the outsider. Carroll might've been rubbing up against Stephanie, the sexual pressure he applied was so explicit and unremitting.

"I've come out here today to explain the Bergers' intentions." Both of them held their breath; finally, sentence was about to be pronounced. "Unfortunately, there's been an increase in art thefts near Princeton, just across the river.

Lately the gang has gotten even more brazen, and for the first time has actually struck while someone was in the house."

Nick interrupted to make his long overdue announcement: "Well, Mr. Carroll, we've had some trouble here, too."

Carroll sat up rigidly upright: "I don't understand."

Nick lied a little: "For about a week I've been chasing what I think is a prowler around here at night."

"Exactly how many times have you been aware of this prowler?" Carroll looked extremely upset.

"I'm not sure, five, maybe six times."

"You must tell me everything you can about these incidents. Be as precise as possible, please."

As Nick explained the sequence of events—the night he saw the shadow and chased it with the flashlight, the footprints in the rosebeds, the drained lawnmower, Massey's secateurs, the broken clay pigeons, the sequence of noises at night—Carroll copied the particulars in a leather diary.

"I don't want to alarm you," Carroll said soothingly. "As I said when I first spoke to you about this position, physical violence is never used. Art thieves have no interest in that. In the single instance of physical, uh, intervention, the Princeton business, a maid was bound but otherwise treated respectfully." Carroll looked at Stephanie, then at Nick. "You should have informed me immediately, you know."

"We really weren't sure until a few days ago, Mr. Carroll." Stephanie seconded Nick's lies.

Carroll went on: "In the first place, we must consider your safety above all else. In the second, it's of utmost importance for us to know everything about their methods and timing."

"Who do you mean by 'us'?" Nick asked. "The police?"

The agent's face assumed its most knowing expression.

"In matters of this sort, quite frankly, the local police are not always the most useful—" He let his statement hang there a moment. "They often aren't sufficiently trained or sufficiently discreet to deal with a number of delicate questions, including the clients' need for privacy. Information must be kept out of the newspapers. When extremely valuable property is involved, secrecy is an absolute requirement."

Nick felt the web of mystification which had shrouded their entire experience in Bucks County being drawn around them again. But this time he refused to sit passively. "Mr. Carroll, if the police are not involved, I'd like to have some idea who's protecting this place. Just how risky is it for us?"

"That's exactly the reason I've come out today." Nick and Stephanie exchanged a quick glance. Both had expected Carroll to go straight to the question of the smashed goddess. "You see, the Bergers were alarmed by my report about the Princeton robbery, and they want to install sound-detection equipment together with visual monitoring devices which will pick up the presence of any intruder. The system employed will be the most advanced and sophisticated available, and it will be monitored by one of the most reliable and discreet of the country's security firms, Property Guard." Carroll flashed his perfect dental palisade. "I'm terribly sorry you've been victimized by whoever this is." Whenever Carroll said "you," he looked at Stephanie, which made her think he used the word in the singular. "But I will have to consider any repetition of this secretiveness a severe dereliction of duty. For your own safety, please let me know anything suspicious that happens."

Stephanie interrupted: "But you told us it was safe."

"And I meant it. These thieves are highly accomplished

173

professionals. Their interest is in the collection, not in harming you."

Stephanie remembered her mother's story about her great aunt, Edith Ohlrich, who loved fabulously expensive jewelry. After one particularly spectacular society party she'd gone to bed wearing a huge emerald and diamond ring. In the middle of the night she'd been awakened by a noise, and after a moment she knew that someone else was in the room with her. As her husband hadn't entered her bedroom in years, Aunt Edith was terrified. She peered into the darkness but couldn't see anything. She lay there for hours fighting sleep and trying to see. Finally, when she was about to drop off, as silently as possible she slipped off the ring and, with the greatest stealth, slowly inched it down toward the bottom of her bed. Somewhat relieved, she fell asleep. When she woke up the next morning, the ring was gone.

Carroll stretched his leg and an admiring sunbeam caught in a polished hollow of his boot. "The alarm system promises a minimum of inconvenience in exchange for a maximum of protection."

Stephanie felt thoroughly confused by his calmness and all the talk of technological safeguards. She couldn't understand his sense of priorities. "Mr. Carroll, can you please tell us what the Bergers intend to do about our accident?"

"Accident? Accident? Oh, you mean your breaking the statuette?" Astounding, she thought. Nick shook his head a little, as though recovering from a blow.

Carroll flashed the philanthropist's indiscriminately generous smile. "The Bergers are quite remarkable, really the most generous and *forgiving* couple. They feel literally bereaved about the loss of that piece which, I needn't tell you, is one of their most prized possessions." To Stephanie and to Nick, the speech sounded memorized. "Still they recog-

174

nize that in spite of one's best intentions accidents do occur, and they're certain there will be no repetitions."

Nick wanted to look at Stephanie, but he restrained himself. Through clenched teeth, Nick thanked the Bergers for being so generous. Stephanie nodded agreement, though the back of her hand kept rubbing her forehead like an eraser trying to clear up the tension and pain. Both felt shocked at being let off so lightly.

"Of course you have every right to consider leaving, but I know the Bergers would appreciate your staying on. They'd be rather hard pressed to replace you, and they take it you are enjoying yourselves."

Stephanie said, "We'll have to think about it."

"Naturally," the agent replied.

On the veranda, Bradford Carroll laid out the blueprints for the electronic installation. They saw the proposed trenches for the cables, the locations of the hidden microphones and TV cameras, and a rendering of the bank of TV screens, which looked, Nick quipped, like a studio control room. Though Nick was impressed by the scope of the undertaking, he also considered the business technological overkill, a further example of the Bergers' astronomically conspicuous consumption. An electronic circus, he thought. A regular Defense Department bonanza brought to you by the people who brought you infrared bombing in Vietnam.

Carroll grew positively rhapsodic as he described the responsiveness of the microphones and the sensitivities of the films. Nick had read enough about the new high-speed, low light-level films to make small talk, and he mentioned in passing, again, how impressed he'd been by Carroll's stereo.

Carroll explained that the installation would take a week or ten days. He apologized again for the disruption.

After the briefing, they took Carroll on an obligatory tour of the farmhouse. Because of the missing horses, both felt nervous, but Carroll barely glanced at the living room and only paid attention to the Giacometti in the sunroom. "I think I have a buyer for the bronze. At a not inconsequential price. Look," he gestured rhetorically, "It's so economical, so simple. Five small figures crossing an open space. Each generalized yet individuated. That's clearly a feminine figure, you see. Each already embarked on his own path, pushing forward in his own direction. The brilliance of the drama is that we see only the moment before us, yet both past and future are implied by the vectors of these figures. What a wrenching momentary convocation." His manicured hand hovered above the small taut grouping. "What an invaluable experience living here must be for you." But again Carroll looked only at Stephanie.

Nick poured two large Scotches for the postmortem. "I don't know, pal. I should feel up but I don't."

"It's as though we got off too easily, Nick. Not that I wanted us to suffer, but they hardly seem to give it a thought."

"That took a lot of balls, Steph. These people have a lot of balls."

Stephanie had another thought: "Maybe the Bergers waited this long as a sort of favor to us, to put the accident into perspective. God, Nick, they must be extraordinary to behave so generously."

"I guess so."

"I mean, would you be so calm about that much money and that much beauty?"

"No way."

Both felt diminished for not believing in such unqualified generosity.

"Look," Nick said tentatively, "about staying on here—"

"I'm not ready to decide yet," she replied. "I want to think about it more."

"Sure." Pause. "You're not scared?"

"Not yet. I guess it hasn't sunk in."

For the next two weeks workmen scurried all over the estate, digging trenches and laying cable and setting up hidden television cameras like rifles in a duck blind. With so many people around, Stephanie had no time to be frightened. But she thought about the estate all the time. She took walks alone and with Nick and let the mellow beauty of the place seep into her. Meanwhile, protective as a mother hen, Massey hovered over every inch of excavated turf, fluttering about and sticking his red beak into everything. He insisted on showing the men from Property Guard at what depth to score the roots of his turf, how long a strip to cut, how to carefully lift the turf out and roll it up. The turf was stored under tarpaulins so that its roots wouldn't dry out. Nick watched Massey carefully, trying to determine if the gardener was trying to obstruct the installation. But Nick could never be sure whether the old man was deliberately getting in the way or was simply exercising his compulsive professional prerogatives. Nick occasionally offered commentary during these delicate operations, and Massey and Nick would've squared off again if it hadn't been for Mr. Carl Meyers, the foreman from Property Guard. Meyers, a sunny, low-key electronics wizard, kept Nick at his side much of the time, explaining the intricacies and virtues of "Your Personalized Surveillance System." If they wanted "a sure thing," Meyers insisted a number of times, they ought to invest in Property Guard stock. (Stephanie made a mental note to pass the information on to her father, if she ever spoke to him again.) Meyers explained about the new generation of detection devices which could sense weight, vibration, smell, heat, and light emanations. He had alarms so sensitive they could be set off by a drop of water, a note of music, a sigh. Meyers and his soft Tennessee accent had traveled all around the world, installing devices for kings and prime ministers, shahs and commissars. Security today, Meyers said rather more imperiously than usual, knew no politics. There were people and things to be protected. That was his job. Most of his work had been with political figures and in museums, galleries and banks. The Bergers' system was one of the most elaborate "home jobs" he'd ever installed.

They liked Meyers, and he liked them, so much so that they could even discuss their apprehensions about the intruder with him.

"If we've got ourselves a real pro, you two got nothing to worry about. Got no interest in people, only very expensive pictures. You didn't ever see him, did you? I say him, ma'am, just because of the stats. But there are a handful of good female ops too."

When Stephanie said that those who demanded such elaborate protection let paranoia run their lives, Meyers looked up with his deep, sad, beagle eyes and explained there were valuable people in the world whom others wanted out of the way. When Nick objected that the Vietnam war had produced the technology that created these electronic surveillance devices, Meyers replied that wars have produced great medical advances too. Nick said that was an ass-backwards way to go about healing people, and the three sadly agreed. Stephanie asked Meyers how the system could help them since the burglars wouldn't know that Property Guard had been installed. Meyers replied with characteristic gentleness, "I don't want to scare you nice folks, that's not what I'm here for, but a good pro's got to know what's going on with all our trucks and digging.

After all, that's his business." Stephanie liked to ask Meyers questions just to hear that soft, sweet drawl. He made her realize once more how unnatural their lives had been in Bucks County—out of touch with friends, with neighbors, with everything they had been accustomed to. Except for Henry, Carl Meyers was the only visitor to the estate whom Stephanie hadn't resented—which reassured her, since it said she wasn't anti-people, just anti-certain individuals.

All three of them, including Meyers, who had talked at length to Bradford Carroll about the security installation and who had been impressed by Carroll's familiarity with complicated technical matters, were surprised that the agent did not appear during the installation. Of course, Carroll had been sent a set of plans and blueprints, which he and Meyers had gone over inch by scale inch and which Carroll had mailed to the Bergers in France.

Meyers seemed particularly intrigued by a new light-sensitive videotape, which Carroll had suggested they try out in the camera for the wine cellar. In the test, he got rather vague images in the dark, so Meyers installed a low-voltage light which went on when the cellar door opened. He said that the little light would make the wine steward's life that much easier.

By working past quitting time, Meyers had all the systems operating at dinner time. They invited him to eat with them. He did. Afterward the three sat in the bedroom sipping beer and watching the television screens gradually take on a higher contrast. Hung from the ceiling at the foot of their bed in a horizontal console were eight screens and twelve microphones. The outdoor cameras moved in long arcs which overlapped at most edges, so side by side they could watch the driveway and carpark, pool and pump house, the area around the barn, and so on.

"Look, kids, I like you both too much not to be straight

179

with you. Don't worry. This is one of the most complete home-protection systems in the country, even in the world. I give you my guarantee you'll be safer now than you've been in your whole lives."

"But I don't understand," Stephanie said. "In order for the system to work you need a sentry watching the screens. I can't imagine one of us sitting there all night."

"No, that's not it, Stephanie. The mikes will pick up noise before the image. If, god forbid, anything was to happen, the audio would probably be your early-warning signal."

After Meyers left, Nick and Stephanie sat and smoked a joint, and Nick put away a couple of cans of Michelob. The grass and booze didn't bring on sleep. They weren't used to nature's amplified chirpings, gurglings, belchings and mutterings inside the house. The TV screens gave off a weird, ghostly light which the bedroom mirrors played back in pale, infinite repetition. Their life felt like a sci-fi movie. Stephanie asked Nick to wake her if he spotted anything larger than a beaver; she fell asleep with her head still tilted awkwardly toward the screens.

Shortly after two Nick finally dozed off. He found himself outside stalking the intruder with the loaded .30-06 in his hands. He followed the man's shadow across the lawn toward the pump house, moving with magical silence; Nick knew the intruder didn't see or hear him. By the pool, Nick crept up on him and shouted, "Stop!" The figure spun around. Nick just meant to hold him there; then the pressure on his trigger finger kept increasing as though someone had placed a hand over his and was squeezing harder and harder. Nick tried to resist, he fought the pressure, realized he was going to lose, was about to shout, then suddenly, "Boom!" Again "Boom!" The man crumpled and fell, and Nick watched dark red blood spread over the earth. He was dead, dead. Nick woke up screaming, "I couldn't help it! couldn't help it!"

Stephanie woke up long enough to say, "Nick, it's OK. It's just a dream."

Later, in that weird light and among those strange, amplified night noises, Nick finally fell back to sleep.

Two days after Nick murdered the nightmare intruder, he tried to persuade Stephanie to practice using the shotgun. At first, she objected. Nick said that he didn't expect their Bucks County idyll to end in a shootout, but there seemed more percentage in both of them being prepared —just in case. "A little target practice might make the master thieves think a little more before barging in here and trying to rip us off. Besides, you told me you used to be pretty good with a .22. It seems silly for you not to do something you used to like so much." At the trap range, Nick showed her how to load the double-barreled shotgun and how to work his bizarre treadle for the trap, then left her blasting away at dark blurs in the air.

Nick, who hadn't slept well since the installation of the cameras, needed a run to tire himself out. He took the long route, a beautiful two-mile loop which followed the stream through the woods. As he ran, the unremitting pressure on that trigger finger began to ease off. On the last leg, instead of sprinting across the flat turf to the trap range, he went up the ridge. The uphill finish would tire him out.

At the top of the ridge, above and to Stephanie's left, he watched her shoot. She was following each flight well, hitting one of three pigeons. A little practice, Nick thought, and she'd get back her NRA Marksman First Class.

As he came down the ridge toward her, Nick stepped on a tangled windfall, and that snapped a thick branch beneath. Stephanie spun around and leveled the shotgun at

181

his belly. For an instant they stood there— Nick didn't see his life flash past, but the nightmare came back. Only this time he was the intruder, and Stephanie faced him, holding the shotgun. He tried to speak but the sounds wouldn't come out. He raised his arm to signal her to stop. At the same time, he could feel the pressure on her trigger finger increasing as though someone had clamped a hand over hers and was squeezing down. Silently he screamed, "Take your finger off that trigger! The trigger!" He could feel the tension growing on that sensitively sprung wire. He wondered if he'd killed himself in his dream.

Finally, Stephanie lowered the gun. "Nick, you scared me. Don't do that, I almost . . ." Her eyes seemed to grow in size until the tears started to fall; uncontrollably, they fell and fell and fell.

The Bait

"But he says here—listen, Peter: 'I've been offered $85,000 for your Giacometti bronze entitled *City Square*, which lends its impressively taut animation to the sunroom. Mr. Lemato, who asks to see the sculpture at our earliest convenience, has proposed flying from Milan to Philadelphia next Thursday, 22 September. I will meet him at the airport. After lunch in town at the club, we will drive to the farmhouse. If the sculpture conforms to his exacting standards, which, of course, we know it will, he is prepared to present you with a check for $85,000. This long-awaited acquisition of *City Square* will complete his collection of the Swiss sculptor's work and make it the most impressive and extensive private holding in the world.' "

Peter turned back to me and finally stopped drumming his fingers on the sideboard. "Lemato is going out there to examine it. Of all people, Lemato. It's such a beautiful job." He made a sound like a snort, then took his head in his hands and groaned, "God, this is awful. We can't let him see it."

I watched the florid, unhealthy flush rising on his face. Such a few minor steps were needed now, just a bit more unwholesome, underhanded courage, a timely shove. Trap set, bait in place— How Peter would've cheered my performance if someone else had been involved. I sometimes believed this capacity itself came from him, that he'd bred it, nurtured it in me. "Almost over," I whispered, almost like a prayer. "Almost over."

"What?"

"We need this money, Peter. The market's been terrible. Your luck in Cannes and your friends at the tables— We will not get a better price, and we must have this sale."

Peter exploded: "Of course I know that." The large vein in his temple pulsed wildly, his color edged toward that blood-drenched vermilion. Odd to witness these explosions without force, all noise and smoke but utterly lacking in detonating power. Peter had come to embody fear. At night I held and comforted him as he quailed in terror, the imagined heart attacks ripping through his body, the vise clamping down on his chest, left arm tingling, mouth gasping for air. At night his nursemaid, watching the coward die those thousand thousand times, seeing him shed tears and plead with a deity who didn't exist and whom he didn't believe in to let him last through the night; by day submitting to the charade of control. Oh, Peter, you were once such a different man.

"The question, really, Peter, is are you up to it?" I keyed in the knife blade. How much longer could one live with such loathing?

Bluff strength took up the insult. "Certainly. Besides, my dear, we have no choice. The pieces must be switched."

"We could tell Carroll, explain to him—"

"No. Absolutely not. No one but you and I must know. Otherwise"—he smiled a weak bitter smile—"we're too vulnerable."

Let it end then. I wanted only the blankness that comes afterward, the anxiety-free fog of the accomplished. How quiet it would become. I wanted the ending, the frame of frames.

"You'll write Carroll the usual sale instructions. I want the standard authorized contract and customary credit check, just for form. I'll be in and out of the farmhouse before Lemato arrives."

"Whatever you do, don't be seen there."

"Don't worry, I'm no fool. Carroll did say next Thursday."

I waited expectantly for last-minute irresolution. It didn't come. "Next Thursday. The twenty-second."

Indian Summer

The near-miss at the trap range left them severely shaken. The slightest sound startled them, the least irregularity—a missing change purse, a misplaced box of shells—threatened to undo them. Their emotional reservoirs had never been so depleted.

Two nights later Nick broke into her fitful doze: "Somebody's out there, Steph. The monitor outside the barn's picked up some weird noise. You stay here. You'll be safe."

"No. Don't leave me alone."

Hand in hand they crept downstairs, the old wide boards squeaking alarms as though broadcasting their deepest fears. Nick removed the shotgun from the double-locked gun case. Stephanie did not object.

At his shoulder, a half step behind, she followed. Nick felt he was reenacting his dream as they skirted their vegetables, went up the hill, cautiously swung open the huge barn door.

They saw nothing out of the ordinary until Nick trained the flashlight on the giant pegboard that covered the sixteen-by-twenty-foot wall. At least a third of the items had been rearranged—rakes rested where shovels should have been, a hoe replaced a post-digger, the damaged secateurs themselves straddled the large staple reserved for the bolt cutters.

"Weird sense of humor," Nick declared. He did not say that the intruder had entered by the back door, which wasn't covered by a camera. There was no camera inside the barn either, and the closest microphone was outside, by the maple.

"Demonic, Nick, positively demonic. It's like someone's toying with us."

They decided to wait until morning to reshuffle the tools and crept back into the farmhouse. She wanted to curl up and sleep, but Nick insisted they have a policy discussion. He poured two large brandies, then sat above Stephanie on the sofa's arm.

"We've got to figure out what we should do." His hand stroked the hair at the back of her neck; his fingers were ice cold.

Total panic struck Stephanie. "I'm afraid something terrible's going to happen here. I feel it."

Nick stroked her neck reassuringly, he massaged the top vertebra. She pulled away. He said, "Somebody's trying to scare us away. I think they want both of us out of the house so they can slip in and out." Stephanie's recollection of the genius jewel thief who robbed her great-aunt took hold of her nerves and started to shake them. Seeing the look on her face, Nick continued: "I'm not saying we ought to behave like heroes, pal. But I don't think whoever's mindfucking us will hurt us. They've had plenty of chances to do that and haven't. No, they want to get in here. And the real question is, do we want to split? It's not like we don't have legitimate objections to this setup."

Her answer surprised her. "I feel we'd be smart to leave, but I don't want to run out. I love this place, Nick."

"You really do, don't you." The wistfulness made him sound as though he spoke from some faraway place and would have liked to join her.

Stephanie thought of the soft upward sweep of the lawn; she could hear the stream in the background. She looked into her kitchen and back at her fireplace.

"I remember my mother once telling me about her mother—"

"Mrs. Archie James."

"Yes. After Archibald died she left Long Island and was living in London during the war. The first night the Germans bombed London she got up at midnight and went down into the cellar she'd had prepared. Everything was there—cots, a small refrigerator, even a hot plate. She stayed down there until dawn, then she went back upstairs. And you know what?" Stephanie's eyes shone with an intensity he found startling, beautiful. "She never went down there again. She said, 'If they drop one on me, that's it. I'm never leaving my bed again in the middle of the night.'" Nick felt respectful. "Something in me really wants to see this thing through. Does that make sense?"

"No," he said, secretly pleased that she thought as he did. "But it sure is interesting.

"I feel drawn to this whole strange frightening mess. I want us to face it and, most of all, I want to face it myself." She looked at him directly. "It has something to do with your not telling me about the prowler in the first place." Nick's face colored. "But it's more than that. I don't want to run away."

Her undemonstrative fierceness couldn't help but impress Nick. Still, it was a complicated moment for him. Nick had hidden the intruder from Stephanie because of his assumption that only he, the street-wise operator, could handle it. During the month-long ordeal he'd often said to himself, If only she knew a little about the world I grew up in. Then I could tell her about the prowler, then she'd really know something about me. Now that his wish had

187

come true, he'd have to consider her an equal. Barging into his myth, she wiped out his role as protector, the built-in, long-term inequality that he'd always considered the linch-pin of their relationship. A moment of desperation followed in which Nick feared he might not have anything else to offer her.

There was yet another fear: Nick felt mystically yet none-theless certain that the intruder was one of the people he might have become—a punk hustler from New Bedford looking for a fast buck in a skilled, dangerous trade.

"Steph, I love you. You're wonderful and very tough." He drew a deep breath. "I've got one more confession, and I hope this'll be the last one for a long long time.

"The night we broke the horse, just before that when I was getting really loaded— What I really wanted to do was detroy all the shit in the room. I kept dreaming just how I'd go after the Kline, just the way he painted it—a long slash, another long slash!" His hand slashed through the air. "And the Rothko"—he pointed at the beautiful painting—"I'd think about slicing it up like a surgeon, moving the sharp-ened straight razor delicately along the edge of that purple bar, watching a white sliver come up behind like some kind of deadly wake behind a ship. I had strategies for each thing —hammer for pottery, saw for wood, a torch for the bronze. Then it was all over. That one crazy evening and the whole thing stopped."

That night they sat in the bedroom glued to the moni-tors, waiting for a vague shifting pattern of black-and-white dots to resolve into the horror. As darkness gathered till late into the night they sat there, straining their eyes to look into the swirling gray snow. A few times Nick jumped up and pointed at nothing, deceived by his blurred tired eyes. A few times Stephanie thought she detected move-ment, then all subsided back into those flat ghostly repetitive planes. Their eyes did all the conjuring. What horrors lurked in their imaginations.

The next night, as Nick was taking a shower, Stephanie saw out of the corner of her eye a shadowy figure move into the corner of the pool-side screen. "Nick, Nick," she called, running toward the bathroom. "Nick, come here. Quick!" The slow night videotape held a continuous soft-edged image as the white figure moved slowly along the edge of the fence. "Hurry!" The blurred, continuous thing seemed to drag a self behind, retaining a stuttering memory of where it had been. It—HE! Stephanie thought—hung in the upper right-hand corner of the screen, feet, legs maybe a face moving in and out of view. Then was gone.

Dripping wet, Nick hustled out of the shower. By the time he reached the bedroom the screen was blank. The gray-white ghostly light threw shadows around the room, the dispersed light seemed to lie everywhere and nowhere.

She gripped his hand: "It's almost like they know where the cameras are."

The thought had occurred to him before, but Nick tried to be reassuring: "Meyers said if they're as good as everyone figures, they'll know everything about the setup. The last thing they're interested in is hurting us."

"Then why are they torturing us, Nick?"

He walked her over to the window. "No point going out there now. He'll be gone."

They sat up another hour and a half, watching, waiting. Nick said that he felt like his grandfather who, when Nick's family finally bought their first television set, used to sit and watch the test patterns for hours.

The next morning, at Stephanie's urging, Nick called Carroll and told him about the intruder.

"Call the police immediately," Carroll said. "I don't like the sound of this."

That evening as Stephanie and Nick sat on the veranda

sipping beers, the police announced their entrance with flashing red lights.

"I'm surprised they didn't use sirens," Nick said.

Two young policemen from Doylestown, one barely out of high school, stood awkwardly in their blue uniforms as Nick invited them to sit down. The older one refused for both. Stephanie offered them a beer. The older one, who talked, said, "Thanks, but no thanks. Can't drink on the job."

The talking policeman asked the questions while the other one wrote down their answers in a spiral notebook. Nick and Stephanie explained when they'd first noticed the prowler, the prowler's usual behavior, and how, recently, he had become bolder. They gave the policemen a tour of the grounds and a look at the inside of the house, even showed them the television screens. The two men left precisely at midnight, when their shift ended.

Nick brought the .30-06 into the bedroom and placed it under the bed on his side. When Stephanie went around to Nick's side to go to the bathroom, she shuddered.

The next evening the two young policemen came back, once more in a blaze of red flashing light.

Stephanie remarked, "There probably isn't a deer or an art thief within twenty miles of the place."

On the third night, the police captain appeared shepherding his young charges. "You haven't had any trouble the past two nights?"

"That's right, Captain."

"I'm pulling my men off the estate for the time being."

"Thank you," said Stephanie. "And thank you both."

Everyone nodded; the men shook hands.

When the squad car pulled away, both Nick and Stephanie were glad to be alone again.

The Nightmare

Mid-September brought a disturbing sweetness, an indigestible, clotted ripeness that strained the couple's already strained tolerance. The Bucks County air felt dense enough to clog the arteries and make their blood bubble. Indian summer's palette made Mark Rothko's colors appear blanched, Matisse's extravagant ripeness look thin. The tomatoes seemed artificially scarlet; even the grass seemed to wear a thick coat of green paint. Gourds poured seeds on the ground, squash burst and late melons cracked and oozed, leaving a saccharine spoor everywhere. Nature seemed to moan from its opiated trance: too much, too much.

That night—September eighteenth—after an hour of concentrated scrutiny of the TV screens, Nick rolled away from the cool white light and muttered, "I'm exhausted." Not having slept well all week, he fell into an unusually heavy sleep. But Stephanie couldn't escape her fears so easily. She played the usual con games with herself, but each time she tried to talk herself to sleep she'd get bored with the approach, open her eyes and see those hateful, dull flickering screens. The air, which wouldn't cool off, lay on her like moist hands.

191

About 1 A.M.—Nick had been asleep for an hour—she kicked off the sheet. She didn't feel excessively horny, only hoped that she'd be able to tire herself out. Sometimes it was the only thing that worked. She touched herself quietly, trying to keep her body absolutely still and getting off on the furtiveness. Yet after she came Stephanie still felt tense, strung out. It was one of those nights when she could have gone on indefinitely without ever being totally satisfied.

After a while, she slipped her hand down onto Nick's groin. At first she stroked the penis quite softly, trying to ease her way into his dream. Then she took away the hand, thoroughly wet her palm with a gob of saliva, and slid her hand back onto it. At the first hint of tension, she slipped down and took his cock in her mouth. As she sucked, it rose; she could feel her mouth lengthening the muscle.

Nick's dream felt good. He hesitated a moment in sleep, then, as worn out as he felt, Stephanie's reality began to overtake his fantasy. Nick hung in that vague erotic mood while she persisted, going at him more intently. Drugged, blissful, half-awake now, Nick lay back like an Oriental potentate. He arched his back, he stretched, the privileged look growing on his face.

She let go of his penis and slowly slid up over him, scraping his chest with hard nipples. Staying on top of Nick, she slipped him in easily. He responded, excited by her treatment of him, by her wetness. Their smell enveloped them; hot night air seemed to knead their bodies. Awake now, Nick ran a hand under Stephanie's buttocks to hold her closer. She hung near climax, Nick's breathing burning in her ears. Then from out of nowhere came a foreign noise which only she noticed at first because it wasn't keeping time with them. She thought Nick wanted to shift positions. As the noise continued, Nick kept pushing, operating under necessity now. He thrust at her as the sound persisted, first a scraping, then what sounded distinctly like footsteps. Stephanie tensed. Her mind intervened, telling her not to look up at the screens.

He was about to come when she struck him lightly in the ribs. "Nicky, Nicky," she cried softly.

With great effort he stopped. He craned his neck up a little to look at her. "Are you all right?" His voice was very tense. Then he heard the noise. Nick let go, shifted her weight to the side and looked up over her shoulder at the TV screens. "Oh my god, somebody's down there."

Slowly Stephanie turned. There, second from the right on the wine cellar screen, dim yet visible, a shadowy ghost slowly dragged along his before-and-after image. As it moved the head blurred, a double, triple arm reached out toward the wall. The figure then moved slowly along the space between the wine racks toward the back of the cellar.

"You call the police," Nick commanded softly. He didn't want her any more frightened. "I'm going down there."

Stephanie looked terrified.

"Don't worry. I won't shoot."

He broke away, slipped out of bed and into his jeans, and pulled the .30-06 out from its place under their bed.

Finally she was able to say, "Be careful."

"I will. You call the cops."

As frightened and anxious as he felt, Nick actually welcomed the coming resolution. He was tired of being toyed with. Oddly, he felt like he had in high school just before a big game. Only this time he didn't have to psyche himself up. That fight he'd lost in Cambridge— No way, he thought; he was ready this time.

Stephanie never took her eyes off the TV screen as she dialed the police emergency number.

Nick reached the bottom of the stairs, crossed the living

193

room and approached the wine-cellar door. She heard him, saw him, watching Nick's screen and the intruder's at the same time.

The phone's ringing stopped, a voice answered, and she blurted out: "We are living at the home of Peter Berger, off Reston Lane, the private road, you know, his housesitters. A prowler's in the cellar, and my husband just went down to stop him; he's carrying a rifle. Please, please hurry."

A delay, another voice, Stephanie was asked to repeat her message. She did—furiously, quickly. The voice asked if she'd said the prowler was armed. "No, my husband," she said.

She lost the prowler behind the freestanding wine rack, grew frantic until she saw his double arm reach out again. He stretched awkwardly around and back, as though working his way down behind something. At that moment Nick clicked open the latch on the cellar door. The prowler made a startled movement—an odd little twisting jump— and turned his head up toward the sound. Stephanie couldn't make out the man's face, but she imagined the fear and anger on it. She screamed into the phone: "Hurry! Hurry, please." But the phone was dead.

The prowler bolted toward the outside steps directly opposite the staircase that Nick was starting down. The man moved thickly in what seemed to be many-jointed parts. The camera made it seem as though he moved through a medium denser than air. Nick lost sight of him behind the wine rack for a moment, but Stephanie watched the figure knead his left arm with a bulbous fist. Then Nick reappeared in the left side of the cellar screen, just behind the intruder, who had reached the foot of the outside stairs.

The man took one step up and suddenly clutched at his chest. He beat wildly on it, ripped opened his shirt. He put an arm up on the steps to support himself, then he crumpled. His body seemed to shrivel up, and he fell to the floor as lightly as a scrap of paper. He lay there gasping, writhing, clutching at his chest.

"No, Nick, don't shoot him!" Stephanie thought perhaps that Nick had fired until she heard the strange disembodied voice ask, "What are you doing here? Who are you?" Nick then moved into camera range.

The man tried to answer but he could only make a series of unintelligible noises. Another spasm—the limbs splayed out, head jerked up then banged down hard on the cellar floor. He stiffened, twitched, then the intruder lay absolutely still.

Nick looked straight into the camera and said, too loudly, "He looks like he's dead."

Dead—the word wouldn't translate into meaning for Stephanie. Dead— Stephanie felt like a child. All she wanted was to bury her head under the pillow and lie there till it all went away. Yet she didn't have the energy to take her eyes off the screen. Still she lay there, knowing that she couldn't leave Nick alone downstairs. While Nick stood over the body like a hunter over fallen prey. Finally, as though snapping out of a dream, Stephanie flew out of bed, threw on a robe and ran downstairs.

In the living room she had to take hold of the sofa to steady herself. The low dark forms seem to threaten; the mammoth fireplace leaned ominously toward her. Stephanie could barely keep herself from crying out. At the door to the cellar she stopped and began to tremble. She snuck a glance down the stairs. Fortunately, she could only see the bottom two rows of the wine racks, a strip of concrete floor. There were no feet, no arms, no grotesquely frozen features.

"Don't come down, Steph!"

She thought: "A dead man is lying on the wine cellar

floor. In our house. Dead." Exhausted, terrified, confused, she sat down beside the door and stared blankly down the cellar stairs.

Below, Nick instructed himself: "Don't touch anything. Remember every single little detail." He knew he hadn't killed anyone, yet a well-dressed, heavy-set middle-aged blond man, his face locked in a horrible contortion, lay dead on the floor. Nick felt no squeamishness, which chilled more than it pleased him. He felt no surprise: After four months of mystery and evasion, this violent ending did not seem inappropriate.

Nick came up from the cellar very slowly and found Stephanie doubled over at the head of the stairs. He helped her up and they limped over to the sofa, where they clung together. They didn't stir until they heard the sirens coming lazily toward them. Stephanie had to keep herself from laughing hysterically. It was like the countless murder movies she'd seen, the spectators sitting inert and dumb—exactly as they had!—blasted into another dimension by the magnitude of the event. All those prerehearsals seemed to have robbed this very real death of its power, its reality. And yet, she realized feverishly, a body lay downstairs.

The rise and fall of the sirens closed in on them, brakes took hold, gravel sprayed, doors opened, closed; another door opened and two men entered the farmhouse. The leader was a brisk thin middle-aged man who quickly flashed a badge and introduced himself as Detective Lieutenant Theodore Scully. His assistant, a smaller rounder man in a cheap brown suit, was Sergeant William Morgan. They looked around in some confusion, then Nick said, "The prowler is downstairs, and I think he's dead."

The lieutenant said, "Excuse us, please." He looked at Stephanie sympathetically as his left eye slowly drifted toward the corner of the room.

The men trooped down to the cellar, leaving Stephanie on the chaise.

Scully felt for the intruder's vital signs. "He's dead, all right. Now tell me, Mr. Young, exactly what happened down here."

Nick went over the story, telling them what he had seen on the television screen, how he went down to the cellar, then the sudden, unexplained, agonized death. As though, Nick said, the man had been frightened to death.

Scully asked, "You touch anything?"

"No, sir, not a thing."

Stephanie had never heard him use "Sir" before. She realized they were moving around on the concrete floor. She heard scraping, thought somebody whispered. She heard Nick say, "She's pretty upset."

The sounds continued to rise up to Stephanie as Nick reconstructed the accident for them. A few minutes later Nick and the two detectives came upstairs. When Scully leaned against the fireplace, Stephanie started to cry. "I'm very sorry about this, Mrs.—or is it Miss?"

"Miss." Stephanie thought, I said Mrs. over the phone. The upsetting thing was to realize she was totally out of control. Why in the world had she lied about that?

"I won't take much of your time because it's very late, you're tired, and you've had a horrible experience." Scully had a soft low voice, a kind expression, and that drifting left eye, which made him appear to see everywhere at once. He made Stephanie confident that the truth would come out eventually. "Nick here has told me you work as house-sitters for the people who own this place, the Bergers. Is that right?"

Choking back tears, Stephanie nodded.

"Do you know the Bergers?"

She shook her head.

"Do you have any photographs of them here in the house?"

"Only of Mrs. Berger—Amanda Berger." Nick spoke for them.

"But none of Mr. Berger—Peter, is it?"

"That's right."

"I'm going to call the coroner, then I'd like you to give me a little rundown on how you two ended up here, what you do for the Bergers, that sort of thing." This demand came in the same relaxed tone, while Scully's left eye drifted toward Nick's favorite photograph of Amanda.

Nick explained how they'd come to Bucks County—the meeting with Bradford Carroll in Philadelphia, the terms of the housesitting job, the prowler's appearance, his call to the Doylestown police and the three-night surveillance which turned up nothing. "There's always been something weird about this job—one of us having to be in the house at all times, our not being able to write to the Bergers directly but having to send everything through Mr. Carroll. Then there was the prowler and the strange noises I told you about, usually the same or very similar sounds, which is the reason for all the TV equipment, Lieutenant. Like I told you, the Bergers wanted the mikes and cameras as added protection against the art thieves." The Lieutenant said nothing, only raised a shaggy eyebrow inquisitively, which sent his left eye roaming again. "Lately there've been a lot of art thefts across the river, in Princeton." As Nick spoke that last sentence, his words came out slower and slower. He had only Carroll's word that there'd been an increase—Carroll's word, and the evidence of the dead intruder.

Scully nodded toward his assistant, Morgan, who jotted something in a blue notebook. A car drove up and in walked the coroner. He was called Pulski, a bland-looking man with a Nikkormat dangling around his neck and a layer of dandruff that covered his shoulders like epaulettes. He was greeted brusquely and directed to the cellar. Scully turned back toward Nick. "When was that equipment installed, did you say?"

"They finished—what, Steph?—a week ago. Last Wednesday, I think. I can check." Nick felt nervous again.

"This was done at the Bergers' request. You're absolutely sure about that?"

"Yes. From what Mr. Carroll told us."

Suddenly for both of them there seemed to be four months' backlog of unexamined assumptions, unanswered questions. Both felt hideously stupid.

Scully didn't seem to change his tone, yet Stephanie felt him leap to the next question: "Did you know the dead man?"

"No," answered Nick.

"You, Miss? You have any idea who that man is?"

"I haven't even been down there."

"The man in the cellar is Peter Berger."

Nick and Stephanie looked at each other with unqualified astonishment. If looks could be graphed, charted, accurately read, their exchange would have conveyed total innocence, so precisely did one's expression mirror the other's.

"Peter Berger?"

"Here? Dead?"

"Yes, yes," Scully said as solemnly as a priest pronouncing last rites. "We had dealings with your employers about a maid of theirs who made off with a batch of silverware. Deported."

Footsteps came up the stairs. Nick took Stephanie's hand. The coroner appeared.

"What do you think Peter Berger was doing sneaking around his own basement?"

"I have no idea," Nick replied. "I can't believe it's him."

"You folks won't be going anywhere for a few days?"

"Of course not."

"I want you here at least until the inquest."

"When will that be, Mr. Scully?"

"As soon as we can get Amanda Berger back from France. Shouldn't take more than three or four days." His left eye skittered away to explore the room. "If we're lucky."

When they were ready to haul the body up from the cellar, Nick suggested that Stephanie go upstairs. The night was warm, yet Stephanie's teeth chattered with fear and fatigue. She wrapped the quilted bedspread around herself and sat dumbly on the edge of the bed. On the TV screen she watched the coroner go out to one of the two police cars, come back in, then, single file, the four men went downstairs. A few minutes later they rolled the heavy body onto a stretcher. With Nick and Morgan in the rear, the coroner at the head, the sheeted figure was carried upstairs, through the living room and out the front door. She tried to turn away but kept peeking, watching the slow ghostly procession hauling the stiffening deadweight. Then she lay down, wrapped the bedspread tighter and pulled the down pillow over her head, but she couldn't shut out the sight.

What seemed like much later, Nick slumped wearily onto the bed. "I can't believe it was Berger. It's so weird. Why do you think he came here?"

"I don't know. All I know is I can't stop shivering." Nick crawled in under the covers. The night was torrid, but she hugged as close to him as she could. "You were great."

"Great? What'd I do?"

"You were great." Stephanie felt too frightened and tired to articulate it.

"I was scared shitless."

Stephanie wanted to say good-night and tell him she loved him but between thinking it and saying it she was asleep. Nick hooked his arm around her waist and kept it pressed against her all night, under the ghostly gray light of the blank screens.

The Inquest

The hall of the Doylestown courthouse was packed with reporters and photographers, policemen and the curious. Inside the coroner's office, Amanda Berger sat perfectly still as Lieutenant Scully introduced Stephanie and Nick. Extending her hand to them in a gesture of graceful sadness, she said softly, "I'm sorry you had this horrible accident. Peter was very ill."

Nick replied, "We're very sorry about Mr. Berger." To himself he said, again, Beautiful. She is really beautiful. How well she fits the style of the farmhouse. And what lousy substitutes, Nick admitted, photographs are for the real thing.

Nick and Stephanie said briefer hellos to Carroll and Carl Meyers from Property Guard. Meyers shook Nick's hand firmly, saying, "Terrible shame." They all stood near Amanda Berger, which caused an awkward moment as each of the four tried to figure out how to move away without upsetting her. Noticing their uncertainty, Amanda simply said, "Stephanie, Nicholas, would you please sit beside me?"

The crowded room held three rolltop desks, various unmatched and overflowing wooden file cabinets, and an extraordinary collection of dried flowers—pale tufts of venerable wayside yarrow, which sprouted from all surfaces, drooping clumps of goldenrod, desiccated sprays of milkweed and baby's breath which left tiny graying petals everywhere, feathery droppings which made circular waves each time someone took a step. The room's clutter possessed a distinctly Victorian air, and its uniform coat of dust testified to the unruffled quiet which had ruled the coroner's office for eighty years.

Having been smitten by Amanda, Nick thought it safest to distrust her. Out of the corner of his eye he scrutinized her for affectation, a false expression, some slight movement of the hand or mouth or brow that would seem rehearsed. Meanwhile, she sat stiffly, staring straight ahead —a composed, dignified queen in pain, her full body straining against the discreet black suit, those expressive eyes. Regal, Nick thought, a word he never used and whose embodiment he always doubted.

Coroner Pulski dolefully intoned the cause of Peter Berger's death: massive coronary occlusion caused by overexertion. There was also an apparent irregularity of the pacemaker.

After the coroner's report, Lieutenant Scully turned to Bradford Carroll: "Mr. Carroll, can you please describe the nature of the instructions you received for the installation of the detection system designed to protect the Bergers' home and possessions?"

Carroll, who wore a black suit and dark tie, kept his seat. "I received a letter from Mr. Peter Berger on— Let me refer to my notes, please." Carroll pulled his black leather diary out of his briefcase and paged back from the present. "On July twenty-eighth, Mr. Berger asked me to have a protective system installed. I did rather extensive research for a few days, and on August second contacted the Property Guard Corporation and was put in touch by them with Mr. Carl Meyers, head of their installation division." Carroll nodded toward Meyers. "We discussed the nature of my clients' needs, and a day or two later Mr. Meyers phoned with an estimate. The estimate fell within the maximum established by my clients, I had another two estimates made, both of which exceeded Property Guard's bid —I have the paper on this when and if you please—and then later that week I asked Mr. Meyers to facilitate the installation of the system by September twentieth."

Carroll checked his notebook again. "On August nine I received a phone call from Mr. Meyers which suggested that it might be possible to complete the installation prior to the date originally agreed upon. Of course, I was delighted."

Nick's glance was already on her when Lieutenant Scully's left eye wandered over to Amanda Berger. Stephanie and even Pulski looked in her direction, too.

Scully suddenly seemed intent: "Just when did you say that installation was completed, Mr. Meyers?"

Stephanie felt relieved by the lieutenant's handling of the inquiry: the tone didn't suggest an inquisition, but she felt certain that, if anything was hidden, it would come out.

"Let me get these dates straight. You said the installation was supposed to be ready to go on the twentieth. But today is only the twenty-sixth. Peter Berger died on the morning of the nineteenth, and by then the system had been in operation for a week or so. Is that correct?"

He's fishing for something, Nick thought. All the blurred and disconnected unknowns that had haunted their stay in Bucks County seemed ready to snap into focus. He sensed that a configuration lay hidden there, just beyond his reach.

Carroll interrupted: "Naturally I informed my clients that

the date of completion was being moved forward. I assumed they'd be very pleased."

In the same leisurely tone, Scully asked, "Did you receive a letter from Mr. Carroll, Mrs. Berger?"

What a pleasure, Nick thought. You could fall in love just by looking at her.

"The letter you refer to arrived a week ago."

His eyes still looking in two directions, Scully spoke softly to her: "Do you know what day that letter arrived in France?"

"I'd have to check to be certain, but I think it was the day after Peter left for Paris. It might've been two days later. I tried to phone my husband that night in Paris at the George V, but he wasn't registered there. This frightened me." The gigantic, tear-engorged eyes commanded everyone's attention. "I called friends in Paris, finally I phoned all the hospitals. Peter was a sick man and I was terribly worried— afraid something had happened to him."

Scully took the part of the kindly uncle: "Did your husband ever go away before without telling you?"

"Not since he'd been ill."

"You had no idea he was coming to the States?"

"No, he said he was going to Paris on business. Oh, and he wanted to see the work of a young sculptor, a Jean Gagnier. Peter was once a sculptor himself, and he enjoyed encouraging young people's work."

"Thank you," Scully said. "I'm sorry this is so difficult." Then quickly, "No idea why he came home?"

"Not then. I do have an idea now." Amanda Berger found it difficult to speak. She turned her head toward Nick and Stephanie as though to draw comfort from them. "It's difficult to speak about personal matters in public, Lieutenant Scully. But I knew we were having financial difficulties —losses in the stock market, substantial gambling debts.

204

Peter did his best to hide this from me, as he always did. But I knew. I would've had to be unfamiliar with his character not to notice. My feeling now is that he went to Bucks County to arrange for a sale."

"He'd been selling work lately?"

"Yes."

"Did you know anything about a recent increase in the insurance on the farmhouse and its possessions?"

Amanda Berger looked perfectly blank. "No."

Scully looked at his notes. "In December of 1976, Peter Berger increased the value on the house and its possessions to three million dollars."

Everyone in the packed coroner's office drew a deep breath. Stephanie, who caught Nick's eye, nodded toward Scully. She was impressed that the Lieutenant had done his homework so well.

"I knew nothing about the insurance, Lieutenant Scully."

"And you were not involved in the selling of the artwork?"

"Not recently. Peter didn't let me have anything to do with his business." Amanda began to speak more rapidly: "I've always wanted to know. Up to a year ago I did help him. But recently—since his illness—he rarely let me become involved. Increasingly, I asked him less and less."

A small luminous drop at the side of her eye gathered into a tear which kept growing and growing until it fell. Only Amanda seemed unaware of its gentle fall down the slope of her cheek. The dusty Victorian room was suddenly very quiet. Scully spoke to her gently, almost deferentially: "But why did he hide, Mrs. Berger? Why did he surreptitiously enter his own home?"

Slowly she regained control of her voice. "I think his ill health embarrassed him. He was frightened of being exposed. Perhaps he had arranged a sale in the States. I don't know."

Scully nodded his head in understanding agreement.

Outside on the steps of the courthouse at a busy four-way intersection in the middle of Doylestown, Nick watched the people gaze up at him as they strolled by. A number of the locals lounged at the foot of the courthouse steps, waiting for a glimpse of Amanda Berger. He realized that he and Stephanie were part of the show. He thought how long it had been since he'd lived in even a vaguely familiar world.

The crowd stirred when Bradford Carroll and Amanda Berger came out of the building. In stride they started down the stairs until, three steps below Nick and Stephanie, Amanda turned and came back up to them. "I'm terribly sorry," she said in her low, clear voice. Amanda looked at them carefully, as though to set their faces in her mind. Then she let Bradford Carroll steer her down the stairs toward the waiting Mercedes.

A Year Passes

That evening Carroll phoned them at the farmhouse to say: Amanda Berger had graciously suggested that, if they wished to stay on an extra week or so, they could. That would give them sufficient time to find another place to live. About two A.M. Stephanie woke up screaming from a horrible nightmare. The next morning Nick phoned Carroll to explain that they would leave immediately.

"Of course," replied the silken voice. "That's altogether understandable."

Nick paused, waiting for the words to come to him. The pause grew so long that Carroll asked if anything was wrong. Stephanie stood rigidly at Nick's elbow, poised as though expecting a blow. Finally Nick started, "I would've said something to Mrs. Berger at the inquest, but it just wasn't the right time."

"I don't understand." Carroll spoke tentatively.

"We have a problem here." The other end of the phone became absolutely silent. For the first time in four months, Nick knew that Carroll was actually listening to him. "We accidentally broke a leg off one of the Han Dynasty bronze horses. Just one leg. It is a clean break." Then Nick exhaled the breath he felt he'd been holding in for a month. Stephanie looked at Nick gratefully, pleased that they'd shared the blame.

If they could have seen the expression of relief on Carroll's face, they would have been astounded, amazed, alerted. But Nick only heard Carroll say, "Oh god. Another accident. This is exactly what Mrs. Berger does not need now."

"We couldn't feel worse, Mr. Carroll, believe me. But I want you to know the horse can be repaired. I can see that."

"You can, can you?"

"Of course we'll pay for the repair. We were thinking about taking the horse down to the Philadelphia Museum of Art. I understand—"

Carroll interrupted, suddenly all graciousness again. "No, no, not at all, Nicholas. I'll have it taken care of."

"You're sure? It would be no trouble for us—"

"No. I've had a good deal of experience with these matters."

"You'll bill us when the horse is mended?"

"Certainly."

The agent arrived at the farmhouse two hours later. Their conversation lasted only a few minutes.

"I'm sorry I'm in a rush, but I've got to get back to town right away. There are so many things to be arranged—"

"We understand," Stephanie said.

"Mrs. Berger has asked me to tell you how sorry she is that your stay here ended the way it did. Mrs. Berger has no feeling but that you, too, were unfortunate victims of circumstances. She insisted I make that clear."

"Mr. Carroll," Stephanie said, "will you please tell her how much we thank her for the thought. It's most gracious."

"Yes," Nick said.

They dealt with the final business details quickly. Stephanie concluded: "You have my father's address for forwarding our mail and for whatever bills we owe—"

"And the bill for fixing the horse." Nick pointed at the bronze horses which Carroll cradled in a padded box in his arms.

"Certainly. I must say good-bye. Sorry to rush off."

"We understand."

Carroll drove away with the Han bronzes.

The guard and his huge attack dog were already on the estate when, two days and two horrible nightmares later, Nick and Stephanie pulled out of the gravel parking lot.

At the top of the driveway near the end of the serried line of pin oaks, Stephanie asked, "Nick, please stop." She craned around and continued, "There won't be any asparagus. Massey will rip it up."

Nick nodded dumbly, knowing that, once the asparagus was gone, it would seem as though they'd never lived there.

Back on the Cape, they found their old apartment had been rented. Stephanie took that as a bad sign. Her superstitiousness annoyed Nick. They rented a bungalow on the opposite side of the same inlet, which made them feel as though they lived their lives in reverse—the sun rose on the wrong side, they couldn't watch the sunset unless they went out into the garden. To make matters worse, Stephanie fought valiantly to stay out of William Harrold's paternal clutch. Every week or so her father would call and invite her "to come home and rest." He wooed her with offers of Caribbean cruises, the Greek islands and "a fishing vacation in Canada like the old days, when Sarah was alive." Her nightmares persisted: She'd be looking up at a blank TV screen, a man would appear in giant close-up, blood pouring from his mouth, his eyes liquefying as they bubbled out of his head. She'd try to turn away but her eyes would remain locked on the man's face until, slowly, row upon row of television screens would light up to endlessly multiply the horrible image.

Stephanie went to see her friend at the plant store, who hired her back after explaining that the dwarf apple trees had languished in her absence.

As long as they had lived in Bucks County, Stephanie and Nick had regarded Woods Hole as their home. Yet when they returned, they couldn't quite settle in. Had they, they continually asked themselves, grown too used to the solitude, the affluence, the beauty? They wondered, too, if they'd become too familiar with the tension that dominated their lives there to return to their quiet old existence. Except for Henry Brewer, whose sympathy was limitless, their old friends kept them at arm's length. It was as though the people they knew had read something into those newspaper

209

accounts of Peter Berger's death. The community seemed to regard Stephanie and Nick as either greatly changed or highly contaminated. Nick fumed, Stephanie resented the others' condescension. One night as Nick was tending bar in the 4-Square Grill, a drunk whom he vaguely knew said, "That guy you knocked off, Young, he was pretty rich, wasn't he?" Nick had to be restrained from jumping over the bar and hitting him.

After that, Nick's pursuit of the loose ends of the matter became relentless. Virtually every day he'd ask Stephanie, "Why *was* Berger in the cellar? It's his own house, he can knock on the front door, even use his key. Yet he broke into the wine cellar like a common burglar. It doesn't make sense." She'd find him poring over what he called "the evidence"—a photograph of a bootprint in the rose bushes, another of the same bootprint at the trap-shooting range, and three photos of the broken clay pigeons. Nick contended that something had been put over on them in Bucks County; something had happened at the farmhouse that they didn't understand, and it was his self-declared duty to figure out just what went on. Stephanie quickly tired of playing amateur detective in the dark. After a month of listening to Nick's vague surmises and false starts, she set up new house rules: no talking about Bucks County until Nick had something new to tell her.

It was Henry who suggested a change of scene: He had a friend who had once rented a cottage right on a dune at the ocean's edge. By then Nick had offended or bored to death everyone they knew except for Henry; and Henry, Stephanie realized, had the advantage of having been to Bucks County and seeing their life there. In mid-November they moved "down Cape" to Truro, a town which actually lay north of Woods Hole. She sympathized with the native Cape Codders' relativistic sense of direction since their

210

own situation was so topsy-turvy. The move was a considerable wrench to Stephanie—away from the plant store, the only real constant in her life; away from their old if not very close friends; away from Henry. By the end of November she was sleeping eleven, twelve hours a day. She had absolutely no energy. Meanwhile, William Harrold kept up his unremitting pressure, reeling Stephanie in like a game fish worn out by the struggle.

The cottage, she kept thinking, would be perfect for summer. Perched seventy feet above the ocean on a spectacular dune. To the north, the dune peaked thirty feet above the roof of the cottage, and the dune to the south rose six feet higher than the cottage floor. But that six feet—just above eye level—cut off the view of the neighbors' houses and made their place feel private, totally isolated. The inside, unfortunately, was less imposing—a gloomy sea-green living room with a patched hideous green floor and cast-off furniture covered by dreary, faded throws. The walls were awash with cheery plastic nets and buoys and anchors; dried starfish were pinned to the ceiling beams. The bungalow's single imposing feature was a huge, racking fireplace devoid of a single right angle. Apart from the wretched masonry, the fireplace had been built without a tumbling chamber, which meant it gave off almost no heat. Stephanie bought an electric space heater, which made life in the cottage like swimming in a freshwater pond—they moved from cold spots to hot spots to cold spots that were continually shifting with no discernible pattern.

The wind had been howling nonstop for eight days now, jiggling windows and whistling strange incessant tunes until Stephanie thought she'd go mad. They had just finished another tedious argument: Nick had tried once again to pump her for information about the day he'd discovered the three footprints in the rosebeds, an event which she could only vaguely recall, as she insisted, because he'd kept her out of it in the first place. Then he'd berated her for not understanding the importance of the event. Nick had scrutinized the time in Bucks County with such obsessive attention, remembered or created so many little details Stephanie didn't recollect, that at times she wondered what the farmhouse looked like and if she'd ever lived there.

Now she stood near the blazing useless fireplace, hot in front and cold in back, trying to keep the blood moving in the tips of her fingers. "Nick," she started, feeling her life hung in the balance, "I say this for your own good. It's not easy." She sounded like her father. "You're going around and around in circles. You're stagnating here. Apart from the goddamn barkeeping job, you haven't thought about anything else but Bucks County for four months, and it's driving me crazy."

Nick looked at Stephanie like a total stranger. The meaning of his existence was too wrapped up in the struggle to understand what had happened at the farmhouse. Since he demanded total belief in his quest, Stephanie's lack of faith seemed both the perfectly targeted insult and the ultimate betrayal. Nick wanted to cry; he had the impulse to kick and scream and slap Stephanie. His right fist tensed, and Stephanie, who had known a few rough moments with Nick in the past, picked up the signal. She had to keep from smiling. So it's come to that, she thought. A tense moment passed. Though neither moved, it was as though they circled around each other. Nick took one quick step toward her and let his fist relax at his side. He couldn't behave like his father.

"You of all people. I thought you would understand." His voice was without resonance. "I have this feeling we've been played for suckers. I can't spend the rest of my life not knowing what went on."

"And I've got to get out of here and get started on my own life. I don't know if it'll be a career or marriage and kids, I don't even know if it'll involve you. You won't ever talk about it." In their three years together, Nick had never mentioned one word about marriage. "I only know I'm twenty-nine years old, and I've got to get out of here before I go nuts."

Stephanie could no longer bear Nick's obsessive scrutiny of the events of the past. He seemed to take no notice of the present, let alone the future. "You're living on another planet, Nick. It has no place for me."

"I always wondered if you'd cop a plea," he said bitterly. "Going home to *Daddy?*"

"*Daddy* isn't what it's about. Or the money. You want to believe that because it makes it easier for you, but you haven't given a shit about me for months. Not since Peter Berger."

"Our precious *us*. What about it?"

"We're not anything now. You're not interested in anything else but what's in your head. And really, Nick, if you thing about it, you don't want me here. You may need me but you don't want me here."

Of course Stephanie was right, but Nick was too angry to admit it. "Listen, baby, if you want to run out on me, that's your privilege. If you're not tough enough to stick this out, then don't. Because I've almost got it. I can feel the explanation out there just beyond my reach."

"You're a fanatic. And don't look smug about it."

"Bucks County sucked, Steph. I hated it."

"For me, it was a chance for us to be together."

"Yeah, on your own terms. A chance to test me out and see how I fit in the approved environment."

"You're like a broken record, Nick."

"Oh, fuck it! There's no point in trying to discuss it with you." Nick thought, She's so much like her father.

"Would you please drive me to Wellfleet?"

"Certainly, Madame. Why don't you take the car?"

"No, you need it more than I do."

"I can always get a bike."

"That's all you need, another motorcycle." She felt like his mother, babying him.

"It'd be great out here, all the dunes. Where are you going?" His tone was softer. It dawned on him that she actually was leaving.

"Home."

"Where's that—Daddy?"

"For the time being."

Nick stiffened: "OK, I'll drive you."

"I'm sorry, ma'am," the bus driver said, "I can't wait any longer. You're holding us all up."

They stood in the middle of the concrete parking lot by Wellfleet's one-story white frame city hall. Nick wanted to cry out, Don't go, Steph. I'll drop this whole goddamn thing. Anything.

She said, "I love you and I'll miss you terribly but I've got to have some time alone. And so do you. Maybe you'll work all this stuff out of your system."

"Maybe it's better if we're not together for a while."

She nodded yes.

For the first two weeks after she left Truro, Stephanie was mad at Nick and furious with herself for running out on him. Life with her father was a strain: too many barely veiled I-told-you-so's, too many references to class differences—people who weren't "our sort"—too many overt shoves toward properly eligible young and not-so-young men. She could have taken all that if it weren't for the squabbling between her father and current stepmother,

214

whom he'd taken to calling "Floozie." Stephanie hadn't been around a bad relationship in a long time; it startled her how ugly, small and wearing domestic life could be. One day she withdrew a chunk of cash from her savings account, left her father a note and caught the next train to Manhattan. She took a room at The Chelsea and looked up an old boyfriend, Edward King. But Edward was involved with a woman and was only available one afternoon. That afternoon was not much of a success. She tried playing the singles scene at a Village bar; to some extent she enjoyed the impersonal sex. But the morning after was too empty and numb. Back to Rye and Daddy for another week, then the two of them flew to an isolated lake in Canada which had been owned by the James family for five generations. Their Indian guide, hired for $100 a day, practically got out of the boat and stuck trout on their hooks. The excess of privilege depressed her; she kept hearing Nick's dictum: "The rich expropriate experience like they used to expropriate property."

On the third day, Manto, the Indian guide, left to pick up another party. At the end of the week he would return and help ferry them out of the woods. William Harrold immediately expropriated the guide's prerogatives, even to the point of showing Stephanie how to tie flies.

"Daddy, Buck Weaver showed me how to tie the breadcrust and the genie may when I was twelve."

"But he never showed you the caddisworm, did he?"

She paid less attention to her father's absurd pushiness than she ordinarily would have, thinking that, while they were in Bucks County, she never once went fishing. At the time she'd told herself that she didn't like ponds. Now Stephanie knew she hadn't wanted to outdo Nick with her handling of the fly rod. If they did get back together, she'd never do anything like that again.

215

As evening began to soak up the day's heat, William Harrold showed her how to build a log cabin campfire, which made her feel like a retarded girl scout. Four hundred miles from the nearest settlement they sat on a sandbar under an overhanging wooded bank, watching the thick pine woods shrink up toward them.

"What sort of a wife was she?"

"Who?" He took a sip of coffee from the telescoping metal cup.

"Mother."

"The finest I've ever known, Stephanie." The reverent tone seemed an evasion to her.

"I've heard that before, Daddy. But what did she give you? Explain to me what she provided that you haven't had since. I've got to know."

Stephanie's insistence surprised her father, who was rarely caught off guard. "She gave me everything—herself, you. She was the person whom I admired most. I hope someday to feel the same way about you and, to be frank, occasionally I think I just might."

Having so rarely received praise from him, Stephanie's first impulse was gratitude. But she was alert enough to recognize the deflecting bribe. Her father hadn't answered her question. "Tell me specifically what made her different, Daddy."

William Harrold looked away into the dark for a long moment. "She taught me how to look at things." The dancing fire-thrown shadows reshaped the fierce blunt face. "I've never said this to anyone before, but in some important ways I was an untutored kid when I met your mother. Certainly I was a successful broker, I had a reasonably good education and a certain modicum of taste, but living with your mother allowed me to see what things of quality were, not from the outside but from the inside. And not just

216

things, but also people, the way certain people behave with character and cultivation, the way they establish their moral and intellectual presence. I sometimes wonder if I would've gotten there by myself. How long it would have taken." He cleared his throat and now the voice was more assured: "Clearly she recognized what I had. I think I offered Sarah a way to revitalize all that she'd received and to recuperate what was lacking in her world. It was a very bold step to marry me, Stephanie. I'm not sure you can appreciate how bold it was."

Stephanie watched the burning log pile slowly cave in, feeling very calm, very much in charge. Making someone in your own image, Stephanie considered, that has its costs. She recognized how important the exchange had been for her father, for his self-respect; she didn't begrudge them this, but it clearly wasn't enough for her.

"What else, Daddy?" Her voice rang loud, importunate. She had never been so demanding of him. "What was it about the quality of your life together that was so wonderful?"

He watched her, sucking on the lip of his aluminum coffee cup. "It's so elusive, Stephanie. It's been such a long time."

He can't explain it, she said to herself. Which means he really doesn't know what their marriage meant or who she was. Stephanie had demanded her birthright, and her father couldn't hand it to her.

Long after William Harrold had crawled into his sleeping bag, Stephanie sat listening to the popping knotholes and watching curving darts of fire disappear into the night. The dark wooded bank leaned protectively down over her. Sarah had been a woman of intelligence and courage. But William Harrold had always been a steamroller, probably even more so then. Her mother, Stephanie concluded,

217

must have been coarser-grained morally than she had wanted to believe. For how fine could Sarah's discernments have been if she made a deal for his vitality and ambition? And his sexual energy. Maybe her mother had died at the right time, before Stephanie could understand who she was. Having overromanticized Sarah for so long, Stephanie was relieved to feel neither angry nor disappointed with her. Together Sarah and William had occupied a niche that Sarah had carved out for them. Her own world—and Nick's world—seemed so much more open and varied than her parents' one had been, so much more interesting and terrifying. She was proud of this, she suddenly realized, and the thought filled her with strength.

Nick's letter arrived a week after she'd returned from the Canadian fishing trip.

My Darling Steph,

What a madman I was to let anything come between us. How much I miss you. My one real obsession now is how much I want us back together. Next to that everything else—everything—is meaningless. You're never out of my mind. I can't go for a run or a walk, I can't sleep or drive into town without seeing your beautiful face. In my head your eyes are always changing color with your mood—when you're angry they're blue; grey when you're warm and snuggly; green when you're deeply in love with me. No matter how much or how many times I say this, I can't tell you how much you mean to me and how much our being apart makes me understand about us. Life without you has no meaning or center for me. Or, as Sonny Liston said after he lost the heavyweight title to a guy called Cassius Clay—the reporters asked him how he felt, did it hurt to lose? And Liston said, "It hurts me more than words can talk." That's exactly how I felt and how I feel since you've been gone.

I think there are a few things we ought to set straight.

218

I'll always resent your father. I'm never going to really want to be with him. He is an incredible prick but I'm also jealous of his closeness to you and his accomplishments. Yet since he is your father I'll face him and deal with him and try to be as good as I can whenever I have to. I'll try to help you with him too, because I know how hard it is.

You were absolutely right about me needing to be alone. I took a real long look at the dark shit inside me —I know, that sounds like macho bullshit but I had to take the last look to find out how much of the street kid remained and how much used to be me. I'm pretty clear on that now, but I'd rather demonstrate that to you than brag about it all before you see it in operation.

Being away from you made me realize that Bucks County was about our honeymoon being over. I resented the fact that the honeymoon could end. But the moral of the story is, honeymoon over, time to get to work on the real life of our love. I didn't see how much you loved that place, how it brought you ease and peace. Because I didn't feel at home, I resented your happiness there. I don't ever want to be so insensitive again.

Two months ago I probably would've said, "Graduate school is for rich dilettantes." Now I think your going to graduate school in art history is a great idea. No, I'm not sucking around. Yes, I'm impressed by how much you can learn in a couple of months. This graduate school business put an idea in my head, and I'd like to talk about it when we get together. Which had better be soon, because I'm so lonely and horny for you I can't stand it much longer. I love your body, your breasts and thighs. I miss our making love almost as much as I miss you.

My nutsiness about Peter's death is just about over. I lived my life like a telephoto lens, with Peter's death in focus and the rest of the world fuzzy and blurred. You gave me room to play out this craziness, and that's another example of how strong and big you are. I hope my playing this out hasn't been done at too much cost to us.

We could get moving separately, my love, but it'd be infinitely better if we did it together forever.

All my passion and love,
Nick

Stephanie was moved and overjoyed; she read and reread the letter. But she didn't go to him yet, partly because she had one matter to take care of herself, partly because she wanted to give Nick time to play out his hand. Stephanie dated, she saw a man for a month with some regularity and had a reasonably good time with him. But she felt too deeply bonded to Nick to get involved.

"Mildred, please!" Stephanie said impatiently. "I'm trying to have a private conversation with my father."

"If it's family business, oughtn't I—"

"No. This is between Daddy and me."

As Mildred was closing the library door, William Harrold looked up from his paper and said loudly, "You are very good with her, my dear."

Stephanie waited until the door shut. "Daddy, you're an unmitigated prick. One of the most vicious, manipulative men in the world." William Harrold regarded her placidly over the top of his *Wall Street Journal*. "But you're also candid, which I want to be with you. I love Nick, and I'm going to go back to him soon. I'm also going to see if I can do anything about mother's will. Her intention—"

"I'm the interpreter of her intentions."

"The hell you are. You just used to be. But I don't think that'll last much longer."

"We'll see," he said and turned back to the *Journal*.

Nick's letter established beyond doubt where her heart resided, but Stephanie still felt too inert, too sore and tired to return to him. For the remainder of March, Stephanie stayed in the big house in Rye, reading and thinking, writing letters to Nick, and even trying to paint a little. Toward the end of the month her father and stepmother left for a Caribbean vacation; she declined their invitation to go along. On April first, as she was pining away for Nick, feeling lonely and horny, Henry called to say he was in the city; could he drive out.

"Hurry up," she said. Henry arrived in early afternoon.

"You've never seen this place?"

"No."

"Let's walk around the grounds. That's the best part anyway."

They strolled down a tree-lined gravel path which opened onto an elaborate rock garden.

"How are you doing?" Stephanie asked.

"The usual. Up some, down some."

"How's the est training?

"It isn't doing it anymore. The old shit's closing in again."

"Sorry to hear that." Ordinarily, Stephanie would've pursued the question of Henry's well-being, but today she had other things on her mind.

Henry suddenly chuckled to himself. "But I'll tell you something. I really did appreciate Nick not jumping on me about est when we came to visit you. I know how much he hates that kind of group stuff. What's he call it, 'Collective hand jobs?' "

Stephanie smiled too, thinking of Nick's settled prejudices. "How's Cindy?"

"Finished."

"Are you sad?"

"You kidding?" Henry looked at Stephanie seriously. "I don't seem too good at liking the women I love."

221

"What do you mean?"

"You know, all these dumb bimbos who end up chasing me because—I guess because I want them to. And then I dump them because they're chasing. I don't know . . . Look, I didn't drive out to talk about my love life. I went to see Nick—"

"He wrote me."

"He's very together, Steph, very fine and clear in the head. What he says about the Bergers makes sense to me." Seeing her expression, Henry said, "OK, let's not get into that. I'm worried about him." Stephanie looked alarmed. "He's lost a lot of weight from eating out of tin cans." Stephanie gave him a sly look and he smiled, knowing she took the sympathy ploy with some irony.

"If it were only the Scarsdale diet, I'd be concerned. But he's got that faraway look that the old loners in Maine get, like they're surprised that they're not the only person in the world. I'm worried—no, not really worried because he's sure this whole episode is wrapped up. But I think it wouldn't hurt if you went out there to have a look in on him. He didn't ask and I'm not pushing you two back together—"

"I know that, Henry." The lump kept expanding in her throat. Stephanie knew how much Henry did want them together. Their good friend had a lot invested in their relationship. He loved her and Nick, their "us."

"I'm just telling you this so you'll know how it is."

"Sure, thanks. Thanks a million, Henry."

She asked him to stay for dinner, but he declined: "I've got a heavy date back in the city."

As he got ready to go, she said, "It really wasn't necessary for you to drive all the way up here, Henry. We could've talked on the phone, you could have just called me."

"Uh, I love to drive, you know that. And I wanted to see

222

you." She looked up into those big gray eyes and thought, not for the first time, what a lovely man.

She saw Henry to the car and waved him off, then went back inside. She picked up the pseudo-antique gold-plated telephone on the hall table and held it in her hands for a moment, staring at it. Then she settled the baroque implement into its cradle. She took a tour of the house—marked out the green-on-green rug in the green sitting room, the green lattice wall paper in the outdoorsy breakfast nook, considered the gold-and-silver dining room. Upstairs, she shook the thick, turned mahogany cornerpost of the canopied bed. She examined her stepmother's decorator's taste with sociological detachment, trying to root out the values implicit there. She found the house too absurd to pose any threat at all; she had no desire to rip apart the settee or bash the curios or furnishings. But Stephanie understood how someone could work up hatred for the style.

All the way from Westport to Orleans, Stephanie tried to calm herself. At the traffic circle she gave in and let the mood take her.

South Wellfleet, Wellfleet, the Truro marker, a right turn off Route 6. Like a countdown. Onto the winding road that picked up the long roll of the dunes, past the sea captain's house with the seven Chinese mulberry trees. She had needed an excuse to return. Why? She just had. And Henry, lovable, understanding, dear interventionist Henry, had provided it.

As she turned off the paved road onto the first slope of the half-mile sand track that led back to the cottage, she realized that Nick had graded the washouts himself. Stephanie imagined him out there with wheelbarrow, rake and shovel, throwing in crushed rock, raking it, rolling it, evening it out. Slowly making his way up the hill, then along the ridge. For me, she thought. The smooth surface kept pulling her closer.

She stopped when she saw the cottage on the other side of the switchback. On the ocean side he'd built a small deck, and a low wall to shelter it; he'd painted and rehung a number of shutters and had scraped down the peeling paint on the windward side. Stephanie watched the familiar whipping motions of the beach grass, the dun and rust and purple bushes bending to the wind. The whole landscape danced, welcoming her home.

They remained tentative at first, Stephanie almost uncertain who this unfamiliar person was: He had a saint's intensity—dark and gaunt with hollow cheeks and slightly distracted eyes. Like the philosopher in Rembrandt's painting, she thought. Like the landscape around them. Nick was more abashed and solicitous than she'd ever known him, offering her a place to sit and tea, coffee, beer, wine all in the same breath. He recognized that he owed her a huge apology.

In bed they met like a husband and wife after a long absence. A few familiarizing touches, a passing awkwardness, then the most gratifying of sensual understandings returned, was sustained. Luxuriously, they welcomed each other home.

They lay in bed watching the shifting multicolored bands of the sunrise tint the gray ocean. Nick said, "Teddy called me while you were away."

"What did he want?" She felt bad about putting it so harshly, but Nick's younger brother was always in trouble. Mercifully for the last year or so Nick hadn't heard from him.

"Three grand."

224

"Three grand? Where in the world would you get—?"

"Oh Christ, Steph, it was terrible. He could hardly bring himself to ask, he was mumbling, I couldn't hear him. Finally, I kind of pulled it out of him. He said, 'Nicky, I feel like a total scumbag, but these two heavies keep coming around the house, and Karen knows something's up!' " Nick shook his head slowly from side to side. "I knew one of them, Big Bobby Bondo, he's called."

"Who is he?"

"Bondo runs numbers, the other guy, Al, is a bookie. Sweetheart"—his voice cracked—"Teddy thought I could hit you up for it."

"Nick, I'm so sorry. Do you want the money?"

"It's too late. Apparently they're going to work it out. Teddy hit a pool and he's giving them $100 a week. For now, it sounds like it's OK."

"That's good."

Nick forcibly changed the subject. "I was surprised how easy it was to become a hermit. Funny, I'd always been so involved with people before, it was like coming in contact with a whole new being. Of course I missed you terribly, all the time. I was whacking off three, four times a day thinking of you. I'd even try not to remember, then I'd be hit by an image—your breasts"—Nick kissed her nipple— "pulling on a stocking and, boom, stiff like a rod. I had the usual symptoms, hair on the palms, pulled muscles in my right forearm. But that was almost my only distraction."

"Distraction?"

"Apart from working on the house." Nick had foamed insulation on the ceiling, cleared away the junk pile that had lain outside the back door for two months, built that little deck for them. "I'd never been able to concentrate like this before, Steph. It was kind of crazy but also so intense, I really loved it in a way." The sun glancing off the ocean bounced sparks off his dark eyes. "For three, four months I pursued the question with every ounce of macho frenzy I could muster, and now I've done all I could. I don't have the answer but I don't feel the time was wasted— except for us. I'm as close as I can be. Let me show you how I've laid it all out. Stay with this craziness for this one last time, then the subject's closed."

A large, standing easel held the center of the living room floor; draped over it was her old plaid baby blanket.

"Visual aids?" She smiled.

"It'd be better with charts and graphs. The big corporate presentation."

"Audio visuals!"

"Those too. But this is a little more modest." Nick smiled almost shyly.

His chart was printed carefully in block capitals. Underlinings set off each heading:

   I. PRE-BUCKS
       1) Why were we picked—after not being picked?
       2) Who were the older couple that couldn't come? Why? Contact.
       3) How long before our coming was the house being watched? Would Massey or the Spanish maids know anything about anything?
   II. THE CONDITIONS
       1) Someone in the house at all times
       2) No contact with the Bergers
       3) Contact only through Carroll
   III. CHRONOLOGY
       1) Massey's damaged shears
       2) Window frame jimmied?
       3) First footsteps; flashlight chase
       4) Mower drained/tracks in rosebed: 2 photos of large bootprint

5) Skeet range, broken pigeons: 2 photos of same bootprint

IV. BREAKING MINOAN GODDESS

  1) When did Bergers receive the letter? Why didn't they write back right away?

  2) Why weren't they more upset?

  3) When Carroll came out to install the detection stuff, we had to REMIND him about the goddess. a) He was more interested in the video and audio; b) said don't trust local police with high-class thieves

    (Here, in pencil, Nick had added: It didn't seem important enough to him!)

V. INSTALLATION

  1) The thief (thieves) knew where the cameras were, their range, etc. How? Just good pros or inside tip?

VI. NIGHT SOUNDS

  1) I think the night sounds came in three basic variations:

    a) Sound of voice or clearing throat

    b) Shoe on gravel, running or scraping then running

    c) Running

    d) Rustling bushes

    (Nick had handwritten this:)

    1.) Stereo journals suggest two possibilities: equipment that projects sound through a voice-throwing device, like an electronic ventriloquist

    2.) more simple: plant amps in concealed places. Plenty of trees, rocks (I kept chasing the sounds all over the place and never saw anybody ever)

    Also could've been a tape loop, activated

by remote control; if so, whoever activated could've mixed the recorded
sounds and added his own.

VII. ART THEFTS: PRINCETON TRIP

    1. CARROLL LIED! No "great increase" in rob-
beries

        a. This year two *reported* big burglaries (jew-
els, paintings, securities); one in May (maid
tied up but not hurt); one in Aug. LAST
YEAR there was one REPORTED ROB-
BERY!

    2. Lt. Wick of larceny squad said that occasion-
ally robberies don't get reported. This makes
insurance more difficult to collect.

        a. Unreported robberies handled by private
eyes or investigators working for insurance
companies. Wick had heard of muscle
being applied in certain special cases, but
this difficult to prove. Most unreporteds involve items on which estate tax not paid or
bought under shady circumstances. These
are usually inside jobs.

    3. Checked with three big insurance companies.
No surprise, they wouldn't talk.

    4. Called three private eyes. Ditto: no talk.

VIII. UNSOLVED

    1. PETER BERGER'S DEATH

        a. How could Peter Berger be the guy running
around the garden if all the time he was in
France? Are there two guys? More? What
does that tell me?

        b. Whoever was or wasn't running around the
garden always seemed to know when I was
home and Steph away. How did they know
where I was?

surveillance
camera(s)
phone tap
plugging into camera/audio system
all of the above

2. Carroll didn't want us to take the Han horse to the Philadelphia Museum. He said it was easier for him, he had better contacts. Seemed in big hurry to pick it up.

3. *WHY WAS PETER BERGER SNEAKING INTO HIS OWN CELLAR?*

4. What's the connection, if any, between art thieves torturing us while we were in the farm-house and Peter Berger's death?

When Stephanie finished reading Nick's chart, she felt brought up short. She checked her first impulse to say, Nick, we knew all that. What the hell have you been doing out here all this time? But she also recognized his pressing need for her response. She felt as though she stood before a friend's painting, unmoved.

Nick spoke first: "I know it ain't all that much to show for four months' work, but I got a lot done around the house." He forced a sheepish smile. "I just felt I had to lay this out in order for me to be OK, which would help us be OK."

She nodded calmly.

"Steph, do you know they've never even sent us a bill for the broken horse?" Nick pleaded hotly, then moved on. "That's my case. It doesn't add up, but it does isolate a lot of questions. I've gone over it like one of those pictures with all the faces hidden in it. I can't tell you how many times I got the feeling I had it, it was about to come clear —I was finally going to *SEE!* But it never happened and I've spent enough time with it now." Stephanie could feel Nick physically pulling himself away from the chart, from the haunting irresolution, from his overwhelming sense of powerlessness and responsibility. "I appreciate your letting me play it out. I had to. I mean, I know how difficult it's been." Unable to dig himself out of that hole, he hurried on: "I'm dropping it, Steph. Going cold turkey. It's all over."

Stephanie stared at the easel, at Nick's anticlimactic, patently obvious presentation and began to smile as the now-familiar mixture of emotions crept up: The world, she had begun to feel recently, did not comply with her wishes; her life was—and always would be—full of uncontrollables that neither good intentions nor money nor good breeding could shield her from. Nick was not the perfect complimentary Romeo to her Juliet, not the perfect anything for that matter. But he was the person she loved, and she felt more certain of that than she ever had before.

"I've been thinking a lot about your going back to school," he was saying. "The more I think about it, the better the idea seems. When I was in Princeton trying to squirrel out statistics about increases in art thefts, I stopped in their art museum and—you know what? Don't laugh—I thought about applying to their museum school."

Stephanie's smile threatened to broaden, but she couldn't let it surface. If she laughed, if only from outright joy, the spell would break. "I started to think—I know how weird this sounds—that I'd be a damned good art restorer. I mean I've always liked to work with my hands, and the technical shit they do now with frescoes and underdrawings is really amazing—"

Before he could finish, the dam of her emotions broke, and Stephanie swamped Nick in her love.

The lawyer believed that Stephanie had a case against her father and agreed to work for $500 minimum plus a 15 percent contingency fee. She wrote William Harrold that she was applying to graduate school in landscape architecture, Nick in art restoration, and that their intentions were honorable. (She giggled writing that line.) She was old enough, responsible enough to handle her own money. Sarah had clearly intended the money to be hers, and Sarah had assumed William Harrold would play fair. Either through carelessness or muddleheadedness, her mother had made the mistake of allowing her father to change the rules at whim. If she had to take her father or the executors to court, she would.

William Harrold's attorney wrote back to say, "Don't be precipitous, my dear. We can work out an agreement." Seizing on their waffling, Stephanie had her lawyer serve William Harrold with a paper. Her father agreed to "grant" Stephanie one-half of the interest from the principal of her mother's estate and a monthly stipend of $300. As usual, William Harrold declared himself the winner, explaining that it would cost unnecessary money to fight in court, insisting that her tactic pleased him because it indicated how much "spunk" she had, that she was her father's daughter, and so on Polonius-like at considerable and tedious length.

Meanwhile, Nick stood on the sidelines quietly cheering Stephanie's determination. He didn't feel he could comment because he would have a healthy share of the benefits. Nick realized just how serious a commitment they had made to one another.

She was accepted at City College in landscape architecture, and Nick took out a loan to enter Princeton's art restoration program. They found a big unfinished loft on Grand Street. Nick went to work fixing up the loft and doing carpentry jobs on the side, while Stephanie, because she wanted to, worked in a Soho art gallery on the weekend. In June they were married by a clerk at City Hall. Nick grumbled lovingly that the only thing worse than being married by a clergyman was being married by a bureaucrat. Only very rarely did Stephanie catch that perplexed, faraway look in Nick's eye; in those moments he reverted to his solitary Truro existence, and, while there, he pondered the mystery of Bucks County.

Sotheby Parke Bernet

On a quiet Sunday in early October, just after the start of the first semester, Stephanie sat at the breakfast table reading the Arts and Leisure section of the *Times*. Finishing the article on Matisse's cutouts, "his great drawings in pure color," she let her eye drift down the column to an advertisement for a sale at Sotheby Parke Bernet. Her hand started to tremble and she glanced surreptitiously at Nick, who was lost in his latest book on restoration. Turn the page. He'll never know, she thought. Although they hadn't really spoken about Bucks County for over two months now, she knew that Nick's obsession merely lay dormant. When Henry had come to visit, Nick and he had closeted themselves for a late-night drunk. Until early in the morning she'd heard their conspiratorial whispers about camera placement and the sequence of Peter's mysterious movements in the wine cellar. Later, their male voices had cut their way into the fearful recurrent nightmare—she'd awakened crying and screaming. Nick had run upstairs as quickly as his drunken state would allow, and, as he hugged and rocked Stephanie, he'd promised never to speak about Bucks County again.

Staring at the ruled spaces at the bottom of the *Times* page, she was tempted to get up and go to the bathroom where she could rip out the incriminating page. She sat immobile, considering what Bucks County had taught her about lying and hiding things. And if that wasn't sufficient, she had Peter Berger's example. Countless times she'd wondered what would have happened if Peter had told Amanda what he was up to: His visit could have been totally out front. They would have welcomed him home; she would have cooked a meal; the most dramatic event would have been showing him the asparagus. Stephanie hesitated a moment longer, savoring the privacy of her thoughts. Then, to her vast relief, she heard herself say, "Nick, you're not going to believe this."

He waved his hand as though signaling, "Wait a minute."

"I'm serious."

Her urgency brought Nick's eyes up from the page. Stephanie handed him the *Times*.

"What? This piece on Matisse?" He sounded annoyed. "I'll read it later."

"Keep going."

The paper seemed to stiffen in his hands. "Oh Jesus." In the large block below the article on Matisse was this Sotheby ad:

IMPORTANT 19TH-AND 20TH-CENTURY DRAWINGS, PAINTINGS, SCULPTURE including property from the Estate of Mr. Peter Berger (sale 3175) Monday, October 5, 2:30.

By the time they stood outside Sotheby's shortly after noon the next day, they'd been over the question of the sale a hundred times. Emotionally, Stephanie insisted, it made sense: Amanda couldn't stand living in the farmhouse surrounded by the artwork; just too many memories of her old life. Nick resisted the ease and obviousness of Stephanie's reasoning: Nothing related to the Bucks County experience had ever been that straightforward. They'd nudged each other a little about their differences, skating, again, around the thin ice of Nick's obsession without, so far, falling in. So both were a bit nervous as they walked through the entrance hall and asked at the information desk about tickets for the 2:30 sale.

Upstairs, on the third floor, they collected their tickets, then followed two older couples into the exhibition gallery. They meandered through a treasure trove of antiquities and primitive art, all of which was to be sold at auction on Friday. As they moved away from an arresting Stone Age "Venus" with a bloated belly and enormous mounded breasts, Nick found himself confronting the tiny pre-Columbian goddess which had adorned the little velvet pad on a glass shelf to the left of the Bergers' stone fireplace. He nodded at it. Stephanie's eyes filled with tears; she shook her head dolefully: "I hate seeing it like this, Nick. Hate it."

"I know what you mean."

The card on the wall next to the glass case identified the piece as pre-Columbian. There was no indication of ownership.

With eyes like automatic zoom lenses, they moved around the room, spotting former Berger treasures wherever they turned: the famous Ice Age necklace made of bone, unearthed in southern France; the gold cup from Scythia with the painstakingly detailed relief carving of the hunt; the tall graceful Mycenaean vase.

"Something so impersonal about it, Steph," Nick said under his breath.

234

"Brutal!"

"Liquidation, pal. Melting down the gold."

They were tempted to ask the attendants to open the display cases so they might touch the pieces one last time, but instead they watched elegantly attired dealers and buyers handling the merchandise. One overdressed man had grossly wide lapels, a pink pleated dickie for a shirt and three rings on each finger. One woman had an extraordinary slit up the back of her skirt which showed her legs up to her thigh; Nick was certain it was designed to allow someone to enter conveniently from behind. The convocation of expensive perfumes confounded his nose and made him a little nauseated.

"Bread," he muttered angrily, "that's all this bullshit's about. Classy investments." But he also realized how deeply he loved these objects, and what lasting changes their Bucks County idyll had produced in his attitudes and in their life. They had come to each other from so far away. Not long ago the distance between them had been almost unbridgeable: That struck Nick with its full, terrifying force for the first time. Now they stood in front of the familiar objects experiencing the same outrage; like himself, Stephanie hated to see their former life stacked up in cases or skewered to tasteful fawn fabric walls.

In the Americana exhibition room they found Berger rugs and quilts, the painted blanket chest from the guest room, the silver and enamel music box in the form of a bird, the trumpeting cherub weathervane Nick had liked so much, even the scrimshaw pie crimper Stephanie had hung in the kitchen. Sad and disillusioned, their proprietary instincts aflame, they passed into the last exhibition room, which held Chinese art. An enormously tall, elegant Chinese gentleman in an exquisite blue velour suit stood in front of a showcase examining a porcelain bowl—Stephanie was taken with his insouciant ease. The man handed the bowl back to a waiting attendant. Stephanie watched the attendant carefully place the green glazed piece in the case, lock it and turn away toward the Chinese gentleman. In the case, next to the bowl, were the Bergers' paired Han Dynasty bronzes.

"Nick," she said breathlessly, "Look."

Nick almost pushed a well-dressed matron out of the way to get a closer look at the horses. The card to the left read:

EASTERN HAN DYNASTY (1500–1100 B.C.)
Wu-wei Excavation
Bronze

The two horses faced each other in positions very similar to those they'd held to the left of the Bergers' fireplace. Around them were exquisite Chinese bowls and cups and vases, a tea service, jewelry and jade and other bronzes. Stephanie dismissed all the other objects and stared at the bronze horse on the right, the one with the raised right foreleg. As though from far away she heard Nick say, "Christ, those restorers did incredible work."

Stephanie's impassioned eyes moved over the flaring nostrils and gaping mouth, over the chest and clung to the vulnerable extended foreleg. She reheard the sickening brittle snap, felt the ancient bronze come away in her hand and, in that instant, the beautifully proportioned foreleg became a useless metal shard. Yet, in spite of the painful clarity of that memory, the case now held what looked like —what was, she decided—a perfect horse.

She remained still for so long that Nick asked, "You all right?"

Stunned and confused, she whispered, "That horse has never been repaired."

236

"But they do this mending you can't see, babe."

"It's perfect," she asserted, her eyes pawing at the fore-leg, trying to find a telltale crack, the minutest shadow.

"It must've been fixed."

She shook her head so violently her shoulders rocked back and forth. "Perfect!" That was all she could say.

Nick turned and walked over to the attendant. He was talking quietly to an overdressed birdlike woman with thick silver rings on all fingers.

"Excuse me, but would you help us? Could you come over here for a minute?"

The attendant, who looked Nick's age, exchanged a glance with the older woman which read: "How tedious." He smiled grudgingly and followed Nick.

Stephanie stood in front of the case, her eyes on the bronze horse.

Nick explained, "We're having this little argu— discussion about whether this bronze horse here, the one on the right, has been mended or not. Do you have any idea?"

"Sotheby cannot comment on the condition of the LOTS, sir." His Anglophile accent projected utter disinterest. He reached into the pocket of his brown velvet blazer and produced an illustrated catalogue of the upcoming auction of Chinese art. He opened to the first page and ran his finger back and forth under this line:

> All lots are sold 'as is.' Sotheby Parke Bernet
> makes no representation as to the condition of
> any lot sold.

Nick responded quickly: "Then we'd like to examine that horse. That one." He pointed. "On the right."

With a show of indifference, the attendant pulled out a set of passkeys, flipped through a great number of similar-looking keys very quickly, matched a number at the edge of the case, and opened it. Quite deliberately, he picked up the bronze on the left.

"No, the other one."

"If you drop it, it's yours."

"Is that the estimated price?"

"Just handle it with care."

When Stephanie finally held the horse in her hand and ran her fingers down the graceful foreleg, she knew that the bronze was flawless. She knew that and no more, for her mind would take her no further.

Examining the bronze himself, Nick felt less certain than before: "You've got to understand what perfectionists these restorers are."

Around them the expectant murmur kept rising as more people drifted into the main auction hall. To pull Stephanie away from the horse, Nick handed it back to the attendant and said, "Let's go in. Otherwise we'll never get a seat."

She nodded dumbly and slowly followed after him.

At the front, in the space formed by the rectangular room's truncated corners, the floor was raised. In the middle of the raised floor, flanked by two ceiling-high, chocolate-brown velour draperies, was the wedge-shaped platform—bare except for a graceful silver easel. The auctioneer sat to the left of the platform in a massive dark-mahogany chair that must have been designed for a Renaissance prince. The chair had unusually wide arms and a high back which angled up into a hood, and the hood extended out over the auctioneer's head. Nick supposed that the angled hood served some acoustical purpose, but principally it let the audience know just who the featured attraction was. To the auctioneer's left, at a long mahogany desk, sat three extremely attractive young women assistants, to the auctioneer's right an equally attractive pair of women, and all five wore the standard-issue chocolate-brown blazer.

238

The auctioneer was a middle-aged blond man with a soft, handsome face and a very cool expression which, Nick thought, might just be his way of inciting the crowd. But unlike Nick, the audience seemed entirely at ease. They were not afraid of lifting an indiscreet finger to scratch an itch and ending up with a $125,000 painting.

Slowly the brown-velour platform began to revolve, and the next quadrant of the pie moved into position. Stephanie's head whipped around toward Nick. Facing them was the huge Rothko they'd lived with for four months—terracotta rectangle on top, a deep blueish-purple bar in the center and a rich luminous blue square below.

The auctioneer spoke quietly: "Lot 1401. One hundred thousand to start this." An instant later: "I have one hundred ten thousand. One fifteen." An instantaneous pause. "One hundred twenty-five."

To the left of Nick a woman with a ravaged face, high green leather boots and a revealingly open white silk blouse leaned closer to her companion, who waved a program.

"One hundred thirty-five thousand dollars," the quick hypnotic voice recorded. "I have one hundred thirty-five against you now."

The auctioneer at the Doylestown American Legion Hall into which Nick had wandered one Sunday had kept up an unceasing chatter, whipping up the bidders as they pursued stacks of chipped stoneware and racking oak chairs. At Sotheby there was no incitement, only attentive arrogance and a knowledgeable, matter-of-fact sense of privilege. As the bidding pushed upwards, Nick grew increasingly incensed. At the same time his right arm tingled and the hand itself seemed to relive its struggle to keep from drawing the straight razor across the bleeding purple edge of the Rothko. A sweat bead formed under Nick's arm, peeled off and made the long chilling journey down his side.

"I have one hundred and fifty for it."

The audience watched every movement, listened for the slightest sound. No one, not even the most disinterested dealer in the room, seemed to sit still: It was as though everyone were moving with a barely discernible momentum, moving in time to the rhythm of that controlling voice. Except for Nick and Stephanie—isolated and immobile, with no knowledge of who these bidders were or how high the bids would go. And yet they were the only ones in the room who actually knew the painting.

"One hundred seventy-five thousand on the right."

A slight collective intake of breath with that bid. For Nick it was like sitting stiff-necked at a tennis match, unable to follow the ball. Up front, a quick-eyed brown-haired attendant tracked down a bidder in the far corner.

"One hundred eighty-five now."

Along the mahogany counter two matching blazers recorded the escalating figures. The three other women nodded to standing male attendants—these dressed in light-brown blazers—who scanned the room, their eyes everywhere.

A lady in the center with what looked like an ostrich feather for a hat raised her index finger, and the bored voice intoned: "One hundred ninety-five thousand dollars."

Stephanie sat silently; Nick wondered how the auctioneer could tell if it was a $5,000 or a $10,000 bid.

"Two hundred thousand for it? Where?"

"In the middle."

Occasionally Nick glanced at the middle-aged woman with the unabashed cleavage. From the back, he realized, she would look beautiful, with that slender body and those firm breasts. He felt excited by those fleeting glimpses of dark nipple outlined against her white blouse.

"Two hundred ten. Two hundred fifteen on the left."

At $210,000 the Rothko reached its estimated market

value, and the audience gathered itself now to see how high the price would go. Collectors, dealers, and the house stood to gain by a new record for an American modern.

"Two hundred and twenty-five thousand. In the center, two hundred and thirty thousand dollars." A beat. "Two hundred thirty against you. Last throw." The rhythm was interrupted; a long pause followed. The auctioneer didn't say, "Going once, twice," but the audience seemed to keep time through the interval. The man sitting in the massive mahogany chair with the angled hood raised his hand over the desk. "Down it goes at two hundred thirty thousand dollars."

No moment of celebration followed, no one got up and strode to the front of the room to collect the fabulously expensive prize. For the uninitiated, like Nick and Stephanie, there wasn't even a clue as to the identity of the buyer. Instead, the stage began its smooth clockwise quarter turn. Ahead, to the left, Nick glimpsed six hands reaching out to pluck the Rothko from its easel; behind, a David Hockney drawing swung into view.

The drawing of a young man was slightly touched in places by colored pencil and beautifully controlled watercolors: a delicate, intimate drawing, a quiet little beauty. Nick had seen the Hockney only in the Bergers' catalogue, for they'd taken it to France. The drawing fetched $3400. Next came a group of three drawings by Picasso, two of which had belonged to the Bergers.

Each time the stage revolved, Stephanie held her breath. She felt depressed and extremely tired; she didn't want to think, just sit there protected by that blank gray mood. Nick kept thinking he was in an expensive automat, with disembodied hands stuffing the slices of pie onto the revolving platform, and other hands snatching the sold stuff away. Clearly, too, the auctioneer had programmed the order of the sale. Fabulously expensive paintings, the blockbusters, were followed by quietly beautiful drawings, smaller watercolors. The intervals allowed the audience to catch its fiscal and psychic breath. The minor beauties were gorgeous tidbits thrown to the more quotidian bidders, followed invariably by the legendary pieces of modern art.

Mostly, though, Nick and Stephanie sat and watched as the paintings and drawings they'd lived with appeared, were bid up and up to outrageous prices, then disappeared forever. The sexy Balthus went, and after it the Pascin, then the familiar banished Avery. A Diebenkorn that the Bergers took to France went for $45,000, a new record. The Matisse cutouts sold for $70,000 each.

Close to tears, Stephanie whispered, "It was a mistake to come here. Please, let's go." But neither of them could bring themselves to move.

The next turn and the Maillol nude appeared, the painting which Stephanie had used to change the subject. Nick stared at that familiar, generous nude, thinking, Stop bullshitting yourself. You've looked at enough welds by now to know there isn't any such thing as invisible mending. That horse was never broken. There's got to be another one.

"Let's go," he said loudly. Heads spun around, eyes fastened on them. Even the auctioneer paused.

His command startled Stephanie. She stood up before she could think, and, with Nick, picked her way down the row. "Excuse me. Excuse me, please." In the aisle it seemed too late to object. Besides, she'd rarely seen this authoritative mood lately. Clearly, this had to be Nick's play, the climax of his Bucks County obsession, and she resolved to let him have this last shot at a resolution.

Big Bucks County Revisited

Driving a little too fast down the interstate, Nick gnawed on his anger, experiencing the emotion simultaneously as stick and carrot. How stupid he'd been, how long they'd fooled him. Finally he would prove to Stephanie that his apparent craziness had really been a sort of sanity.

"There have to be two horses, Nick, or maybe even two sets. So why don't we go straight to Carroll and ask about the broken horse?"

"Because I'm in no hurry to tip our hand. I want to go to the farmhouse first and see if that'll tell us anything.

"You have to put this question of the horses together with the thing that's been bothering us for so long: Why was Peter Berger sneaking around in the cellar when he could've gone straight to the living room for all the goodies he presumably wanted to grab and sell? Why didn't he just sneak in the front door, get them and sneak out? Something important had to have been in the cellar."

"It makes sense."

"One more thing, love," Nick continued. "We're going to have to take a chance. My guess is that the guard and the dog are gone since everything valuable has been moved to Sotheby's. But it is a chance."

"I understand."

They spoke infrequently, the words more like shorthand than conversation. It's going to be over, Stephanie told herself again and again, the thought becoming more credible the more she repeated it as on they drove through the increasingly familiar countryside.

Only a year before the softly sloping lawn had placed the farmhouse in an exquisite living frame. Massey's manicured turf was now totally obliterated, and the eye was left on its own to wander about. The flawless lawn had been invaded by extravagant clumps of weed and nettle. Blackberry bushes edged in from the woods, and already a few scrub hemlock broke up the former smooth undulations. In the midst of this anarchic growth, the farmhouse looked shrunken to them. A single window in the pump house had been smashed. As yet, no one had dared touch the farmhouse. But Stephanie felt the vandals poised just beyond the ridge, ready to descend.

Nick moved quickly up the flagstone walk toward the front door, and Stephanie ran to catch up. She didn't want to be left alone even for a minute. They found the front door locked. She took his hand as they walked around to the back door. Again, locked. Nick looked around but didn't see any sizable rocks, so he stuffed his trouser leg into the top of his low boot. Gripping the porch posts, he hoisted his lower body up and kicked in the pane of glass adjacent to the door handle. Stephanie uttered a startled little cry. Nick turned quickly and said softly, "There's nothing to be afraid of. Nobody's here." Then he kicked out the rest of the glass. He wrapped his hand in his handkerchief and carefully reached in and turned the key in the lock.

They walked through the sunroom, past the spot where Giacometti's *City Square* had sat, on into the kitchen. The house was bare, dim and formless. It looked almost ugly to her. Even the fireplace seemed too large for the low, dark room, and the house had the worst of musty, unlived-in smells. He tried a light switch, nothing happened. Immediately he went to the fuse box in the broom closet and flipped on the power. A single lightbulb in a wall sconce came on in the living room.

The key to the wine cellar was missing from the hook above the sink, so Nick went back to the broom closet and pulled out the spare key ring. The big wooden cellar door opened easily. He tried the light switch at the top of the stairs. Below, nothing happened. "Surprise," he muttered ironically to himself.

"Is the bulb burned out?" she asked nervously, listening to the terrible resonance of her own voice in the empty house.

"They took it out." For the first time in the long long year, whoever had been manipulating them no longer moved a step ahead of Nick; he matched them stride for stride now.

With Stephanie trailing behind, Nick went quickly back into the living room and took the single working bulb out of the sconce. He found a second live bulb in the bathroom. Then, holding her hand, he cautiously started down the cellar steps.

The wine cellar was utterly empty. The historic unplaned beams, the crumbling stone walls and primitive aggregate floor no longer seemed the least bit picturesque. The three parallel metal wine racks, once stuffed from floor to ceiling with vintage stock, stood like dreary skeletons. The chart of the vintages' location was still pinned to a beam: Burgundys, Red, bins 1-6, to the right; Burgundys, White, bins 7-12, to the left. While Stephanie and Nick had lived in the house, the cellar had hummed with the sound of refrigeration and humidity-control devices. Now all was silent.

Stephanie had half expected to find a bloodstain on the floor. There was none. Yet she squeezed Nick's hand so hard that he gently tapped her wrist and said, "Ease off or it'll fall off." Still she didn't let go of his hand until he screwed both lightbulbs into their sockets and opened the outside cellar door toward which Peter Berger had made his desperate run.

"Stephanie," he said, "you've got to remember everything you saw that night, and me too." Nick stood solidly in front of her, forcing her to look into his eyes. "I have an idea of what happened to Peter, but we've got to be able to put together what we saw. The smallest detail might make all the difference."

She nodded, still uncertain.

"What was it you saw first?"

"I think the first thing was the shadow moving across the floor."

"From where to where? Show me."

Stephanie started uncertainly from a spot beside the outside wine rack. She took a few steps and stopped. "I lost him here."

"Where was I then?"

"On the way down, maybe halfway across the living room."

"All right, where did you pick him up again?"

It wasn't easy for her to be precise, and at first she was afraid she might be inventing it all. Then she got her signpost: Peter had momentarily placed his hand on the middle wine rack, as though steadying himself.

Nick didn't interrupt her, and Stephanie moved on to the far rack, where she paused again as Peter had done. The reel in her mind reminded her that Peter had reached downward then. She stuck her arm out on the empty metal rack.

"He did that?"

She nodded.

"What was that about?"

"Don't have the slightest idea."

"Reach around there, Steph, fish around."

She did precisely what she'd seen Peter Berger do, running through the blocking as tentatively as an actress on an unfamiliar stage. She reached out into the middle shelf of the wine rack; again she groped around but nothing fell within her reach.

"How tall was Peter Berger?"

"I don't know, pretty tall." Then he got her suggestion. Nick replaced Stephanie, and by dipping his shoulder into the rack and squeezing his torso halfway into the shelf, he finally got his hand to touch the back wall. Nick felt along the stone until he ran into the metal strut that supported the wine rack.

"Anything?"

"Just the frame." Nick withdrew his arm and stood up. "Shame we don't have a flashlight. Let me really get in there." He went in headfirst this time, squeezing his head and upper body between the shelves and feeling along the stone wall with his hand. He found nothing. "Got to be something there," he insisted as he ran his hand along the wall, trying to cover every millimeter. With his wrist jammed into the tiny space between the wall and the metal frame, his palm was forced up against the back side of the frame, and there it brushed something. "Something here. Maybe a switch."

"Switch?" she said.

"Lightswitch, maybe."

Nick threw it. It clicked but nothing happened. Frantically he clicked the switch back and forth. Still nothing.

Stephanie shut her eyes slightly, trying to meld this

image of Nick's arm squeezed into the wine rack with her dim, elusive memory of the TV screens that September night. For a long moment Nick remained her only image, then the shadowy figure seemed to move alongside him.

"Nick, I got it. He did it again."

"What?" The cramped position caused Nick's voice to crack.

"Peter reached for something twice. Not just once. I remember. Come out of there and I'll show you."

She moved to the far corner of the room, accompanied, she thought, by Peter Berger's ghost. Aloud she said, "Peter reached in here at the far end of the wine rack and did it again. He could have been flipping a switch."

It took them a moment, but once again Nick located the switch on the inside of the metal stud that held up the wine rack.

Nick hugged Stephanie: "I think we're home free, pal."

Ceremoniously he threw the switch. Nothing happened. He told Stephanie to go back and throw the first switch. Nothing. They tried the two switches in ON position. Nothing. Then one ON and one OFF, the other ON and that one OFF. Still nothing.

A year's frustration settled on Nick, which exhausted him, defeated him, left him without the strength to continue: "We've blown it, Steph. I've blown it."

Nick slumped down to the floor and sat silently. Stephanie waited. Suddenly Nick jumped to his feet angrily: "OK, let's try all the other switches, every one in the house if we have to."

They turned the light switches and the lights merely went off and then on again. At the bottom of the stairs Nick threw the switch he thought controlled the bulb at the top of the cellar landing. When the switch flipped on, they felt a sudden draft and heard a slight creak. In the wall behind the wine rack they made out the dark outline of a door.

The Room

Neither doubted that the room behind the wine rack would hold the key to the mystery that had been tormenting them for more than a year. They didn't rush in but moved forward slowly, savoring the rare delicious instant before their shared belief would become a reality. Breathlessly, they looked into the pitch-dark space —and saw nothing.

Nick took one cautious step, a second less-cautious step, and stumbled down a short flight of steps.

"You all right?" she asked.

"Yeah. But I can't see a goddamn thing."

Stephanie searched the wall to the left of the entrance way for a light switch, found it, then suddenly, out of the dark, in a flash of light, Giacometti's miniaturized *City Square* lay before them, which they'd last seen in the sunroom. Next to the Giacometti stood a polished steel piece which looked like a David Smith, and on a shelf against the far wall was a Matisse bronze of a reclining woman. A second David Smith, identical to the first, stood in the opposite corner. As their eyes adjusted to the glare, Nick and Stephanie picked out several more sculpted pieces and their finished or partial duplicates.

No natural light reached the room, which was long and narrow with a surprisingly high ceiling. Someone had spent enormous effort digging down into the dirt and bedrock to create such clearance.

In the middle of the room stood a long scarred table littered with plaster dust, dried clay and metal shavings. The furnace occupied the corner, its metal vent pipe making a sharp right angle into the dirt wall. The floor at the foot of the furnace had been burned repeatedly by a welder's torch. As Nick shifted his feet, he scuffled metal scraps and pieces of broken molds.

"At the inquest didn't Amanda Berger say that Peter used to be a sculptor?"

"Yes," she said, "there was something about his visiting a young sculptor in Paris."

"Peter Berger used to be a sculptor. That was before he became a forger."

Stephanie moved forward, crunching as she went, and laid a hand on the Matisse sculpture. How thrilling to run her fingers along the woman's back, to count the rhythmic irregularities of the sinuous spine. This beautiful thing, she realized, might be an almost perfect lie. She said, "That's why he was down here in the cellar, not in the living room. For some reason he must've raced back from France to protect this room, to protect his forgery operation."

Nick pursued her thought: "Maybe he wanted to sell something that was in here—one of those Matisses. Or maybe the Giacometti." He moved his fist toward the Giacometti as though he were going to punch it. "We know there was a buyer for it."

"That's what Carroll said." Stephanie paused, concentrating on the Giacometti. "But is this the one from upstairs in the sunroom? Or is it a forgery?"

"I don't think it's the sunroom piece, Steph." Nick forced his mind ahead step by step. "If it is, then somebody would've had to move it down here. And that somebody would have had to move it after Peter's death!"

Stephanie picked up Nick's thought: "Suppose there are two Giacomettis. There are certainly two David Smiths down here. But which one is the fake?"

Nick examined the figures in the open space. "From the little I know about his casting marks, these look right." He spoke uncertainly, as though he hadn't yet found the right professional tone. "Wait a sec— If the one upstairs was the real one, there wouldn't be any reason for him to come down here. But if the one upstairs was the fake, he'd have had to switch them before the sale. That's got to be it. Peter came home to switch the two Giacomettis. That's why he was sneaking around down here. He couldn't let the fake upstairs get sold to that buyer."

"Then this has got to be the real one." As she spoke, Stephanie considered how vulnerable they were: She strained her ears to hear rapid footsteps pounding across the wine-cellar floor. The door would be kicked in and someone—Stephanie's mind would not let her ask who— would burst in with a gun. Yet, terrified as she was, she knew, for the first time, that Nick had been right all along.

In the car, racing to the neighbors' house to use the phone, Stephanie said she was afraid that the secret room would close up, that the second time their Open Sesame wouldn't work, that the incriminating sculptures they'd just touched would vanish before they returned. They phoned the police from the neighbors' place, then drove too fast back to the farmhouse.

She thought about Nick's explanation for the vent. There was something about these technical explanations that was so satisfyingly neat. "Peter had to exhaust the metal smell away from the farmhouse," Nick had told her, "which is why the forgery room is on the side of the house near the stream. The pipe probably does come out somewhere along the bank. But it's also probably very well concealed." With the police on their way she felt quite relaxed. It was as though, after an interminable intermission, she was about to hear the final chord of a great symphony.

Nick and Stephanie welcomed Scully and Morgan like old friends. But with a perfunctory nod, Scully pulled professional rank: "I got to tell you kids you're trespassing."

Stephanie replied quickly: "We understand that, Lieutenant, but we really have something very important to show you. Something that might resolve the mystery of Peter Berger's death."

"I didn't know there was much of a mystery," Scully said.

Standing in the high, narrow room, surrounded by the incriminating sculptures, Nick announced: "Peter Berger was a forger, Lieutenant. That's why he came in through the cellar that night, not through the front door into the living room where all the artwork we knew about then was on display. He wasn't after anything in the living room. Our guess is he came down here to switch this Giacometti"—Nick touched the sculpture—"switch it with the fake that was in the sunroom. That's why he had to come back. We know that Peter Berger had a buyer for the piece, probably someone who would know the difference between the real thing and a fake. My guess is that Peter had to get back here and switch the pieces before the fake got sold by mistake."

While Morgan's flashbulbs flooded the room with fleeting sheets of white light, Scully's left eye blinked and darted about. The lieutenant asked Nick and Stephanie a lot of questions about what they had been doing and where they were living and why they had come back to Bucks County, and they explained at length about the Sotheby sale and their accidental run-in with the unbroken Han Dynasty bronze horse.

When they'd offered Scully all the background informa-

252

tion they could, Stephanie said, "It would be easy enough to tell if we're right about these forgeries. We can find out when the Giacometti's going to be auctioned off at Sotheby's. The one at Sotheby's, which came out of the sunroom, ought to be the fake. And this one should be the real thing. If you call Mr. Carroll, presumably he should be able to tell you when the other piece is going to be sold."

"Unless," Nick added, "they already sold it to the buyer they had."

They showed the policemen the paired David Smiths and argued that one of the sculptures was probably a fake. They pointed to the furnace, the welder's torches, the files, rasps and chisels lined up in graduated sizes on the pegboard—" "Once a compulsive, always a compulsive," Nick exclaimed. "This is set up just like his tools were in the barn."

Scully listened patiently to all of their theorizings, Scully wrote notes in his notebook, Scully agreed he ought to go to Philadelphia the next day to speak with Bradford Carroll; Scully even used the police radio to make a reservation for Nick and Stephanie at a small inn just outside Doylestown, where they were to spend a few days while Scully followed up on the questions they'd raised. But just before they drove away from the farmhouse, the lieutenant said, "I hate to get heavy with you kids, but the next time you better be more careful about trespassing on somebody's private property."

"Cops have no imagination, Steph. I've told you that a thousand times. You can't trust them to think."

"I don't think he liked us scooping him. That crap about private property— How else could we crack this case?" She giggled.

Their low-ceilinged, beamed room at the inn reminded

them of a tacky version of the farmhouse—flowered wall sconces, a fake fireplace. Instead of getting the good night's sleep they needed, Nick and Stephanie lay on their backs holding hands and talked and talked.

"I'm proud of us, Nick."

"Me too."

"Especially you."

"Mmm."

"Are you happy? I am," he said hesitantly.

"But what?"

"Not sure yet."

"Do you mind going through it all again?"

"No. It's like counting sheep. OK, we can assume that Sotheby has the real Han horses." In the dark she nodded. "We think that maybe the Minoan goddess I smashed was a fake."

She picked up the thread: "That's why the Bergers didn't get more upset. Why they didn't write back right away."

Nick growled, "Boy, that pisses me off. Those fuckers— When I think about all the bullshit reverence—"

"We also know that there are two pairs of Han horses."

"At least."

"Don't complicate the issue, Nick. Here's a simple question: Tell me, where is the broken horse?"

He said, "Carroll. Bradford Carroll! That guy seems to crop up in the middle of all the simple questions."

Stephanie insisted they wait until dawn before phoning Lieutenant Scully, and she prevailed, though Nick was afraid Scully would already be on his way to Philadelphia. Just after 7 A.M., after an interminable delay at the inn's switchboard, Nick reached the lieutenant's home. Scully's very sleepy wife answered.

Nick thought, Not much action for a cop around here if his wife picks up the phone.

254

After profuse apologies to the wife and a less elaborate apology to the lieutenant, Nick explained that they had thought of a few more questions for Carroll; "Can you ask him what he did with the broken Han Dynasty horse? And also ask him where's the Giacometti sculpture that was in the sunroom. Is that the same one as the one we found in the cellar yesterday? Or is there a second Giacometti? There's got to be a second one. So the question is, which is the real one and which is the fake? All the fakes were upstairs, Lieutenant. Peter must've left them up there just in case we got clumsy and broke something. OK, our guess is that the Giacometti in the cellar is the real one. Unless someone moved the fake from the sunroom and switched it for the real one in the cellar. You following me? We checked the Sotheby catalogue and the Giacometti's not listed. So it's probably already been sold to the buyer. If the buyer has got the real one, then I think something's seriously wrong.

"Lieutenant Scully, I don't mean to tell you your business, but I think you ought to question Carroll in a way that doesn't tip him off to what you know. I mean, he might have helped Peter Berger with the forgeries. Or he might even have been the one who switched the real Giacometti for the fake if it was switched. Because one thing we do know for sure: he had the broken Han Dynasty horse in his possession."

The lieutenant replied slowly, perhaps still a little sleepy or just befuddled by the names and details: "Let me get this straight: You think Bradford Carroll had something to do with the forgeries?"

"I don't think anything yet. But could you just let him volunteer the information and see what he comes up with? Two more things," Nick continued. "Could you find out Carroll's shoe size?"

"Shoe size?"

"I showed you those photographs of the bootprints."

"OK, OK, what's the other thing?" Scully was clearly losing patience.

"Do you think it would be possible for us to go along with you to Philadelphia? I don't think we can stand the suspense."

"Absolutely not. This is official business."

As though to placate Scully, Nick said, "You just might turn up something down there, and his office alone is worth the visit. While you're there, Lieutenant, check out his stereo. He built the amplifier himself and it's a real gem."

Two days later in the Doylestown courthouse behind the opaqued-glass door which bore the title DETECTIVE LIEUTENANT THEODORE SCULLY, Stephanie sat and Nick stood as Scully clicked on the tape:

"THIS IS NOT AN INTERROGATION, MR. CARROLL, JUST A REQUEST FOR INFORMATION. OF COURSE THERE'S NO QUESTION OF SELF-INCRIMINATION, BUT IF FOR ANY REASON YOU'D LIKE TO HAVE A LAWYER PRESENT—"

"NOT AT ALL, LIEUTENANT SCULLY." Carroll's suave voice smoothed away the procedural detail.

"I'D LIKE TO ASK A FEW QUESTIONS ABOUT PETER BERGER THAT HAVE COME UP RECENTLY, AND I'D LIKE TO RECORD OUR CONVERSATION."

"CERTAINLY. ANYTHING AT ALL I CAN DO TO COOPERATE—"

"DO YOU KNOW ANYTHING ABOUT A SECRET ROOM IN THE BERGERS' HOUSE?"

"I'M SORRY, LIEUTENANT, I DON'T UNDERSTAND."

Stephanie and Nick strained to hear the slightest dishonesty in Carroll's reply.

"WE'VE JUST LOCATED A HIDDEN ROOM BEHIND THE WINE CELLAR. DO YOU KNOW ANYTHING ABOUT THE EXISTENCE OF THIS ROOM?"

"NO. NOTHING."

"THERE IS ALSO EVIDENCE IN THIS ROOM THAT SUGGESTS THAT PETER BERGER WAS A FORGER OF SCULPTURES."

Nick thought, Oh Christ, he's giving Carroll all the answers beforehand. Why did he have to tell him about the sculptures?

"I KNOW NOTHING OF HIDDEN ROOMS OR OF FORGERIES, THOUGH I WOULD IMAGINE THAT IF HE HAD PUT HIS MIND —OR HAND—TO IT, PETER BERGER COULD HAVE MADE QUITE A TOLERABLY IMPRESSIVE FORGER." The voice sounded so relaxed, so in control that even Nick found it persuasive.

"A GOOD FORGER?" Tension thinned Scully's voice.

"AT ONE TIME PETER BERGER WAS A VERY TALENTED SCULPTOR."

"I UNDERSTAND FROM MR. AND MRS. NICHOLAS YOUNG THAT YOU DROVE OUT TO THE BERGERS' PLACE TO PICK UP A CERTAIN DAMAGED CHINESE BRONZE HORSE."

"ACTUALLY, IT WAS TWO HORSES."

"ONE OF THOSE WAS DAMAGED AND NEEDED REPAIR."

"YES, THEY BROKE ONE. THEY ARE VERY SWEET BUT THEY PROVED MUCH CLUMSIER THAN WE HAD HOPED."

Stephanie looked at Nick, who cursed softly to himself, "That arrogant son of a bitch. For all I know those goddamn things were fakes."

"AND WHAT DID YOU DO WITH THAT BROKEN HORSE, MR. CARROLL?"

The hesitation was brief, but it brought Stephanie upright in her chair. She was sifting every syllable Carroll uttered, waiting for the false tone.

"AT FIRST I DID NOTHING— THERE WERE SO MANY DE-

257

TAILS TO ATTEND TO AFTER PETER BERGER'S DEATH THAT, FRANKLY, THAT MATTER TOOK VERY LOW PRIORITY. I KEPT THE HORSE RIGHT HERE IN MY DESK AND RATHER FORGOT ABOUT REPAIRING IT UNTIL WE WERE ASSEMBLING THE COLLECTION FOR SALE. WHEN I DID REMEMBER—IT'S AMUSING, LIEUTENANT—I GOT OUT THE PIECE AND TOOK A THOROUGH LOOK AT IT, AND, BECAUSE THE LEG WAS BROKEN OFF, IT WAS POSSIBLE, IF YOU KNOW ABOUT THESE THINGS, TO SEE THAT THE PIECE WAS A COPY: AN EXCELLENT COPY, MIND YOU, BUT NONETHELESS A COPY. I COULD SEE IN THE CROSS-SECTION OF THE LEG THAT THE PATINA WASN'T GENUINE. THE COLOR CHANGE WAS TOO ABRUPT, IT HAD BEEN 'WORKED UP.' "

"WHAT DID YOU DO THEN?"

"NATURALLY I INFORMED MRS. BERGER. AMANDA WAS PUZZLED AND ASSURED ME I MUST BE WRONG: SHE HAD THE HORSES AND THEY WERE PERFECTLY WHOLE. THAT IMMEDIATELY TOLD US THAT THERE WERE TWO PAIRS, A REAL AND A FAKE."

"DID YOU PURSUE THAT LINE?"

"NO, LIEUTENANT, I DIDN'T SEE ANY REASON TO. AT THE TIME THERE WAS NOTHING TO PURSUE."

"BUT YOU WEREN'T CURIOUS ABOUT THESE TWO PAIRS OF HORSES?"

"TO THE EXTENT THAT I THOUGHT ABOUT IT, I ASSUMED THAT PETER HAD PROBABLY PURCHASED THE FAKES FOR SOME REASON OF HIS OWN. COLLECTORS ARE OFTEN WHIMSICAL PEOPLE. PERHAPS HE INTENDED TO PLAY A JOKE ON SOMEONE. I DON'T KNOW."

"WHAT DO YOU THINK HAPPENED NOW?"

"WELL, FROM WHAT YOU'VE SAID ABOUT FORGERIES I'D SUPPOSE THERE'S A GOOD CHANCE THAT PETER HIMSELF MADE THE HAN FORGERIES."

"WHY WOULD HE DO THAT?"

"Perhaps he intended to sell them. Perhaps he just enjoyed the work for art's sake. I really can't say."

"What did you do with the broken horse?"

"Actually, that's quite funny. Once I knew it was a fake, I didn't bother to get it repaired. For a month or so I kept the Han bronzes, broken leg and all, on my desk. I was curious to see the reactions they'd evoke. And they did receive quite an interesting reception. People who thought they knew a little about such things congratulated me on my good taste. One client asked if they were for sale. I quoted him an outlandish figure and then told him I couldn't part with them for any price."

A pause. "Does the discovery of this hidden room mean anything to you? Did you ever have any hints that it existed?"

"No."

"The existence of the room means nothing to you?"

"Are you asking me to play detective?"

"Would you mind?"

"Not at all. I suppose it's altogether conceivable that my deceased employer wanted to make copies of pieces in his collection. He was a fine sculptor, and perhaps this was his way of staying in touch with those skills. But that's only a guess. I really can't suggest anything else. Certainly nothing sinister. Is that what you're interested in, Lieutenant Scully?"

"I only want to know if you have any information that might help us understand Peter Berger's sudden death." Scully clearly sounded defensive. Stephanie imagined his left eye drifting about the art deco set, searching for an emotional grip. "For instance, were you in possession of a piece of sculpture of a man by the Swiss Artist Jocko Medi? Our information tells us

259

THERE WAS A BUYER FOR THAT SCULPTURE, CALLED *City Square*."

"INDEED, I WAS HOLDING IT FOR A BUYER."

"HAS THE SCULPTURE BEEN SOLD?"

"NO."

"IS IT ABOUT TO BE SOLD?"

"PETER'S DEATH PUT THE SALE ON THE BACK BURNER UNTIL CERTAIN MATTERS OF THE ESTATE WERE SETTLED. A FEW MONTHS AGO, WHEN WE WERE FINALLY READY TO SELL, THE BUYER HAD WHAT HE CALLED A 'CASH FLOW' PROBLEM. THAT BROUGHT US UP TO THE SOTHEBY SALE." Nick and Stephanie sat up attentively. "BEFORE THE SALE I ADVISED AMANDA BERGER, SINCE A NUMBER OF THE ESTATE'S FINEST PIECES WERE CONTEMPORARY SCULPTURES, AND SINCE THESE WERE TO BE SOLD AT AUCTION, THAT SHE WAIT AND SEE WHAT THE MARKET WAS LIKE BEFORE PARTING WITH THE GIACOMETTI."

"SO THIS JOCKO-MEDI WAS SOLD AT THE SOTHEBY AUCTION?"

"NO. IT WASN'T. AMANDA BERGER INSISTED THAT, SINCE PETER PLEDGED THE PIECE TO THE BUYER, SHE WAS BOUND TO HONOR HER HUSBAND'S PLEDGE. I SIMPLY ADVISED HER TO WAIT UNTIL AFTER THE SALE TO SEE IF THE PRICE OFFERED WAS REASONABLE."

Nick interrupted excitedly: "Have you checked with this buyer of theirs?"

"Not yet. I just got back. But we will. Everything in time." Scully switched the tape recorder on again.

"ANOTHER QUESTION. COULD YOU PLEASE TELL ME YOUR SHOE SIZE?"

"SHOE SIZE?"

"YES. IT'S PURELY PROCEDURAL."

"TEN-D. BUT I DON'T SEE—"

"THANK YOU."

Quietly Nick said, "Shit. The footprints are a twelve or thirteen."

Scully asked a few more desultory questions about the kinds of functions Carroll had performed for the Bergers, when he had last written to Peter Berger, and if he still handled matters of the estate for Amanda. Carroll answered yes to the last question. The interview ended with the same formal cordiality it started with.

Nick said, "I had a few more questions for Mr. Carroll. I'd like to ask him why he didn't tell us that the broken horse was a fake. It could've saved us months of agony."

"Well," Scully replied, with the estate so up in the air, it must've been hard for Carroll to worry about details."

"Details?" Nick replied. But an alarmed look from Stephanie quieted him before Nick became too obstreperous, and Nick and Stephanie parted from the lieutenant amicably enough.

Back in their room at the inn, Stephanie insisted that Nick stay out of a war of egos with Scully. "We've got to keep him on our side, Nick; we need him. We really need him."

"You're right. But when I think of that bastard Carroll not telling us about the horse— What kind of gentlemanly bullshit treatment is that?" He took a slug from his glass of Black Label.

"This shoe size thing's really got me. Those prints I have the pictures of are a size twelve. A twelve!"

Stephanie wrestled with that one. "Nick, it's altogether possible that those prints were left there for you to see. What was it, four bootprints? Maybe somebody carried along an extra pair of boots and made them to throw you off?"

"It's possible. But Scully's not going to buy that."

"True. You know, I was just thinking: If Sotheby's has only the real sculptures, then someone must've gone through the living room and picked out all the fakes. I can't see it any other way. Unless there were only two fake pieces in the entire house."

"That doesn't figure. Look, we lived with the sculpture for four months thinking they all were real. And beautiful. And products of great artistic imaginations. Shows you what ignorance gets you." Once again, Nick summarized the state of their current knowledge. But he felt he was falling back into an interminable bad dream: "The broken Han horse that Carroll conveniently took away is definitely a fake; the Minoan I broke is probably a fake too. We're not sure if the Giacometti is real yet, but we'll know as soon as that insurance appraiser gets done examining the piece we found in the hidden cellar. Besides, if it isn't the real one, *and* if the one in the sunroom wasn't a fake, then our theory of why Peter Berger was sneaking into his own cellar goes right down the tubes. But there's something else that's weird: Carroll rushes out to the farmhouse to pick up the broken horse. Then, after all his high-speed cornering, he never bothers to get it fixed. Why the hell did he rush out here? It doesn't make sense."

"I don't know," she said. "He can always say he just wanted to get it out of our hands before we messed it up any more. We don't have much of a record in the handle-with-care department."

"True, and he can say that afterwards he was just too busy. But there's another possibility: That smooth Mr. Carroll knew it was a fake before he saw it, knew there were two pairs of horses from in front, and he drove out here to keep us from taking the horse to a museum."

Stephanie looked at Nick uneasily, wary of where the gathering weight of their conjecture was heading.

"If Carroll knew the horse was a fake beforehand, where's that get us?"

"Look!" Stephanie was excited. "If Carroll knew about the fakes, he'd be in the same bind Peter was in. He couldn't give Sotheby the fake because their appraisers would spot it. So he had to withhold it from the sale."

Nick grew animated: "That's good, Steph. Maybe the buyer did have a cash-flow problem, but that was only a lucky break for Carroll. It bought him time." Taking Stephanie's hand, Nick gripped it tightly. "Now try this on: If Carroll knew that there were fakes, maybe someone else did too."

"Amanda?"

"Right."

They puzzled over that for a while, but it was late and they were tired, and that night they could go no further.

A Phone Call

 "They've discovered the workshop."

"Who?"

"Scully of the Doylestown Police. Those kids led him to it."

"How?"

"It was the Han horse at Sotheby's. They realized that they'd broken the fake."

A tongue clucked softly against the palate. "Let's not panic. Let's think this whole thing through. The question is, just what will the workshop tell them. First, that Peter was a forger. That doesn't suggest we knew anything about the forgeries or the workshop. Second, what's in the workshop: a Matisse, a pair of David Smiths, I think. What else?"

"The Giacometti."

"Oh. The real one." Pause. "The kids might guess from Sotheby that they broke the fake horse. What else did they break?"

"The Minoan—"

"Yes. So now they'll know there are two Giacomettis." Longer pause. "But since the real one is downstairs, and since we haven't sold it—God, that was lucky."

"—then there's nothing that we can be accused of. All the discovery will do is support the theory that Peter went home in a hurry to cover his tracks. It's perfect. Gives them something meatier to pursue."

"Will it stop there? What about those kids? Can they get any further?"

"I don't see how they can touch us."

"As long as we don't deviate from the story. Not one iota."

"I covered us well. When Scully came to the office to interview me, I told him I discovered it was a fake and told you and that we just assumed Peter had bought it or had it made on a whim." She laughed. "I also said I kept it on my desk as a conversation piece."

"I always thought that was mad."

"It turned out well. Oh, did I tell you, in the midst of our conversation, Scully mentioned a sculpture by Jocko Medi." A short humorless laugh. "You were right about not selling it. I'm grateful."

"We're both grateful."

"I told him that the Giacometti buyer couldn't come up with the cash."

"Good. Nothing but the truth. We were lucky, Brad. Suppose Lemato had been able to come up with the money? Then we would've been forced to switch. Those kids would've walked in and found the fake, and eventually someone could've figured out what happened."

"No looking back. I miss you."

"So do I. We'll talk soon."

Illumination

Not unexpectedly, the drive drew Nick and Stephanie closer and closer to the farmhouse. They parked the car by the bridge where they'd paused so long ago just before plunging into the Bergers' world. They leaned on the railing, looked down through the thick oak woods and watched the dense, frothy water below. Across from them, on the facing ridge, a breeze laboriously swayed the broad symmetrical crowns of the white oaks.

"If you assume that Amanda and Carroll knew nothing about the forgery room or the forgeries, you can't get any further. Peter's the villain and the victim. As soon as you assume they knew something, all hell breaks loose. If Sotheby only has the genuine stuff, then someone had to pick over the living room goodies pretty carefully."

"That someone being Amanda or Carroll."

"Or both, Steph, both."

"Did Amanda know anything about that big fat increase in the insurance on the farmhouse?"

"She already said no. But let's ask her again. Dear Amanda, Would you please kindly—

She smiled sourly. "There are just too many coincidences." The mossy banks of the stream, the rotting leaves on the ground gave off a rich damp smell which reminded Stephanie of the dank close smell in the underground forgery room. "Coincidence Number 1: The letter from Carroll arrives just a little too late. Which leads to Coincidence 2: Peter comes home without knowing that the cameras and microphones he allegedly ordered are working. And Coincidence 3: We just happen to be monitoring his every move, so that you can go down to the cellar and scare the"—she was about to say 'life'—"scare the shit out of him. His perfectly good pacemaker suddenly fails in his own basement. What's it all add up to?"

"Suppose someone wanted Peter out of the way?" The statement was struck into the air like letters on a linotype: The message hung shimmering in the moist air as though lit up in block capitals.

"If I'd wanted Peter Berger out of the way," Stephanie said after a moment's hesitation, "one way to do it would have been to lure him home."

"How?"

"You might tell him there was a buyer for something and make sure that that something was one of his fakes."

"The Giacometti?"

"And I'd make sure that the buyer knew enough to tell the difference between the real thing and the phony."

"So they recruit the perfect young hothead for the job of housesitter/killer. Then they torture that poor clown—and

266

his woman friend—until he's just about out of his head. Send Peter in on cue and, true to type, the hothead's supposed to wade downstairs with the .30-06 and blow his employer away. Only in that elegant set"—Nick jerked his thumb over his shoulder at the Bergers' estate—"I got civilized. So Peter knocks around his basement like we're deaf and dumb for the simple reason he doesn't know all the multiple monitors are plugged in."

"But what happens if you don't shoot him?"

"That's the big question, pal. Whoever's setting him up can't afford to let Peter go back to France. Then he'll know that the buyer and the fakes were only lures to get him down into the wine cellar, that the TV cameras were running, and that this hothead was out stalking his ass. No, this is a one-shot—excuse the pun—deal. Somebody had to figure out how to drop him without a shot being fired. They had to have a fallback position just in case I didn't squeeze the trigger, just in case I missed." Nick proceeded cautiously now. "I've been wondering if there's any way to make a pacemaker fail."

"Can something like that be shorted out?"

"I don't know. But we're going to find out real quick. I think I remember something about microwaves and pacemakers. But that was a while ago: It's very vague."

Nick's eyes left the turbulent pool and moved up the sloping, shaded ground, examining the gnarled roots and giant convoluted boles. The twisted oaks looked absurdly ferocious, like pathetic monsters hamming it up. No threat lurked in these woods. Nick wondered if they'd ever know the truth about Peter's death.

"But why did Amanda want Peter out of the way?" Stephanie asked.

"Amanda!" Nick sounded astonished. "It's got to be Carroll who did it."

Unraveled

Standing at the east end of the white, open loft, Stephanie could feel the winter cold seeping in through the eight-foot-high casement windows. The floor remained unsanded, and it badly needed a coat of urethane; a four-by-six hole in the ceiling still remained unplastered. Still the entire space had been sheet-rocked and painted; the kitchen, while it was not Bucks County elegant, was functional and it, too, fit her well. Livable, she judged. And reasonably handsome. She felt a detached proprietary interest in this loft: no landowner yet but someone with an investment in a place.

Someday, Stephanie realized, they would come to the inevitable question of having children. And she knew that her answer would be yes.

Her hand rested on the fluting of one of the fourteen-foot columns that punctuated the length of the ninety-foot space, when the phone rang. Answering it, she heard the roar of the subway in the background. Nick shouted: "Got to catch this "D" train. But, Steph, you got to know: HE SAID IT COULD BE DONE!"

Forty-five minutes later Nick stormed up the steps and into her arms. "Dr. Martin Pantry came through, pal. He said the odds were long but that it could be done if it was set up right."

She led him to the round oak dining-room table, sat him down and fetched two beers. "Start at the very beginning, please."

Nick told her about his tour of the operating room and Dr. Pantry's patient explanation of how various pacemakers work. Dr. Martin Pantry was in fact the heart surgeon who had implanted the pacemaker in Peter Berger's chest. "He showed me all these glossy pamphlets put out by the manufacturers." Nick produced a handful of pamphlets from his bag. "He broke down the electronics: Peter's pacer was unipolar—"

"Which means?"

"There are two kinds: In the unipolar the cathode's planted in the heart, but the anode's in the pacer box. I think that's right." He thumbed to a place in his pocket notebook and looked at a small sketch. "Yeah, that's right. The unipolar device is just what you would've wanted if you didn't particularly like Mr. Berger; it's more vulnerable to interference than the bipolar. In that one, the anode and the cathode are both implanted in the heart."

"Next you'll be applying to medical school."

"Someone who wanted to fuck up a pacemaker would have to buy—or MAKE—a radio-frequency device that could transmit impulses like the ones the pacer is programmed to recognize as heartbeats, normal heartbeats. In this case that would've been easy enough—Amanda could've written Carroll to say what frequency Peter's pacer operated at, or Carroll could've found out himself by consulting the literature. Anyway, Peter's pacemaker was set to go on on demand, Dr. Pantry said. Oh, this is very important: Peter was dependent on his pacemaker. Couldn't live without it." Stephanie did not smile. "Peter's pacer was set

269

to turn on whenever his heartbeat dropped down below seventy-two pumps per minute. All that they had to do was electronically fool the pacer into thinking that Peter's heart was beating. To do that they had to activate their transmitter at a rate faster than the pacer itself, then the pacer would be fooled into thinking Peter's heart was beating normally, that everything was OK, and then the pacer would automatically shut down. Peter's heart either stops or, probably in this case, beats erratically and develops something called arrhythmia. A little arrhythmia, he has a seizure, and boom. Dead. That's the easy part."

Watching the glowing points of light in Nick's pupils, she found his excitement contagious. Odd, she thought, to feel so triumphant when talking about such horror.

"Carroll knew enough to whip together the transmitter. What's hard is getting the antennae close enough to do the job to the victim. My guess is that Carroll stashed the transmitter in the forgery room— He might've been in there too that night, but I doubt he'd take that chance. The transmitter had to be powerful enough, say five millivolts. He might have been able to off Peter through the door with something that powerful. But he couldn't miss if he lined the wine cellar with antennae. On the ceiling he had the conduit for the wires for the TV camera, so he could've hidden antennae there. On the floor he had the wires for the mikes, and the floor had just been dug up. All he had to do was bury the antennae a half inch in the ground, string up the overhead antennae, and wait for Peter. After that, wait a little longer until I barged in."

"What if someone saw the antennae?"

"Unlikely. They figured nobody would see and they had to take the chance. No one's going to inspect the place very carefully after a very sick man drops dead of what looks like a heart attack. Only later, when somebody figures it's weird for a perfectly good pacemaker to go bad just at the right moment. So they took the chance and got away with it. Until now. They put Peter Berger just where they wanted him—stone cold dead."

To back up their theory that Peter Berger was murdered by remote control, Nick first underlined, then xeroxed all of the relevant parts of Dr. Pantry's pamphlets. He added excerpts from his textbooks and all the literature he'd collected on pacemakers and radio transmitters. He pasted that material along with the transcript of his interview with Dr. Pantry in a notebook labeled "EXHIBIT NUMBER 1."

They assumed that Carroll had been their tormentor, the demon who, night after night, had haunted the Bergers' estate. But the haunting was usually accomplished by remote control—Nick assumed that three or four microphones were hidden in the trees near the farmhouse. The noises that had so often unsettled Nick's sleep came in three basic arrangements, which argued that Carroll had three interchangeable tapes, and that each in turn could be activated by a timed radio signal. If so, the microphones had by now, of course, been removed. If the tape system worked the way they supposed it did, Carroll had to be on the grounds only a relatively few times:

1) to chip the blades of the secateurs
2) to drain the oil out of the lawn mower and plant the three giant size bootprints
3) to break the clay pigeons and plant the single bootprint
4) to rearrange the implements on the pegboard in the barn
5) twice to run around at the edges of the cameras' range (though with this Carroll might have been assisted by a neighbor, an animal, or even real art thieves)
6) the night of September 18.

"On August fifth, Carroll called Meyers to accept Property Guard's bid. The orginal completion date they gave Carroll was September twentieth. Peter died early on the morning of the nineteenth. So Carroll called Amanda to tell her the execution date was moved up, and Peter Berger was sent home without knowing the cameras were working. All they had to do was lie about the completion date; Amanda had to let Carroll know what flight Peter was on. Fortunately, our buddy Meyers gave me another key, Steph. He said that Carroll could've tapped into the cable and monitored both the microphones and the cameras. Once his monitoring system was set up, Carroll only had to watch the basement screen on the last night.

"A week after Peter's death—murder—Amanda returned to play the innocent bereaved widow. The only thing missing was the veil."

"Plus," Stephanie added, "we know there wasn't any GREAT increase in art thefts. Two thefts in Princeton don't exactly create an epidemic. Of course Carroll will probably deny he ever said that."

"I know," Nick answered bitterly. His fingernails were bloody nubs. "It's our word against his. What odds we were up against, what incredible odds. Figure what chance we had of catching that Sotheby ad in the *Times*."

The colossal irony, she thought, was that before their time in Bucks County they never would have noticed a Sotheby ad. "We did have one other chance to catch on, Nick, though I don't see how we could've known what they had up their sleeves then. If we had taken that bronze horse to the Philadelphia Museum, they would've told us it wasn't worth fixing."

"Yeah, makes you understand why Carroll burned up the road to get out here that afternoon." Even though it was a few miles away, Nick could feel the weighty presence of the farmhouse.

272

"They would've burned the farmhouse down?"

"That's the way I figure it. Peter's plan went as follows: Buy a heap of insurance a year and a half in advance so it won't look suspicious. Sell off most of the good pieces in France and all over Europe to private collectors who know the difference between the real stuff and fakes—or can hire someone who does—and also know enough to keep their mouths shut when they're getting a good deal. Meanwhile, make a matching fake for each real piece you sell, then fill up the farmhouse with the phony beauties. One night a log accidentally rolls out of the fireplace and—poof!—your beloved two hundred-year-old farmhouse goes up in a flash along with millions of bucks of art work. What a scam. Peter gets to collect at both ends."

Only Peter never got to collect. They got him first." Stephanie continued. "We were perfect setups for them."

"Such innocents."

Show and Tell

"But you've got to give yourself a chance to see it this way, Lieutenant, because this is the way it really happened." Nick banged his fist at the chart on his easel. Lieutenant Theodore Scully tried to mask the condescension in his smile, but Nick caught it, Stephanie caught it.

The coroner's dusty office was crowded. Next to Stephanie sat a vice-president of Metropolitan Mutual, the Bergers' insurance company, and next to him sat the president of Property Guard, who seemed bemused by the cluttered Victorian office in the center of the small town set. Morgan and Pulski stood in the narrow aisle like seconds on the apron in a boxer's corner.

"We've been over all this before, Mr. Young." The detective's voice was equal parts reason and fatigue. "I advised you not to insist on this meeting. We know you're right about the most important thing, and we're all very indebted to you for your—uh—detective work." Scully turned a bit sheepish. Morgan laughed a loud, dumb laugh, then silenced himself.

The vice-president of Metropolitan Mutual Life Insurance Company, moving his facial muscles with Spartan economy, summarized his company's position: "We now have proof that Peter Berger did forge works of art, that he actually imitated some of the artwork in his own collection. Whether Peter Berger sold any of these forgeries in France, we do not know. Mr. Young believes that Peter Berger sold off the originals to knowledgeable collectors who were both discreet and intelligent enough to appreciate a good buy, or to those who paid for the works with what Mr. Young labels as 'dubious' money. Mr. Young also says that it's possible that Peter Berger sold a forgery or two to those people who didn't know the difference. Mr. Young believes that Mr. Berger's plan involved eventually selling off all the originals and replacing each of them with a forgery, then burning down the farmhouse with those forgeries inside. Peter Berger then would collect the sizable insurance premium on these works of art. This elaborate structure is based upon practically no evidence whatsoever. Quite apart from that, the primary difficulty, as Met Mutual sees it, is that we really have no interest in prosecuting a dead man for a crime that hasn't been committed."

"As to your wilder suggestions—" Scully began. Stephanie thought how much she had wanted Scully to be their savior, to put the final, official seal of approval on it.

"I just can't understand if you follow us to the first point why you can't see the rest of the plot."

Nick's frustration was about to choke his lucidity, so Stephanie intervened: "But isn't it conceivable that the entire plot was hatched before the Bergers went to France and before they chose the housesitters? We're trying to show you how we were used. Isn't it possible that they waited for the right gullible young couple to come along so that they—Nick and I—could perform the dirty work? They may have even rejected the other couple because they were afraid the other couple was too smart or too skeptical. Or perhaps they just pretended another couple was interested to sink the hook."

Nick took over again, calmer now. "Bradford Carroll is an electronics expert. You saw the stereo tuner he built by hand." He pointed to Roman numeral IX on his expanded chart. "Plus the coroner's office has Mr. Carl Meyers's letters about Carroll's familiarity with the camera and radio system. Remember, Bradford Carroll had a full set of drawings and blueprints of the system. Property Guard's president studied the view out of the window. "Carl Meyers said that Carroll could've set up a transmitter in the forgery room with antennae on the ceiling and floor. He could've snuck into the Bergers' estate any night."

"Look at it from our point of view," Scully began with laborious patience. "It gets so absolutely wild here—bootprints intentionally faked by larger boots, tape loops activated by remote control, microphones hidden in trees, nightly electronic tortures, someone monitoring TV screens and then—most outlandish of all— a transmitter on the same wave length as Mr. Berger's pacemaker and antennae strung up on the floor and ceiling like Christmas tree lights—" Even Mutual's vice-president managed a small smile.

"All technologically possible. You have the opinion of Dr. Martin Pantry, of Mr. Meyers, an expert from Property Guard itself—"

"And we've taken police time to check all this through. We even spoke to Mr. Lemato, the gentleman who bid on the Jocko Medi, and he confirmed that he had to hold up buying the sculpture because of other financial commitments. All that you say, Mr. Young, is possible. But so are a dozen other wild scenarios. The problem, as I have told you repeatedly, is that there is not a single piece of evidence to support your theory of the motive or the means for murder." Scully seemed pleased with this unusual flight of alliteration.

Trying not to sound melodramatic, Nick announced: "But premeditated murder has been committed."

"I don't think you want to say that."

"But I do, I do." Nick's face was aflame; he could feel his audience slipping further away, could feel Scully preparing to terminate the interview. "All I ask is for you to listen and follow up on what I say. After all, you're supposed to be an officer of the law, interested in justice."

Scully interrupted, short of patience now: "Nicholas, we do appreciate what you've done for us. Really we do. You proved that Peter Berger was a forger, and you correctly suggested he had a client who knew the difference between a fake and the real thing. So Peter came home from France to switch the two sculptures. He died of a massive seizure caused by failure of his pacemaker. That's as far as anyone in good conscience can go with you. Any further, and you'd just be asking for trouble."

276

Stephanie thought: the minute an explanation becomes official, it's frozen in their bureaucratic minds. We dislodged the first one, which only makes them all the more stubborn about this one. We've laid the entire plot out for them and they can't see it. They don't want to believe! Her mind flooded with possibilities: Someone could subpoena Bradford Carroll's bank records to see if he had purchased components for the transmitter; someone could go to France and see when Carroll's letter about the completion date of the surveillance equipment had reached Amanda; someone could subpoena the telephone records to see when Carroll called Amanda or Amanda called Carroll; someone could keep an eye on both Carroll and Amanda to see when they finally met again; bug their phones and wait for the tiny lethal slip. Stephanie knew that she and Nick were right. It's so clear. It's as though Amanda and Carroll underlined it for us! But only for us! If a person hadn't lived it all, then the sense of being set up and teased and tortured, which read like paranoia to an outsider, might seem an invention; the technology would surely sound like science fiction, the plot implausibly far-fetched. Yet it was the only explanation that made sense.

Scully was saying, "We have no reason to suspect that Mrs. Berger knew a thing about her husband's coming back to Bucks County. She knew nothing about the forgeries. We've checked all aspects of it, and she's clear."

Nick muttered furiously: "I can't believe you smug bastards." His cheeks were a blotched, fiery red, as though the skin could not soak up enough of the blood that coursed through his face; the veins of his neck pulsated wildly. In front of his small audience—every eye stayed locked on him now—Nick slowly began to dismantle the easel. He pulled out the pin, slipped the legs up the groove; he slid the carefully lettered chart into his portfolio, then stood there blankly for a moment.

Scully asked Morgan a question, and they struck up a conversation which was meant only to fill the time.

In the old days, Nick thought, when he was still street smart and street tough, they never would have gotten away with it; he would have sensed the plot before they'd worked out their cover-up. Certainly Stephanie had played the largest part in wooing and weaning him away from the old world, for lowering his guard against people like Amanda and Carroll. Yet the process of civilizing him had also restrained Nick when he'd ached to slash the Rothko and the Kline, and it had made him lift the vase out of Stephanie's hands when she wanted to play romantic anarchist and smash it. Most important, the civilized Nick Young hadn't dropped Peter Berger dead in his tracks. That fellow had left Amanda and Carroll to finish Peter off themselves. Almost from the beginning, Nick realized, Stephanie had projected an image of him that Nick admired and appreciated. She had fabricated a tale of what he might become, a tale with more scale and seriousness than he himself ever would have considered. What struck Nick now was the realization that she couldn't have been that far wrong. He had become surprisingly like the man she thought he could become. And since Nick felt reasonably at home with what he'd grown into, even at this moment of complete humiliation, he couldn't blame her for the changes because he had obviously wanted them to happen too.

Just then Stephanie stood up and leaned hard against the claustrophobic little railing. "You people have no idea what went on with Peter Berger. The official version of life." Stephanie understood what was about to happen: Scully would clear his throat, direct a half-baked apologetic nod their way, and gratefully dismiss everyone. Case closed.

Stephanie began screaming: "I can't bear your smugness. Since you can't see it, can't imagine it, you don't ask the right questions. They murdered him, and you're going to let Amanda and Carroll get away with it." She wouldn't allow them to humiliate Nick or herself, wouldn't let them escape the room unscathed. Scully and his two-man gaggle stood open mouthed. Property Guard's president was already anxiously moving toward the door. She realized that this was the first time she had ever raised her voice in public. She thought of the phone call she would make to her father, of having to listen to the cool relief with which he'd greet her news that there would be no further investigation. For William Harrold, as for the men who were now moving anxiously toward the door of the coroner's office, only official confirmation mattered. Her father would say, "Yes, Stephanie, I know what you two believe, but if the authorities don't agree, you can't really insist you are correct."

With his hand hovering inches from her elbow, Scully was saying, "You really ought to calm down, Mrs. Young. This will get you nowhere."

She cursed herself for having believed that mysteries actually did get solved, that endings were really resolutions. The lieutenant's appeal to courtesy infuriated her; she began screaming at him: "How can you let them get away with it? You won't even question them. You just assume they're innocent." Nick looked on in dazed wonderment. "We won't take this lying down," she yelled, knowing she was being absurd. "We'll catch them if you won't." The two executives slipped through the door.

Scully seemed embarrassed, deferential. "Really, Mrs. Young. Calm down."

Nick moved toward her with his easel and portfolio. "Let's get out of here. It's over. He's not going to do any more than he did before we discovered the forgery room. It's over, Stephanie."

Outside they stood on the courthouse steps and watched the cars awkwardly trying to maneuver through the five-way intersection: first this Chevy, then an old blue Cadillac tentatively slid foward, braked sharply, edged on. Her hands trembled, tears bloated her eyes, but she would not cry. Not for those bastards.

Nick felt an acute sense of relief, as when the dentist finally stops drilling. "We couldn't convince them. We could've stood on our heads and without a smoking gun it wouldn't have worked." Nick looked intently at Stephanie, but she was staring at the disappearing cars. "This shit probably happens all the time. Almost nothing ever gets solved."

"I got so angry," she said.

"I loved it. You were great." This time she'd stepped in, she'd refused to let them be ignored without a fight. The smile she could not see was muted—realistic concession to defeat and also, perhaps, a small nod to a victory. Inside the Coroner's dusty office a strange mystical transfer had occurred: Stephanie had taken on a portion of his anger; he had absorbed a measure of her poise and decorum. Decorum—he'd always hated that word. Yet it was that quality which allowed Stephanie to admit that another person's position might legitimately exist. Decorum provided the ground on which empathy might grow, and empathy was a next door neighbor of love.

Nick knew Amanda and Carroll were now free to walk hand in hand into the sunset. Realistically, he told himself they'd never send those killers to the electric chair. Stephanie and he would have merely the assurance that they'd solved the mystery, if only for themselves. An audience of two? Nick turned and looked Stephanie in the eye, his smile still lifting his lips slightly. He felt closer to her than he'd ever felt. It was a closeness he sensed would endure, a kind of gift from Bucks County. Stephanie, calmer now, turned to be hugged. She looked puzzled as Nick muttered into her hair, "We didn't do so bad. Not so bad."

ABOUT THE AUTHOR

Robert J. Seidman was born in Philadelphia, Pa. and graduated from Columbia University, where he was also in the Ph.D. program. He was awarded a Carroll A. Wilson Fellowship to Oxford University where he earned his Masters degree in English literature. Mr. Seidman is the author of *Notes for Joyce: An Annotation of James Joyce's Ulysses*, coauthored with Don Gifford, and *One Smart Indian*. He lives in New York with his wife and daughter, and is at work on a third novel.